WATER RIGHTS

JESSICA McCLELLAND

I0616849

RED SKY INC.

This is a work of fiction. Names, characters, places and incidents are of the author's imagination and are used fictitiously and not based on actual events, or persons, living or dead. Any resemblance to actual locals, organizations or events is coincidental.

Red Sky Inc.
Grand Junction, Colorado.

Copyright © 2018 Jessica McClelland
ISBN- 978-0-9980319-6-5

All rights reserved. No part of this book may be used or reproduced in any manner without written permission, except in the case of brief quotations.

First printing: 2017
Second printing: 2018

WATER RIGHTS

PRAISE FOR THE KILLDEER SERIES

You'll be compelled to race through North of the Crazies by Jessica McClelland's easy and addictive prose, but that means you'll lose the detail and the accuracy that make her a truly fine writer. Her knowledge of the contemporary West and her abilities as a storyteller makes her a welcomed addition to the new class of crime fiction authors.
-Craig Johnson, author of the Walt Longmire Mysteries, the basis of A&E's hit series Longmire

Jessica McClelland's Snow at Midnight bursts out of the chute with a fresh new voice an authentic Montana sense of place, and a flawed but endearing protagonist readers will cheer for. Welcome aboard, Marley Dearcorn.
–C.J. Box, New York Times bestselling author of Force of Nature.

Ms. McClelland's gritty and endearing heroine takes you for a wild ride through the Montana countryside filled with murder and intrigue.
—Sam Morton, Winner of the Wyoming State Historical Society Award for Historical Fiction.

BOOKS BY
JESSICA McCLELLAND

SNOW AT MIDNIGHT
DRAWN TO THE MEAN
THE JADE ARROWHEAD
THE BUFFALO FENCE
NORTH OF THE CRAZIES
JIM CREEK HILL
WATER RIGHTS

CHAPTER 1

I saw the cloud of dirt before spotting the two men on the ground. At first glance it looked like a dust devil tossing up a haze of dry prairie soil. But as I drove closer, the familiar outlines of Ned and Vern Houston came into focus and I slowed down to get a better look.

The earth around them was scarred from the fight, gouged and pockmarked. A cowboy hat lay on the churned soil a few paces away from them, knocked off during the struggle.

I stopped my SUV and squinted through the early morning sunlight. The brawl continued in spite of my arrival so I watched the fight for a few moments to see who would give up first.

Behind them, a couple of four-wheeler ATVs sat nose to nose a few yards away from the head gate of an overflowing irrigation ditch, and a discarded shovel lay beside it. Mounds of mud were piled beside the head gate, the result of a couple hours' hard digging. One of the brothers had been working all morning to clean out the ditch, and the other had interrupted the work in order to express his dissatisfaction about something. There was no way to tell which brother had been digging and which one had gotten upset about it. Considering how foul-tempered they both were, it could have gone either way.

New grass and blooming wildflowers provided a pastoral backdrop to the scuffle. Sunlight painted the grassland a golden hue, and birds sang from the trees.

The alfalfa was sprouting, the rivers had thawed, and the Houston brothers were fighting.

Spring had officially come to Killdeer Valley.

Ned Houston, the older of the two, was slowly gaining the upper hand. He managed to trip Vern with a swift kick and landed on top of his younger brother with a stomach-turning thud. Ned crammed one knee on Vern's chest and held him down. As Vern squirmed and fought for freedom, Ned pulled a pistol from his belt and pointed it at his brother's face.

They seemed oblivious to me, so I rolled down my passenger-side window.

Ned cocked the pistol and kept the barrel trained on Vern's nose.

I leaned forward a bit and called through the passenger-side window, "You boys alright?"

Ned looked up then, his left eye swollen shut, his good eye blinking through a haze of dirt and rage.

He looked at me with scorn. "This don't concern you, Marley."

His red face dripped sweat and the knuckles of his left hand were white from squeezing Vern's throat. It was taking everything he had to maintain his grip, because Vern was putting up one hell of a fight.

Vern tried kicking him off, but Ned clamped down and grunted with effort to keep his hold. The pistol didn't waver.

"We're fine," Vern said through clenched teeth. His words were a bit garbled due to the pressure on his windpipe at the moment. "This is a family discussion."

I stared at them. My eyes wandered back and forth between the pistol and the chokehold. "Uh-huh."

Being an only child, I'd never known the joy of sibling strife. I'd read in a psychology magazine once that being an only child was supposed to make you spoiled and disagreeable.

"You both want me to leave?" I asked.

The least I could do was give Vern another chance to ask for help. After all, he did have a pistol pointed at his face.

They started wresting again and a fresh cloud of dust exploded into the air.

Vern grappled with one hand, flailing madly, and managed to snag the pistol. He struggled as he jerked it away from his brother and chucked it as hard as he could. The pistol sailed into a stand of buffalo grass and disappeared from view.

Unencumbered by the pistol, Ned took the opportunity to hold Vern down with one hand and punch him with the other. "Son of a bitch was stealing my water."

"Oh, you're fighting over water," I said. "Well, I'll just leave you to it, then."

I rolled up my window and drove away.

Vern would tire in a minute. Ned would pummel him. It would get sorted out the way nature intended. The bigger, heavier one would kick the smaller, lighter one around until he apologized.

It was the same with horses, chickens, and school boards.

The Houston brothers were legendary fighters. Had it been anyone else, and had the pistol still been a factor, I probably would have intervened. But most folks around Killdeer had come to accept that when anyone from the Houston clan was swinging fists it was best to stand back and wait for the storm to pass.

I glanced in my rearview mirror as I drove away and could see that the standoff was degenerating into a juvenile wrestling match. Vern never could beat Ned at wrestling. In a minute he would get his payback for the black eye he'd inflicted. Other than check on the two of them when I drove back this way, there wasn't much else I could do.

The Houston family had always relied on violence to solve their disagreements. Since that had been the case for over four generations, I doubted there was a whole lot I could do to change things. Plus the fact that I was a woman who topped out at 120 pounds soaking wet, and both brothers could bench press a spring steer. I could hardly grab them both by the scruff of the neck and shake them like two scrapping cats. And if history repeated itself, in a couple of hours the two of them would be back at work again, pretending like the whole thing had never even happened.

I switched on the radio. Linda Ronstadt was belting out "Poor Poor Pitiful Me" and I couldn't help but think it was appropriate. If the Houston brothers weren't actively determining the correct level of violence to apply to a current situation, they were wallowing in the belief that everyone in Killdeer Valley was out to get them.

I had better things to do than worry about two men nature would probably select for extinction soon.

Dust billowed behind my SUV as I drove down the washboard road out to the old Wilson

4

ranch. The ranch was deserted. Harvey Wilson
didn't live there anymore. Now it was owned by a
used car salesman who'd swept in and bought the
entire spread on the cheap. I'd purchased an
Icelandic pony from Harvey, back when he was still
the owner of the place seven months ago, but now
the new owner was phasing out all of the old
equipment and leftover horse tack. He'd called me
and told me there was a saddle for the pony still at
the ranch, and a bridle. I was welcome to them
anytime, he'd said.

The ranch was now a tiny ghost town.
House, workshop, outbuildings and barns sat silent
and empty, and yet fully functional. All that was
missing were hands to work the place.

I parked in the huge lot in front of the
deserted workshop. The house was vacant and the
new owner had told me he wouldn't be around
today so I could help myself to the tack. He'd said
that he had left it on the front porch of the house.
Late May in Killdeer sometimes brought unexpected
rain so he'd stowed the saddle someplace dry.

I went up the steps leading to the porch and
tested the screen door. It opened without protest and
I went inside.

On a whim, I tried the second door leading
to the house. It was also unlocked. The used car
salesman probably half-hoped someone would break
in and steal the furniture so he wouldn't have to
auction it off, but this far out in the middle of
nowhere burglars were unlikely.

The house was stale and smelled of mold.
An old sofa sat against the wall, covered with a tall
stack of ancient vinyl records. Several boxes sat in
the middle of the ancient wood floor and various
odds and ends were piled haphazardly around them.
Some of the wallpaper had started to peel. I felt

5

uncomfortable as hell creeping around the old empty house, but cell phones didn't work predictably in the valley. Sometimes we could get a cell signal, but most of the time it was impossible. This was the closest reliable telephone. If it was still connected, that is.

I lifted the receiver on the black rotary telephone in the kitchen and was rewarded with a dial tone. From memory, I dialed the number of the sheriff's station back in Killdeer. The dispatcher answered on the second ring.

"Sheriff's office."

"Valerie? It's Marley Dearcorn. Listen, Ned and Vern from the Lazy Ox Yoke are trying to kill one another again. Normally I wouldn't call, but Ned had a pistol so I thought it best to let Loy know."

A moment of silence was followed by a heavy sigh. "Pistol, huh? Ned had it?"

"Yes."

"You know what they was fightin' over?" she asked.

"What else?" I asked.

"Clear Creek water rights," she said, answering her own question. "I'll radio the sheriff. I see you are calling from the Wilson ranch?"

"I am."

"Well I want you to stay put until I can get law enforcement moving. The Houstons will be long gone by the time Loy gets up there, but just in case, you know?"

"Sure, I can do that," I said with a sigh.

I hung up the phone. A wave of relief surged through me as I left the house and shut the door. I'd had bad dealings with Harvey Wilson last fall and simply standing on his property was unsettling. Far better to wait for the sheriff outside than sit there in the old creepy house with the heebie-jeebies.

Back on the front porch I saw a smaller than average hand-tooled saddle draped on the back of a broken wooden chair. A pony-sized bridle was coiled on top. It made me smile.

The tack was half normal size and it was designed for my Icelandic pony, Lil Nipper. The pony had suffered from a thrush infection when I'd first brought him home but now he was healthy. Still, I had no intention of letting anyone ride Lil Nipper. The tack was coming home with me simply for decoration. That, and I couldn't stand the thought that the used car salesman would most likely toss the saddle out as rubbish if I didn't take it.

Besides, I'd bought Lil Nipper strictly as company for my paint horse, Peanut. Peanut had been a mustang caught wild, but for some reason he hated to be alone. I'd been hesitant to get a smaller horse as companion for Peanut, worried the mustang might bully the pony, but it hadn't been a problem. Lil Nipper spent his time bossing the mustang around and letting him know every twenty minutes who was in charge.

I hefted the saddle, loaded it in the back of my SUV with the bridle and slammed the hatch.

Nothing left to do but wait for Loy. If it was a busy day for him the wait could be considerable.

It had been a wet May so far, at least in Killdeer Valley. There was the promise for a good hay crop this year and everything looked lush and green.

I sat on the bottom step of the house and stretched my legs out, letting the warm sun melt the chill away. The temperature didn't get above forty until at least ten in the morning, and usually I had the sense to wear a jacket when I left for work, but today I'd forgotten one. My black slacks and red cardigan were not quite sufficient to keep me warm and the sunshine was just enough to make the cool bearable.

My shift at the little branch library up in Fable didn't start for another three hours, so I had plenty of time for this errand. At least, I would if Sheriff Loy Shucraft showed up eventually.

Winter had been a struggle for me. My husband Leif had died in a plane crash last October and the prospect of facing the long winter months alone had weakened my spirit considerably.

My father, and my best friend Irene Baker, who happened to be involved in a torrid love affair with each other that everyone in town but them had seen coming, both hovered over me until I'd become exasperated enough to beg them to stop. They took turns calling me each day to make sure I was still climbing out of bed and eating. Seven months of mourning were behind me now, giving me some of my strength back. Grieving was a wobbly process for me, and I wasn't completely healed, but I finally felt like the worst was over.

Seeing the spring flowers blossom on the mountainside was something I could appreciate once again. Living in a valley with so much beauty helped my healing process greatly. That and having Lil Nipper and Peanut depending on me. Between the sunshine and having fifteen hundred pounds of cheerful horse around nosing me for hay every day, my spirits were starting to lift.

The breeze shifted and I pulled the rubber band off of my strawberry blonde hair and let it fall to my shoulders. After my husband's death I'd cut it pixie short for ease and after a long winter it was finally the right length for a ponytail again. I stowed the rubber band in the tiny pocket of my slacks and leaned back to take in the sunshine.

Where was Loy?

The sound of a gunshot pealed across the prairie and sent an echo reverberating up the slope of the mountain.

I stood up, my heart thumping.

"Oh, Ned. You didn't."

A second shot tore through the air and I listened to the echo, straining. It wasn't the short crack of a pistol. It was the ring of a rifle of some kind. It sounded like it came from the same place I'd last seen Ned and Vern, but I couldn't be sure. Gunshots tended to bounce and echo off rock faces and gullies until they wore themselves out and sometimes it was hard to tell exactly where they had come from.

Living in rural Montana, I might typically hear two or three gunshots a day after the first spring thaw. The only thing that alarmed me was the fact that I'd just left two of the Houston boys nose to nose in conflict.

A third rifle crack reverberated across the valley and the echo bounced off a cliff face far behind the house. Less than a minute after, another three shots sounded in quick succession.

I relaxed and sat back down. It was unlikely the Houston brothers were shooting at each other. They were both accomplished marksmen. If one of them really wanted to kill the other he could do it with two shots, at the most. Whoever was firing probably didn't have a thing to do with the Lazy Ox Yoke Ranch. More than likely it was some deer hunter blowing the winter dust out of his rifle, or someone target practicing, or sighting in a new weapon.

The last echo of gunfire faded away. Another moment passed while the valley creatures held their breath. Even the birds had stopped chirping to listen to the gunfire. Another couple minutes drifted by in silence, and then squirrels started scrabbling in the trees, birds resumed their squabbling and things went back to normal once again.

At least another ten minutes dragged by before I saw the nose of a truck edge around the bend.

A brand-new sliver-tone king cab pickup truck with low-profile light bar and the seal of Killdeer law enforcement on the door eased to a halt behind my vehicle.

Loy Shucraft stepped out and adjusted his gun belt, wearing a smug expression on his wide face. He beamed when he saw me staring at the truck.

I was on my feet, my mouth gaping. I looked it over, bumper to bumper, with astonishment. "Where did you get that?"

The sheriff ambled to the front bumper of his new truck and placed a palm on the hood like a proud father. "Department of Homeland Security. I signed up my deputy for anti-terrorist training and we got a portion of the federal funds to support our new, heightened security capabilities."

"You mean you blew the Feds' cash on a new set of wheels," I said.

"Precisely."

"I see it's got leather seats," I told him.

"Wendy thinks it's sexy," he said.

"She does, does she?"

"And what Wendy thinks is important. Which leads me to my request," Loy said, looking at me with a determined smile.

I self-consciously ran a hand over the butt of my slacks, thinking it was already too late. They were probably filthy by now from sitting on the old wooden steps. "What request?"

"Wendy is moving out of your dad's little caretaker's cottage. She is moving in with me day after tomorrow and that means I have to kick Finn out of my spare bedroom."

Wendy Martinez and Loy Shucraft had been dating for months. Her moving out of my father's little house wasn't a surprise, but the fact that it had taken this long was.

"And?"

He smiled brightly. "And now my deputy needs a place to stay."

"So what?"

Loy looked at me sideways. "You're kidding, right? You know what."

Loy Shucraft and I had known each other since high school. We had dated very briefly, back when we were little more than kids, and much to Loy's blatant and vocal disappointment I had kept our relationship platonic thereafter. It didn't stop me from shamelessly abusing his old affection for me by inserting myself into his criminal investigations from time to time. We shared a familiarity that went beyond that of two people who were old flames. We were dear enough friends that verbal abuse went with the territory.

"Loy, I hate to bring up your job and all, but did you see the Houston brothers trying to twist each other's heads off when you drove up here?"

"No, and you are changing the subject," he said.

"I don't care if Finn moves into the caretaker's cottage," I told him. "And what about those gunshots just now?"

"If I had seen Vern pointing a gun at his brother do you think I would be standing here talking to you?" he asked.

"Why can't your deputy go rent a house in town?" I asked.

"Because your dad already offered him the caretaker's cottage," Loy said.

I felt my lips tighten. "So this is more of a see-how-Marley-feels-about-it conversation than you actually asking permission."

"How do you feel about it, Marley?" he asked, his eyes twinkling.

I looked at my hands. "It's fine."

Loy shuffled his big frame to the foot of the steps. His wide shoulders blocked out three-quarters of the light from the low sun. "You're sure? Don't mistake this for Finn trying to wheedle his way back into your life."

I looked him in the eye. "I said it's fine."

He looked unconvinced. "Finn swore up and down to me that he's got no intention of being anything other than a good friend to you."

With so many well-intentioned male friends hanging around it was a wonder I hadn't already gotten remarried.

Not that I was even close to being ready for that again.

"I don't mind, Loy. It might not be a bad idea to have a cop living on our end of the valley for a change. It might curb the high school kids' beer parties down at the old culvert."

The sheriff studied me for a moment, probably trying to gauge my tone. His scrutiny made me squirm.

Then he frowned and looked over his shoulder down the valley. "What gunshots?"

"You didn't hear them? Just as you were coming up the road?" I asked.

He massaged the back of his neck, looking embarrassed. "I was screwing around with the radio and didn't hear a thing."

"Valerie must have reached you just fine. You having problems with your signal?" I asked.

"Not that radio. This truck has a ten-disc CD changer in it and I was listening to the Bangles."

I tried not to laugh and failed.

"It's Wendy's CD," he said. "I was adjusting the bass. It's high-definition Dolby and you have to tweak it just right. Anyway, I didn't hear shots. You sure that's what you heard?"

"I'm sure."

He looked down the valley again and squinted into the bright sunlight, his jaw muscle working. "Maybe I should go over to the Lazy Ox Yoke, just take a look around."

"I doubt it was them shooting, Loy. I know they were fighting again but do you really think they are crazy enough to actually kill each other?"

He gave me a look. "Do you know why it took me so long to get up here?"

"You couldn't find the power step-lift on the driver's side of your new truck?"

"When I started up this way, I passed by the trailer park, and I saw Bethany Carmichael dragging a huge dead raccoon across the road with a rope around its neck."

"You're sure it was dead?"

He sighed. "She was heading straight for Randy Newman's property."

"Is he making his famous chili again?"

He shot me a curt look. "I stopped. Asked her what she was doing. You know, sheriffy stuff."

"What did she say?"

Loy shook his head. "She said that the raccoon got clobbered the night before by a cattle truck and instead of taking it to the dump, she was dragging it over to Randy's place and was going to leave it in his driveway."

"I'm sure she had a perfectly good reason," I said, deadpan.

"His calves keep getting out and they are eating her tulips. She said that unless I can get Randy to keep his calves in, every time someone hits a skunk or a raccoon she is going to haul it over to his place and throw it in his driveway."

"Good fences, good neighbors," I said.

"Montana is a fence-out state," Loy said.

"And you pointed that out to her, didn't you?"

He shrank slightly. "I don't think she is going to vote for me again."

"What's that got to do with the Houston brothers?" I asked.

"You said you didn't think they would be stupid enough to kill each other," he told me. "Look how mad Bethany Carmichael got over a bunch of flowers. Now, think about what the Houston brothers are fighting over."

I swallowed and dropped my chin a bit. "Water rights."

"So can you see why I'm a bit upset this time?" he asked.

"I'm sure those rifle shots I heard didn't have anything to do with the Houston brothers."

"But someday they might," Loy said. "The whole thing chaps my ass. I know their crazy daddy plans to divvy up the ranch between the three boys evenly, but you'd think they were ready to kill one another over it right now."

"I hope not," I said.

Loy's jaw clenched. "Makes me hopping mad just thinking about it."

"So I can leave?" I asked.

"Course you can leave. As long as you don't have anything to add."

"You mean about Finn moving into my father's caretaker's cottage?"

Loy let his shoulders slump. "I mean about the fight between Ned and Vern. I'm officially taking your statement."

"Then, no. I don't want to add anything. It was typical Houston brothers, as far as I could tell. Vern threw the pistol away, and then I drove off. They were both alive when I left."

"Dammit those boys are a pain in the neck," Loy said, irritated. "Even the youngest one has had his fifteen minutes of fame down at the sheriff station."

Ned and Vern were older than Loy and me by a handful of years. I thought that Ned had to be forty-two by now, at least. Vern was probably forty. It didn't stop Loy from referring to them as boys every chance he got.

Peter was the youngest son, and we had been in the same class together in high school. Peter was less obnoxious than his older brothers, but he did what he could to try and keep up. Peter was prone to pick fights more in defense of his little sister, Felicia, than from any slight made against him. But his overprotectiveness of her sometimes made trouble where there was none.

The three of them had terrorized the valley since they were old enough to walk.

"At least Felicia is mostly a normal human being," I said.

Loy grumbled. "Probably comes from being a lot younger than the boys."

"It probably comes from being the only girl with three older brothers," I told him. "There had to be someone in the house civilized enough to answer the door when the neighbors came to see what all the noise is about."

"Those goddamn delinquents think it's some sort of sport to pound on each other." His face twisted with anger. "Well, I've had just about enough of them."

The sheriff climbed in his truck and slammed the door so hard the antenna whipped back and forth.

He started the engine and leaned out the window. "I'm going over there and if both Ned and Vern have bruises I'm busting them. I'll haul them both in and charge them with domestic battery. Maybe the rest of the family will get some peace for a while."

He spun the rear tires and was gone.

I stood on the porch and watched him until the rooster tail of dust faded away.

If Loy really was going out to arrest one of the Houston boys I dearly hoped he would call Finn, his deputy, for backup.

Finn. What was I going to do about that?

As if there was anything that I could do.

Angus Finn and I had shared a very short, tumultuous fling before I'd eventually put an end to it, moved on, and married Leif Gable. Though there had been no shortage of passion between Finn and me, we'd struggled through our torrid love affair. His freakishly protective streak had always caused problems, and his lack of communication skills hadn't helped matters. Since he was not American, but had been born and raised in South Africa and had spent half his life working as a professional bodyguard, Finn could charitably be described as odd.

Our breakup had been smoother than our relationship. Finn had all but told me directly that he simply wasn't the man for me, but after Leif had asked me to marry him, Finn had reacted with surprising anger and had practically begged me not to go through with the wedding. His reaction had come as a total shock. I'd been operating under the assumption that his feelings for me were neutral at best.

I still didn't fully understand what went on inside Finn's head. Probably, I never would.

Since Leif had been killed in the plane crash, Finn had changed his behavior, again. Somehow he always managed to find a way to engage me in conversation about a mundane topic, or find a reason to stop at the library when I was working to inquire about the latest book by some obscure author. If I didn't know better I would have sworn he was hovering around me while trying with all his might to look like he wasn't hovering.

It wasn't a coincidence that he was moving into the caretaker's cottage down the road.

Still, I had better things to think about than the motivations of a man who said three or four words to me in any given week.

I glanced at the clock on the dash of my SUV as I climbed inside. There was still time for a quick breakfast before my shift started at the library and I headed back to Killdeer at top speed. I could grab a bite at Lil's café before heading up the mountain to the branch library to start work for the day.

When I drove by the trailer park I couldn't help but scan the roadway in front of Randy's house. A narrow trickle of blood drew a dark gash traversing the road between Bethany's yard and Randy Newman's driveway.

I frowned and felt a stab of worry.

Loy was right. If one small woman could get that upset about the destruction of a few tulips, then what were two wildly violent brothers capable of doing when it came to fighting over the most precious resource in the West?

After seeing the red scar of raccoon blood on the road, something occurred to me and I felt a momentary pang of guilt.

Maybe they really were crazy enough to kill each other.

And more to the point, maybe I shouldn't have driven off and left them alone so they could do it.

CHAPTER 2

I hadn't even sat down yet when Irene leaned over the café counter and grabbed my hand. Her blue eyes blazed with the thrill of fresh gossip and I could see she was bursting to share.

She hissed in a low whisper. "They are closing Area 49."

I paused. "The weather station up in Fable?"

One eyebrow shot up as she regarded me with satisfaction. "It's not a weather station."

I eased onto the center stool at the counter of Lil's café. Irene Baker, my best friend and the largest archive of local gossip in Killdeer, who also happened to own Lil's, slid a cup of piping hot coffee in front of me and practically vibrated with anticipation. She clearly couldn't wait to hear what I thought of her news.

The breakfast crowd was thinning already. Spring weather fueled a mad rush to the fields and only a few customers remained. Nobody sat close enough to hear our conversation and Irene was obviously frantic to talk.

Area 49 was a small scientific station hidden in an isolated location on the mountain above Killdeer Valley. It was relatively new, having appeared slightly more than five years previously. It had always been shrouded in secrecy, and the lack of information concerning the goings-on at the station had fueled the notion that the facility was actually a secret government compound. Since it was too small to rate an Area 51 moniker, the locals had taken to referring to it as Area 49 instead.

"I just heard from Nick Wilcox that he is out of a job as security chief. Don't you want to know what it is they really do up there all day?" she asked.

I sipped the midnight-black coffee, made a sour face, and poured in about a half a cup of cream. "It's a SETI monitoring facility."

Irene stared at me with an irritated expression. "You take all the fun out of everything. And just how the blazes do you know that, Missy?"

I shrugged. "Leif knew a guy in Washington."

Irene's sharp blue eyes softened. "I should have guessed. That Leif Gable was a force to be reckoned with."

My husband had been anything but average, there was no doubt about that. When not busy running international currency exchange companies, Leif had worked for the government from time to time as something called a forensic accountant. It had been a part-time side job for him. He had built two successful companies that I knew of, traveled extensively all over the world and was connected with all the right people in government and in business. He had been adept at tracking down large sums of money that moved across international borders illegally. When he was moonlighting for the government, his job had been to expose the money trail of wanted criminals and help recover funds or freeze assets. Even this many months after his death, I was still getting condolence letters from people I had never heard of who lived in places like Colombia, or Oslo.

I stirred in sugar and took another sip of coffee. "Leif said the weather station was really a SETI project that got private funding to operate. The staff there were instructed to tell everyone it was a weather station because they didn't want any wing nuts coming around vandalizing the facility. They must have finally run out of cash. Do you know when they are shutting it down?"

Irene reached for a small stool beneath the counter and propped herself up on one hip. For her, it was the closest she ever came to sitting down on the job. "About five weeks. But it isn't being shut down. Loy told me the people who own the facility are selling it to some guy who plans to use it as a data storage building."

"That's a good thing. Might mean a few jobs for us," I said.

Irene smoothed her short blonde hair with one hand and made a face. "Not for anyone local. How many folks around here are qualified to work for a data storage facility? You need a degree in computer gibberish to handle a job like that."

"I think it's called computer science," I pointed out.

"Science my ass. Marley, all of those hacker types get so good at computers so they can look up porn on the Internet and not get caught doing it. Everyone knows that."

I suppressed a grin. "Not for the betterment of humanity? You know, archive the valuable information of the ages for future generations?"

"Please," she said with a snort, "how many kids these days can even find the switch to turn on a vacuum cleaner?"

"Vacuums being central to the humanity issue?" I asked.

"The future generations thing," she said. "The way kids are these days, we don't have much of a future. They are so damn lazy and spoiled it's a wonder the human race still exists at all."

She was in a rotten mood for no reason that I could think of. I glanced around the café and noticed it looked slightly understaffed. Lil's usually had two waitresses running their heads off. But today there was only one. Realization dawned. "Judy Isley quit again, didn't she?"

Irene sagged. "She bugged out yesterday. I'm shorthanded again and spring is here. You know how hard it is to find a good waitress in Killdeer?"

She stared at me without blinking.

"I have a job," I said.

Irene crossed her arms. "I said a good waitress."

"Fine. I won't tell you my gossip, then."

She leaned in. "Yes you will. Or I won't tell you mine."

"Oh really? What's better than Bethany Carmichael using roadkill to make a point about her tulips?" I asked.

"Oh everyone already knows all about her and the dead raccoon," she said. "What they don't know about is the new cell phone tower going in up the valley."

I blinked. "What new cell phone tower?"

She rolled her eyes. "It's going on your land."

"Where on my land?"

Irene grinned with satisfaction. "It's being built on the hill behind your father's caretaker cottage."

"You are making this up."

Her head rocked back and forth sharply. "God's honest truth. Nathan was approached by a site acquisition agent and they said they would pay him eight hundred a month to lease land for a tower."

I frowned. "He doesn't need the money."

"Yes, but Killdeer needs a cell tower. It turns out that hill above the caretaker's cottage is ideal to allow coverage for practically the whole valley. So, he's agreed to it and they are building it."

For some reason I felt sour about the prospect. "When?"

She shrugged one shoulder. "Sometime at the end of the week. Watch out when you go home. There are going to be some big trucks coming up and down the road while they build, and with the thaw, rain and all that, it's going to be a muddy mess."

"That's just terrific," I said.

She shoved her stool back under the counter and shot me a sassy look. "Well it's for the betterment of humanity."

I snorted.

Irene nudged the coffee mug with one finger. "Well, what do you think?"

"About?" I asked.

She rolled her eyes. "The mugs. I had all of them painted with my new logo. Snazzy, right?"

For the first time I actually looked at the coffee mug I held in one hand. It was an ordinary white restaurant cup emblazoned with bright red letters painted in curly script. The letters read "Lil's Café" on the face.

"It's nice."

"Nice? It's a trademark. That's going to put me in the category of a branded commodity. And all you can say is, it's nice?" she demanded. "I've arrived, Honey. I've got a logo now."

"Can I actually get some food this morning?"

"You are having eggs Benedict," she said.

It was a rare occasion that I got to order my own meal at Lil's. Irene took it upon herself to set dishes in front of me at random, either because another customer had ordered something that was fixed incorrectly or because she wanted me to try a new recipe.

I'd never seen eggs Benedict on the menu before.

Today was new recipe day.

Andy, the gunslinger-quick short-order cook was already ringing the bell at the pickup window. They had obviously discussed my order before I'd even walked inside because it was already finished.

"I don't like soft yolks," I said.

She glared. "I know you don't. But you'll eat 'em how I give 'em to you."

Irene set a plate before me and I was relieved to see that Andy had broken the yolks and cooked them through.

She left me to eat and set about driving her remaining waitress mercilessly. Nobody was harder to work for than Irene Baker, but no other café in the valley offered a waitress better tips. It was a trade-off.

I chewed thoughtfully. The implications of the weather station closing would be catastrophic for the people who worked there. Nick Wilcox, the former deputy sheriff of Killdeer and current security chief at the station, was now out of a job. That wasn't good news. Not that Nick and I had ever gotten along. Alright, we hated each other, but I was sorry for him nonetheless. Two of the guys who worked at the station were friends of mine. Will and Seth. They were astrophysicists, or some other ridiculously mind-blowing type of scientist, and as such they were both out of place in cattle country. But whenever I saw them we chatted amiably. I would be sorry to see them go.

And now the valley was getting a cell tower? On Dearcorn land?

It was almost too much. I'd never handled change very well, and anytime something big occurred in Killdeer it jangled my nerves. Now there were two reasons for me to be unhappy.

I finished breakfast and left money on the counter. Irene seldom let me pay for my meals but once in a while I managed to sneak cash under my plate before she could stop me.

I gave her a wave over one shoulder as the door eased shut behind me, and a flash of sunshine forced me to dig around on the floorboards of my SUV for sunglasses. On a whim I pulled out the cell phone I kept from inside the glove compartment and turned it on. Staring at the display didn't magically induce more bars to appear, and as usual the screen let me know politely that we had absolutely no hope of service. Sometimes a cell phone call would connect, but usually it was impossible unless you were willing to climb a hill and hope that the wind blew in just the right direction.

Killdeer always did seem like it was twenty years behind the rest of civilization. The people of our valley were notorious for disdaining anything modern. But now it seemed we were slowly being dragged, kicking and screaming, into the twenty-first century whether we liked it or not.

I turned off the phone and stowed it back in the glove box. Not that Killdeer didn't need a reliable cell phone tower, and I could see the value of having the convenience of being able to make a call, but why did it have to be built on my family's land?

Dearcorn Ranch was technically my father's land, but I felt like it was mine too simply by virtue of my last name. When Leif and I had gotten married my last name hadn't changed. I'd kept my maiden name simply because Leif had said it made paperwork much easier. No social security card changes, or bank account changes. Shortly after his death in the plane crash I had been stricken with guilt that I hadn't insisted on changing my last name to Gable, but now that seven months had passed the decision didn't weigh quite so heavily.

We had been married for only a couple of months, after living together for a little more than a year, before Leif had died. We hadn't spent every day together for the last twenty years like some couples, but I still missed him terribly. At least I wasn't crying myself to sleep anymore.

The sunny day and memories of my short but happy marriage to Leif occupied my thoughts as I drove out of the parking lot to work, and with so much cheerful bird and butterfly activity around I figured it was impossible that the Houston boys had caused each other serious harm after all. I reassured myself that nobody could commit murder on such a glorious morning.

Not quite a municipality, not quite a subdivision, the town of Fable sat high on the spine of the mountains above the valley, hidden in the thick forest of lodgepole pine trees that stood in stark contrast to the rolling hills below.

Fable was always ten degrees cooler than the valley, and always the first to see snow in the fall and the last to see the snow melt in the spring.

Taking the twenty-minute drive up the twisting turns of the mountain road was like stepping back in time.

When I pushed through the front door of the little branch library, my boss, Rose, glanced up from her desk and frowned at the clock.

"You're early."

"Finished breakfast and I didn't have anything else to do besides go back home and stare at the walls for half an hour."

She tossed her stack of papers on her desk. "Well in that case, I'm leaving."

"Everyone has cabin fever."

Rose waved a hand around the tiny, absolutely deserted library. "That's a true statement."

"Can you blame them?"

She stood up, stretched long and hard, and snagged her coat from a hook by the front door. "I'll come in a half hour earlier tomorrow to make up for it."

She flicked her wrist at me in a salute and sauntered down the front steps. Rose was the most laid-back boss I'd ever had in my life. Half the time Rose's hair was either streaked with purple or hot pink accents, her skirts and blouses were a kaleidoscope of color ranging from blacks swirled with jade green to lip stick red, and sewn together like an old quilt, and I'd never seen her wear anything but Keds canvas sneakers.

I watched through the window as Rose fired up her Subaru and tore out of the parking lot. Her mountain bike swayed precariously in the rack on top, and I figured she would make it about three-quarters of the way down the mountain before it gave way and fell off the back.

My shifted ended at five and I had a lot of work to catch up on before then. Since it was spring we had decided it was time to do all the nasty jobs that piled up over the course of a busy winter season. During wintertime there wasn't a lot to do in Fable, unless you were an avid trapper or enjoyed snowshoeing, and our shelves always got quite a workout from folks desperate to beat the winter blues. Now that it was May we could concentrate on cleaning, discarding old books that had broken spines, and placing orders for new titles by popular authors.

Today, there would be plenty of uninterrupted time in the library to dedicate towards maintenance.

After a couple hours of heavy lifting I'd managed to get one entire bookcase wiped down and organized, a stack of books discarded and two sections of nonfiction realphabetized.

The bell tinkled over the front door, announcing my first patron of the day, and when I stepped from behind the bookcase I saw Deputy Angus Finn hovering in the entrance.

"Oh," I said. "Hey."

He surveyed the library with his ice-blue eyes systematically. Satisfied of something, he took a step towards me and looked me up and down carefully.

I noticed that he was back to wearing all black again. For the first few weeks after Loy had hired him as Killdeer's deputy, Finn had maintained his professionalism and worn the brown uniform stoically. But that had gradually waned and soon he was wearing black shirts on casual Fridays, then he had moved on to wearing nothing but black, head to toe, as was his custom. At least he was still wearing his official brown deputy's baseball cap. His badge was clipped to his belt casually. Other than that, it was impossible to tell he was even in law enforcement.

Well, there was the gun.

"Marley, I'd like to have a word."

The first time I'd ever heard Finn talk I'd assumed he was British. His accent was pronounced, and hard to pin down. It had taken me several days after meeting him to figure out he was actually from South Africa and not England. It was still an oddity to hear the sound of someone from literally the other side of the planet carrying on a conversation in tiny Killdeer, Montana, where normally the most exotic accent we ever heard was when someone from Wyoming ventured across the border.

I dropped into the chair behind my desk, rubbing the ache between my shoulders. "Loy already mentioned that you are moving into the caretaker's cottage."

He propped one hand on his sidearm, exactly the way the sheriff did whenever he was about to deliver bad news. The resemblance amused me.

"It isn't about the cottage." Finn said.

"Look, I don't care about the furniture. It can stay as far as I'm concerned. But Wendy did a really good job keeping the place nice and clean. You aren't a slob or anything are you Finn?"

His expression looked set in concrete. "The sheriff indicated to me that sometime this morning you heard shots fired in close proximity to the Lazy Ox Yoke Ranch. Is that the case?"

My stomach did a slight flip-flop. "What about it?"

"Did you hear shots fired or not?" he asked.

"Oh God, the two of them didn't kill each other, did they?"

Finn sat down slowly in the chair opposite the desk. "What time, exactly, did you hear the shots?"

I sat up straight, my eyes wide. "Finn, Ned didn't shoot his brother, did he?"

"Vern Houston is alive and unharmed. Can you remember how many you heard?"

I leaned back and shook my head. "Those two jackasses suffer from a severe case of male-pattern stupidity. I knew that someday one of them would twist off and use the other for target practice."

Finn closed his eyes slightly. "Nobody was shot. The time? Do you recall that?"

"It was right before I went to Lil's for breakfast."

He folded his hands on the desktop. "You notified our dispatcher at 8:32 that you had seen a fight between the Houston brothers, and you phoned that in from the former residence of Harvey Wilson."

"What's going on?" I asked.

"Please," he said.

I spun the chair back and forth a few times. "Okay. I called Valerie, hung up the phone, and got the saddle off the front porch."

He took a notebook from his hip pocket and scribbled. "Saddle?"

Something wasn't right. Even for Finn this conversation was incredibly formal.

My stomach tightened up again. "I went out to Wilson's ranch to pick up a saddle and a bridle for my pony. You know, Lil Nipper? So I hung up the phone, grabbed the saddle and put it in the hatch. Then I went to the porch and sat down on the steps."

"And that is when you heard the shots fired?" he asked.

"No . . . it was at least a couple minutes after. So, if I called Valerie at 8:30—"

"It was 8:32."

My lips tightened. I started again. "So if I called her at 8:32, by the time I heard the rifle it was probably a quarter to nine?"

He jotted a note in the book then glanced up. "Why do you say it was a rifle and not a pistol?"

"Come on, Finn. Are you going to tell me what's going on or not?" I asked.

"How many shots would you estimate you heard?"

"I don't estimate," I said. "I heard six."

"Are you sure?"

I leaned forward. "Positive. Now what the hell is going on?"

Finn stood up and shoved the notebook back in his pocket. "I might need to ask you a few more questions later. Will you be at home?"

I was on my feet. "Of course I will be at home. Finn?"

He turned to leave.

"Hold on," I said. "Is there something I need to know about?"

He paused and glanced briefly over his shoulder. "This is an active investigation, so I can't give you any details."

"Active investigation into what?"

He turned towards me, his expression looking like a toss-up between worried and frustrated. "Loy and I are looking into a suspicious death out at the Lazy Ox Yoke."

"Dammit," I said. "What happened? If Vern is alive, does that mean he killed Ned?"

"It was the youngest brother. Peter Houston."

My legs wobbled. "Peter's dead?"

"He is."

My chest tightened with shock. "But how?"

"That's what we are trying to determine."

I suddenly felt sick to my stomach. "Did he try to break up a fight between his brothers?"

Finn's forehead wrinkled slightly. "It was nothing like that."

"Is there anything you can tell me?" I asked a little bit too desperately.

He made an exasperated face. "I questioned you about the time simply to begin the process of establishing a logistical map for everyone's alibis in case the coroner's report comes back looking suspicious."

"You think it will?"

He grimaced. "I think it might."

"Because of the shots I heard?" I asked.

"Because Peter's skull was caved in."

I leaned both hands on the desk. "Oh."

"I will get in touch with you later. Since you will be able to verify the location of the two older Houston brothers shortly before the incident, it would be appreciated if you made yourself available in case we need to speak to you about this in more detail."

He gave me a nod and left.

I sat down slowly, my chest heavy with shock.

Now I had to admit I'd been wrong about the beautiful day after all.

It was apparently perfect weather for a killing.

CHAPTER 3

"Kiddo, you know I wouldn't ask you to do this unless I thought it was important."

I stared at my father with disbelief. "You realize what you are saying, right?"

His cheeks colored and he ran a hand through his mostly gray hair. "I realize. But it's Irene we're talkin' about here."

I fiddled with my coffee cup and didn't reply right away.

My father and I sat across from each other at my kitchen table, and I could see he was upset. He fidgeted and could hardly stay in his chair.

I didn't want to sound like I was picking a fight so I asked the question as gently as possible. "Dad, do you know how many times you have told me, very specifically, not to get involved with murder investigations?"

He slugged back the rest of his coffee and slammed the mug on the table. "Dangit, Marley. It's not exactly getting involved with the investigation, is it? And she can't do this on her own."

I traced my finger over the wood grain on the tabletop and tried to keep my expression neutral. "I'd agree with you there."

Since I'd come home to Killdeer from Helena, I'd managed to get involved in a number of

Sheriff Shucraft's investigations, sometimes by accident and sometimes by design, and the subject was a sore spot between my father and me. Usually his policy was clear. He would order me to stay as far away from a criminal investigation as possible and hound me relentlessly if I didn't. But today was different. Today he was practically asking me to do the exact opposite.

He ranted on, waving a hand as he spoke. "You know she doesn't even like to talk about it. She keeps it quiet that she is related to them so she won't have to be associated with the Houstons."

"Yeah, I know," I said.

He charged on, undaunted. "And now the youngest, Peter, well it's a damn shame there's no doubt about it. But I can't say I'm too surprised. Someone was going to get themselves killed out at that Lazy Ox Yoke one day. I'm just sorry it didn't happen while Irene and I were out of town or something."

"Why does she have to be the one to go out there? Can't the boys take care of Peter's things for him?" I asked.

But I already knew the answer to that question.

Irene was a first cousin to the Houston clan and she did everything within her power to conceal that fact. But those of us who were close to her knew the backstory. Irene's mother, may she rest in peace, had been sister to Barbara Baker-Houston, the mother to the four wayward Houston kids. Both women had died young, struck down by cancer in their fifties. But while the sisters were still alive they had spent hours together at the ranch, during the summer months, kids in tow.

Irene had grown up traipsing all over the Lazy Ox Yoke with her mother when she was only a girl, and because she was a few years older than the four Houston kids she had been relegated to babysitting duty. Irene had practically raised Peter and Felicia, the two youngest Houston children. She had managed to survive Ned and Vern through crafty evasion. Irene was family to the wayward horde, and being family, she was first in line to assist them when tragedy struck.

"So I take it then that Felicia is too upset to handle this alone?" I asked.

"She hasn't been able to get out of bed since yesterday," my father told me. "How can she even think about packing boxes when she's in such a state?"

"I still don't understand why they feel like they have to clean out Peter's cabin so soon," I said.

My father dropped his eyes. "Butch. He gave the word. He wants it done, and he wants it done yesterday."

That explained it.

Of course I would help Irene do what needed to be done. But as far as I was concerned, the Houstons were toxic. Particularly the father, Butch. Volunteering to go out to their ranch during such a difficult time wasn't something to be taken lightly.

Old Man Butch Houston made no secret of the fact that he planned to divide his big ranch equally between his three sons. He'd made the announcement a scant two years ago and the battles had been raging ever since. It was a terrible idea, but Butch was determined the Lazy Ox Yoke would survive and so he wanted to make his sons equal owners of the land before he died, in an attempt to preserve his legacy. Nobody, not even the four siblings, knew when Butch planned to go through with his scheme. That left the three brothers in a perpetual state of uncertainty and now it was clear what that tension had led to.

Reasonable human beings could have managed such a transaction with no bloodshed, and possibly even thrived because of it. The trouble was, the Houstons were not reasonable human beings.

And now Peter, the youngest son, was dead. But how? I still didn't know if it had been an accident or if it was deliberate. Finn had given me so little in the way of details. I really had no clue what I'd be walking into when I volunteered to help Irene.

Butch had apparently ordered his son's cabin cleared of personal belongings immediately. Why? Maybe he wanted to remove any painful reminders of how bad everything had gotten.

Or maybe it was something else.

"When is Irene going out there to start working?" I asked.

My father gave an unhappy sigh. "As soon as you can get to Lil's to meet her."

"Dad, you couldn't have called me or something?"

He stood up and snatched his battered straw cowboy hat from the table. "Irene and I argued about it all last night. I know I've spent the last few years practically dragging you out of trouble by the ear, but for just this once, can you go with her and give her a hand?"

My eyes softened. "Of course I'll do it. But someone was killed out there, Dad. You can't lose your temper if I end up asking folks a few questions."

He shifted his feet. "I suppose."

I'd had my share of murder and mayhem since I'd come back to Killdeer Valley five years ago. For whatever reason, my curiosity always seemed to lead me places a smart person wouldn't dare go. But somehow I'd managed to figure out more than a couple of unsolved local murders, and because of that, whenever there was some kind of trouble my father usually stepped squarely in my path and tried to keep me from getting involved.

It must have pained him to ask me to do this. But he was a smart man, and he knew how hard this would be for Irene to do alone.

"Does she need me to pick up any boxes?" I asked.

"She's got a whole passel of them at the café. She just needs someone to go with her and keep her from falling apart. Peter was like a little brother to Irene and, well, she's taking it hard."

"Let me get into some work clothes and I'll head down to Lil's right now," I said.

His shoulders eased into a slump. "Thank you, Marley."

"Dad, she means a lot to both of us."

He left and I shuffled upstairs to change. I rummaged in the dresser drawer for grubby clothes and didn't have to try very hard to find them. I knew my life was a study in contrasts, but for the time being I wasn't motivated to do anything about that fact.

The home Leif and I'd originally lived in had been completely destroyed by a fire the previous fall. Leif had purchased a new home the same day. This house was located right down the road from our old place. I'd moved in with only the clothes on my back and my wedding ring. Everything else had been a total loss in the fire. Since the new house was completely furnished I hadn't been forced to shop for much. But considering the grandeur of the house, I knew I looked wildly out of place living in it.

To begin with, it was two stories high, with five bedrooms, a massive den, and an office, and had Italian tile kitchen floors. And I'd recently discovered a third bathroom that I'd thought for six months was a closet. The exterior was crafted of heavy logs, and a row of tall windows looked out into the thick forest of pine trees like a high mountain ski lodge. Or an exclusive resort.

It was considered an event if I wore something besides Wrangler jeans and boots when I wasn't at work. Most days I felt out of place rattling around alone in the big empty house.

Leif had more than seen to my future security concerning financial needs, and by my standards I was a very wealthy woman due to insurance policies and bank accounts he'd left me. But I certainly didn't dress like one. A highly paid prosecuting attorney would match the décor of the massive home more closely than me. I wasn't sure living in a magazine-cover abode was really what I wanted. Or maybe I simply had to change the way I looked and dress more like a woman of means. Someday I would make the effort, but not today.

My car keys were still sitting inside my SUV where I'd left them overnight and I chided myself for being careless. I lived in the middle of nowhere but that didn't mean I should forget to lock my car at night. That was a habit I'd have to break.

I drove down the rutted dirt road towards Killdeer, noticing a few more pine trees were rusty red from beetle damage. Since the land surrounding my place was under the purview of the Forest Service, I dearly hoped that they would start a pine beetle mitigation program soon and begin removing the dead trees. If not, the fire hazard for my end of the valley would soon reach critical mass. My home was surrounded on all sides by thick forest, and thinking about a wild land fire was enough to keep a person up at night. There wasn't a thing I could do about the devastation from the pine beetles, and I had bigger problems at the moment, so I put it out of my mind and kept driving.

By the time I pulled up at Lil's the sun was high and it was nearly nine in the morning. Not the best way to get started on a big project. If Irene had called me the night before to ask for my help I would have insisted we start at seven at the latest.

When I pushed through the door into the café Irene was snapping her fingers at a frazzled waitress and barking orders. She was about to leave her café and that meant relinquishing control for a few hours. Something I knew she hated to do.

She motioned me to the back of the café with a jerk of her head and we slid through the swinging doors, past the kitchen area, and through the storeroom while the cook and a terrified busser ducked out of her determined path.

Irene threw open the back door and started flinging boxes out into the parking lot.

"He can't leave it alone for a decent period of time, can he," she muttered. "Has to go and pitch all Peter's things before there's even a funeral scheduled."

I watched her with concern. "Why can't the two boys handle this, again?"

She stopped dead and gave me a hunted look. "When have any of the Houston boys ever picked up so much as a sponge to wipe a teaspoon of jam off a countertop? You think for one second they can deal with packing up all of Peter's things and not end up just taking everything to the dump?"

"I know it's a lot for Felicia to do alone."

She resumed throwing boxes out the back door like they were hand grenades. "That poor girl. Living out there all by herself with Old Man Butch hounding her to take care of him and still telling her how worthless she is all the time. And on top of it, the boys get to benefit from the ranch, but Felicia? No, no, Butch wouldn't dream of letting a woman have a fair share of the family legacy. Peter was the only advocate Felicia ever had. Now what's she going to do?"

I stood beside her and put a hand on her shoulder. "Irene, you're not alone."

She slumped against the doorframe and wiped away an angry tear. "And that cabin filled up with all those old family heirlooms? Those beautiful pots and such from the Southwest? That all came from Aunt Barbara's grandmother from when she moved here from Taos. There's some gorgeous historical things in Peter's cabin but I can't imagine Butch gives two sniffs about any of it."

"Don't worry," I said. "We will take care of it together."

"He won't dare haul those things to the trash while I'm still around," she said.

At least twenty large boxes were tumbled in a pile behind the café. Irene surveyed the mound and nodded with satisfaction. "That should do."

"You want me to meet you out there?" I asked.

"We are taking your car," she said. "I've got your father coming by here in a few minutes to round up these boxes and bring them along in his horse trailer. We can pack everything up inside the trailer and bring it to my garage so I can sort it out later."

"We won't need my father to help us pack," I said. "You and I can handle it."

She waggled a finger at my nose. "Are you kidding me? I don't want your father out there to haul boxes. I need him there to keep Butch in line. You know he won't listen to a word that comes out of a female's mouth and if the old man starts to make trouble your father can talk him down."

I dropped my chin to my chest. It was promising to be a fun day.

She spun around, marched inside the back room and grabbed her scuffed brown purse from a shelf without breaking stride. I trotted after when she headed through the café and out the front door.

She pulled up the handle on the passenger's side of my SUV and when she realized it was locked her eyes flashed.

"I'm coming, I'm coming."

The SUV chirped as I hit the button and she climbed into the passenger's seat and slammed the door.

We drove the long trek out of town in silence, which was perfectly fine with me. I knew Irene was feeling overwhelmed and her way of dealing with feelings of helplessness was to get angry. For twenty minutes she didn't utter a sound.

We turned off the main road towards the twisting dirt track that led to the ranch. I'd driven to the ranch before, but it had been years since I'd last seen the place, and once again I was struck with how remote it was. The road snaked around the shoulder of the mountain and we drove past the spot where I'd seen Ned and Vern engaged in combat the previous day. As we veered towards the east, the road became rougher, and in order to accommodate the encroaching mountains it looped around like a horseshoe, folding in on itself twice in sharp switchbacks.

If we had been on horseback we could have cut straight through the trees and saved ourselves ten minutes of driving. But at long last, the homestead came into view.

The Lazy Ox Yoke Ranch had been in the Houston family since the early 1900's from what Irene had said, and the buildings still standing on the old property looked it. The family house was painted a tired-looking white, but the wood underneath suffered from decades of neglect, and the thin paint only managed to make the house look a bit on the shabby side.

We pulled up in front of an old cabin and Irene nodded towards it. "That's Peter's place. Park here."

The cabin was surprisingly small. It was worn, but rustic in an eccentric way. Before I could stop the vehicle Irene was grabbing for her door handle and started to jump out. I slammed on the brakes just as her feet hit the ground and I watched her dart towards the cabin frantically.

I scanned the area between the main house and the cabin and saw what had made Irene move so fast.

A woman was hunched over a wheelbarrow, trying, and failing, to muscle a heavy load on her own.

Irene ran to her side and waved the woman away with good-natured scolding. I recognized Felicia Houston at once.

Felicia was beautiful in a soft way. Her brown hair was thick and curly and hung to her shoulders in waves. Her dark eyebrows made her look exotic, but her fair skin burned too easily for her to work outside. Like many women who grew up in the West, she wasn't big enough to carry an eighty-pound calf by herself and couldn't rely on brute strength to survive the day. It was no secret that Butch disdained all things feminine, and that included his only daughter. Her worth as a human being was based on the amount of work she could produce, and since she couldn't buck a hay bale into the back of a pickup truck, she'd been relegated to kitchen duty her whole life.

Sometimes I mourned the fact that there wasn't much forgiveness for soft things in rural Montana. Unless it was hard, it tended to perish early. That was true for people, too, for the most part.

Felicia was trying to muscle a heavy load of old books out of the main house with a rickety wheelbarrow, but she'd stacked the load too high and it threatened to topple. Her small frame was far too slight for such a burden.

Irene shooed the girl away and took over.

I raced to lend a hand and grabbed the front end of the wheelbarrow to help steady the contents.

"Where are you going with this?" Irene asked.

Felicia's voice was soft and high-pitched from hours of crying. Her cheeks were still puffy.

She gestured towards the house. "I got them from the closet upstairs. All these books are Peter's and I don't want Daddy to do something foolish."

I glanced at the family house and saw a flicker of movement from behind a curtain. A face peered at us through the window and I realized someone was watching. A man, who looked to be in his late sixties, squinted through the rippled glass, his pale eyes piercing us with obvious disapproval.

Butch Houston. The old patriarch.

I caught myself staring and managed to look down just as his eyes pivoted towards me. When I glanced back up he was staring straight at me with a hard glare.

His face was tanned, lined and rugged, like a grizzled old felt hat left in the sun and rain too long. He turned his gaze away from me at last and glared openly at Irene's back, cast an unreadable look back at me, then turned and vanished inside the house, dropping the curtain back in place to hide his retreat.

The wheelbarrow nearly tipped over and I had to strain to stand it straight.

"Let's put it by the cabin door, then we can load it into the trailer when my father gets here and we won't have to move it twice," I suggested.

Felicia tried to help us but Irene waved her off and I groaned with relief as we stopped and parked the wheelbarrow beside the cabin. There had to have been at least a hundred and fifty pounds of books in the stack.

Irene wiped a palm on her old blue T-shirt and hugged Felicia to her tightly. "Honey, don't you worry about a thing. Marley and I have it all under control. You just sit back and tell us what goes and what stays, and we can take care of all the packing."

"You don't need to do this, Irene," Felicia said weakly.

"Now, don't argue with me, young lady. I'm not leaving till all this is taken care of. It's for Peter, after all."

I felt useless, watching Irene comfort her cousin, not knowing what to do with myself. To give them a moment of privacy for their grief I headed inside the open door of the small cabin and took a long look around.

"Good grief."

The cabin was rural, to put it kindly. The floor was rough concrete and the walls were constructed of simple planks. The ceiling, like as in all ancient structures around the valley, hovered barely six inches above my head and was made of plywood. It was utilitarian, but clean. The furniture was old, as in fourth-generation homesteader old, but everything was arranged neatly. Peter had obviously been a man of simple needs. I noticed on the tiny shelf above the sink there were only four plates, four bowls, four glasses and one small carafe for drinking water. Nothing extra. Nothing that wasn't absolutely necessary.

But the sparseness of the cabin and Peter's meager belongings wasn't the striking thing about the interior. What caught my eye was the mountain of artifacts and objects carefully stored on the far wall behind an old leather sofa.

The entire wall was filled floor to ceiling with heavy shelving that supported folded blankets, what appeared to be very old Native pottery, several examples of worked stone tools and easily a dozen picture frames loaded with arrowhead points. Something that looked very much like a spear with long feathers was propped against the wall, and beside that was a wooden apple box filled to the top with beads. Not just any beads. They looked very old. The colors were vivid and they were strung carefully on long threads, coiled and set inside the box reverently.

Peter obviously had a treasure trove of Native artifacts and now I could understand Irene's urgency. From the look of it, the stash had to possess some real monetary value.

I sensed movement beside me and turned to look at Irene with a stunned expression.

She surveyed the back wall. "It's amazing, isn't it? Can you imagine all this getting buried up at the landfill?"

"I wonder what it's worth?" I asked.

Felicia had come in to stand next to us. She sighed deeply. "Not much. Mother had a woman from the little museum in Killdeer come out and take a look at it a long time ago. She wasn't really an expert or anything, but she said there wasn't much here that was worth getting insurance on. It's more historical than collectible. But it meant a lot to Peter, so I want to make sure it goes someplace where it can be looked after."

The three of us paused as we took stock of the task ahead.

Irene, true to form, took charge.

"Alright ladies," she said gravely. "Let's get started."

CHAPTER 4

We worked diligently for five hours. Irene took over the responsibility of packing the Indian artifacts, and when she needed an extra hand to lift something heavy I went to her aid.

My father had arrived but he kept his distance, wise enough to know when to stay out of the way of furiously cleaning women. He hauled boxes into the horse trailer when commanded, but otherwise his only job was to make sure Butch didn't interfere. Simply having my father posted at the door seemed to do the trick and we weren't bothered by the angry old codger.

Every now and then I glanced over at the porch to see if Butch was glowering at us, but he never made another appearance. Vern and Ned, looking like a couple of dogs that had just been left at the animal shelter, showed up an hour or so before we were finished. They propped themselves side by side on the porch of the old house and watched us with mute expressions. Both men were sweaty and ragged. The strife that had sparked the previous day's conflict was snuffed out by their brother's death, and they stood together stoically and watched us work.

Vern was a slightly smaller version of his brother Ned, but both boys stood a couple inches above six feet. Where Ned was pale with ruddy cheeks and fair hair, Vern was tanned nut-brown with dark hair. They were heartbreaker handsome, and always seemed to have a girl or two willing to tolerate their tempers. Vern in particular seemed to have discovered early on that the words "I love you" sometimes meant "open sesame" to a woman, and never seemed to lack female companionship. But any relationship the boys started always seemed to end spectacularly at some point. As far as I knew, neither one of them had ever contemplated marriage. They were both already married to the ranch, after all.

I was backing through the narrow doorway, staggering under the weight of a huge stone bowl, when I almost tripped over a stray footstool left in my path.

A man darted from beside the horse trailer and held out a steadying hand as I wobbled. "Careful."

I hadn't noticed him before. It was as if he appeared from nowhere.

My smile was automatic and I clutched the bowl tighter. "I got it."

The man took the dark stone bowl from me without asking and handed it inside the horse trailer to my father. It was all I could do to lift the thing, but he handled it like it was hardly a burden.

He gave my father a warning nod as he passed the bowl over. "It's heavy," he cautioned.

He bent to retrieve the footstool and returned a faint smile. "I'm Jackie. Jackie Miller. I work for Mr. Houston."

"I'm Marley Dearcorn."

He brushed his palms on faded gray pants and shook my hand with a gentle grip. His sleepy blue eyes lingered on the cabin door. His face softened noticeably. "How is Felicia?"

I heard a catch in his voice as he spoke.

"She's on the couch. Irene told her she can't work and made her sit there with a cup of tea. We ask her what goes where, but Irene thought it would be better if she didn't have to carry anything."

He nodded approvingly. "Do you think it would be alright if I went in to pay my respects?"

It wasn't my place to give such permission, but I didn't see the harm in it. "I don't see why not."

He removed his hat and eased inside the cabin. I followed him in and scrambled to snatch another box Irene was holding out towards me, and as I adjusted my grip I saw Jackie sit down beside Felicia with his head bowed.

"Two more trips to the trailer and we are finished," Irene told me.

I nodded to her and headed for the door again. As I navigated the uneven exit I glanced back and saw Jackie lift his hand tentatively. He set his palm carefully on Felicia's shoulder as if to pat her reassuringly, but instead of patting her arm, his thumb stroked her shoulder gently, with obvious familiarity. The gesture had been inadvertent and I saw him look to me with sudden concern, perhaps a little fear. Obviously, he was the type of man who knew the hired help should not make a habit of touching the boss's daughter. But the pain in his eyes told me at once he could no more stop himself from comforting her than he could stop from breathing.

And Felicia did seem comforted. Her face relaxed when he spoke to her. She turned her shoulders toward him and leaned in with something akin to relief. Felicia showed without words she was glad he was sitting with her.

I gave Jackie an understanding smile and ducked my head so he would know I had no intention of calling him out for his mistake. It was none of my business what went on between the two of them, and it was good to know that Felicia had an ally.

I handed the box to my father.

He carefully set it inside the trailer with the others. "How close are we to being finished?"

My back was sore and I stretched cautiously. "A couple rugs, the damn couch, and then we scrub the floors."

"It's concrete," my father pointed out.

"I know. But Butch said everything has to get washed down and cleaned out. Irene said if it isn't up to specs, she wouldn't put it past him to just bring a torch out here and burn it to the ground."

My father snorted. "I bet he would too. I don't get why we have to haul the furniture out as well. I thought Felicia said he's turning the cabin into a bunkhouse like the other buildings? Don't he want something for his hands to sleep on?"

"She said he is planning on moving some of the furniture from inside the house out here. The bed, chairs and such from Barbara's room. I guess it still has all the stuff in it from back when Barbara passed away. Maybe he's finally ready to let it go."

"Marley, can you come here a minute?" Irene asked. She was leaning outside the cabin door, her face pensive.

I frowned and followed her inside. "Don't tell me you found another box of books?"

She snagged my elbow and hauled me to the back of the cabin. Felicia and Jackie sat together, their heads bent in conversation. They were oblivious to us. Irene watched them carefully for a full half minute before turning her sharp eyes on me urgently.

"What do you make of this?" she asked, grabbing my hand. She cupped a tiny leather pouch and spilled the contents into my palm.

Perhaps a dozen blue-, green- and lavender-colored stones tumbled into my hand. They were small and rough, but I could see instantly what they were.

"Irene, these are sapphires."

She rocked back on her heels. "That's what I thought. Holy jeepers creepers. What was Peter doing with a bag of sapphires hidden in his freezer?"

"They were in his freezer?" I asked.

She nodded vigorously. "Wrapped up inside a pack of Legerski sausage. I was going to pitch the sausage, but just in case it was still good, you know? I checked it out, and there they were."

"They are still a little dirty," I said.

"It looks like they could have come out of the creek an hour ago," Irene told me.

I gave her a speculative look. "Maybe not quite that recently."

She glanced back at Felicia. "We have to tell her. If Peter found sapphires on the Lazy Ox Yoke Ranch, she needs to know. Do you think Ned and Vern knew about this? There is no way Old Man Butch knew, or he would be tearing this place apart looking for them."

"Hold on, hold on," I said quickly. "We don't even know if these came from the Lazy Ox Yoke."

"Well where the hell else would they have come from?" she asked.

"I don't know, maybe over in Philipsburg? Maybe Peter went over there to do that day-dig thing and got himself a little bag of sapphires from the Gem Mountain site. It's a big tourist attraction you know."

Irene shook her head and hefted the bag. "This is not what you'd expect to get after a day playing in the dirt at some mom-and-pop operation."

I took the leather pouch away from her and carefully tipped the stones back inside. I handed her the bag. "Give it to Felicia. It belongs to the Houstons and she can decide what to do with it."

Irene stared at the bag for a moment. "I suppose you are right. Come on. Be my witness, then."

She stomped over to Felicia and handed her the leather pouch.

"What's this?"

"Open it," Irene instructed.

Felicia shook a few of the pebbles into her hand and let out an involuntary gasp. She looked up at Irene, stunned. "Where did you get these?"

I noticed Jackie turn two shades whiter when he saw the sapphires. His eyes darted between the pouch and Felicia quickly but he didn't say a word.

No one else seemed to notice his reaction. It seemed odd to me. Something told me that he had known about the stones already.

"It was in the freezer," Irene told her.

Felicia marveled over the stones, flicking them over and over in her palm, and a tear trickled down her cheek.

Jackie stood up abruptly and crammed his hat back on his head. "I must go back to work now. Felicia . . . Miss Houston, I'm sorry about your brother."

He ducked his head to make it through the doorway and disappeared like a ghost.

Irene watched her cousin carefully, her mouth clamped shut. She obviously wanted to pump Felicia for information or offer advice about what to do with a bag full of uncut sapphires, but considering the circumstances, she obviously thought better of it.

She sighed and tore her eyes away from the pouch and squared her shoulders with determination. "All that's left now is the sofa. It will take all four of us to get it into the horse trailer."

"I'll go get my dad," I said.

As much as it pained Irene, she gave every impression that as far as she was concerned, the sapphires were none of her business. She went to stand by the huge sofa with her arms folded impatiently.

When we were all in position at the four corners, Irene scanned her cousin carefully, looking for the pouch, her curiosity driving her mad. But it had been stowed away somewhere in a back pocket or inside Felicia's jacket, and for now the matter was officially closed.

"Ready?" my father asked.

The four of us bent and hefted the sofa together. It was an ancient brown leather monstrosity with many scrapes and stains. And it weighed a ton. The door to the cabin was low, but strangely, it was wide enough to accommodate the old couch without necessitating tipping it on its side.

The sofa still had a few items sitting on top. An old horse blanket and a couple of woven pillows tumbled around on the cushions as we wobbled to the door, but we managed to get the thing loaded into the horse trailer without spilling them to the ground.

We set the sofa down at the top of the ramp and everyone heaved a sigh of relief.

One of the pillows was threatening to tumble off the sofa and Irene snatched it up with one hand. She lifted the old horse blanket off the couch and ran a hand over the fabric.

"Nice. Too bad it's a little beat up. But it's still a good blanket," she said.

The horse blanket was rather plain, and looked very old. It was nothing like the other blankets in Peter's collection. The others were dazzling with red, white, yellow and gray star patterns and complex chevron designs. This old blanket was basic and dull. It was a simple stripe pattern and made of only three colors. Black, white and blue. But it was heavy and probably made of good wool, and Irene hefted it a couple of times, admiring the weight.

"You could probably use it as a saddle blanket," she said.

Felicia raised an eyebrow and shrugged. "I don't care. As long as it gets some use."

"I've got a horse," I said.

Irene tossed me the old blanket. "Here, it's yours."

I draped it over my arm and backed out of the trailer. My father lifted the ramp, closed the gate and locked the handle down.

"That's all, then. Where do you want me to take everything?" he asked.

Irene wiped her hands on her pants. They left a couple dark smudges on the tops of her thighs. "Take it to my house and park it in front of the garage until we figure out what to do with it. If I leave it at the café the waitresses will want to go through it like it's their own personal yard sale."

"I can't thank you enough for this," Felicia said, hugging Irene hard.

Irene held Felicia out at arm's length and gave her a careful examination. "You look beat. Let's get the floors scrubbed and then we can call it a day."

"No, no. I'll do that," Felicia said absently. She stifled a sob as she looked back at her brother's cabin. "You all go on ahead. It won't take me long. I'll just run a mop and some soapy water around the floor and it'll be finished."

Irene started to protest, but the look on Felicia's face made it clear she needed the time alone.

"Alright, but if you need anything you call me," Irene said.

As they gave each other a peck on the cheek, I tossed the blanket in the backseat of my SUV.

There was nothing left to do and I couldn't wait to leave. The Lazy Ox Yoke was an oppressive place.

My father wordlessly climbed into his truck and started the engine. A cloud of black smoke shot out the tailpipe as he gunned the motor to life. As he ground the old truck into gear I noticed the front porch of the old house and my heart sank. The two brothers weren't alone now. Old Man Butch Houston glowered down at us from beside his two sons.

My father drove a tight loop and pulled the trailer away, leaving Irene and me to face the three Houston men alone.

It was like feeling a trickle of cold water drip down the back of my neck.

"I still don't know how he died," Irene said absently.

A deep voice spoke behind us. "He fell off his horse."

I glanced at Ned, who had answered. The oldest brother was watching me with blazing eyes. "And I don't recall us giving you permission to take our brother's things."

I watched as my father drove away with the trailer. It was too late to stop him now.

"Leave it," Butch snapped. "I don't want nothing from that cabin around here. They can have it all."

And that was the end of it.

Ned cowed slightly and dropped his gaze.

Jackie Miller was watching the entire exchange from the corner of the cabin, doing his best to look busy with coiling an old rope. He kept glancing towards the cabin where Felicia was still cleaning, but then his eyes fell on Butch and he ambled towards the bunkhouses, passing by the cabin door with his head bowed.

Irene had turned to face Butch and was puffed up with hostility. "He fell off his horse?"

She brazenly walked to the porch and stared up at the men fearlessly. Their contempt radiated down at her, but Irene bore it straight on. "Peter didn't even like to ride."

"Loy was standing right here, on this spot," Butch said caustically, "when Pete's gelding came dragging him back to the house."

"Dragging him?" She folded her arms.

"That's what I said," Butch told her. "Loy said you"—he pointed a gnarled finger straight at me—"told him you heard someone shootin' and he came to make sure we hadn't poached a mule deer. Which was a lie. You told him my boys were fightin' again and he came out here to nose into our business."

I kept my mouth closed tight.

Butch pointed down at the spot where the trailer had been parked. "Right there we were standing. Loy and I was talking. We heard Pete's horse a-comin', and moving slow. When it came around the cabin it was draggin' him."

"His foot was caught in the stirrup?" I asked.

Butch glared. "Course his foot was caught in the goddamned stirrup. How the hell else could the nag have been dragging him?"

Vern was strangely silent. His dark hair was disheveled and he stood like a willow bearing up underneath too much heavy snow. He kept his eyes down and wouldn't look at me.

Butch lifted a heavy wooden cane and shook it at me. "It was a goddamn fool accident. Loy saw it with his own eyes. Pete's head all caved in like that? Saddle all sideways like it had tipped over? What the hell else could have killed my son?"

Everyone looked away, even Ned. The boys seemed embarrassed by the outburst.

The old man's lower lip shook. He wiped it with the back of one hand and glared at everyone in turn. He shuffled away from the porch railing and hefted his heavy cane with one gnarled hand. The knuckles were arthritic and when he moved, it was obvious he was in pain.

Butch's rant came to a swift end and he shuffled back inside the house, letting the screen door bang shut behind him. It was clear that Butch wouldn't be able to move very well without the help of the cane. Not an easy thing, for a proud man like him, to be brought low by bad knees and too many years carrying an entire ranch on his shoulders.

I had no idea what the loss of a son would do to someone like Butch. I knew he had to be hurting, in his own way.

Not far from Peter's cabin I saw two bunkhouses off in the distance partially hidden behind a stand of twisted cedar bushes. The bushes were twisted and bent from years of abuse by howling spring winds. The cedars were crabbed and mangled, so they didn't completely conceal the two bunkhouses, and when I focused on them I saw movement. Two figures lingered in the doorway of the closer building. Even from far away I thought I recognized them. A couple of winters ago I'd had a run-in with one of Butch's hired hands. A man named Willy Pittman. Willy had a knack for getting himself into trouble and dragging others down with him, and as far as I knew, the hotheaded kid had recently been released from jail after serving seven months for a probation violation. The violation had been reported to Loy by my father, and because of that, there was no love lost between Willy, his entourage, and my family.

The two figures watching me from the bunkhouses were the leftovers of Willy Pittman's gang. I only knew their first names, Barry and Eric. Obviously Willy was no longer with the Lazy Ox Yoke, but these two had managed to hold onto their jobs. In the bright spring sunlight I made out Eric's shock of red hair. And the cinder-block shape standing next to him was unmistakably Barry, who, like a great many hired hands around Killdeer, made a living with his muscles instead of his brain.

I wondered how long the two of them had been loitering there, watching us empty out Peter's cabin. They'd been standing there long enough to see us struggling with the sofa, there was no doubt. Why not step up and offer to lend a hand? Not a chance. They wouldn't get a dime extra on their paychecks for doing something nice for someone else. Besides which, it was common knowledge that any friend of Willy Pittman hated the Dearcorns on principle.

Everyone except Felicia seemed hostile towards Irene and me, and I couldn't stand being there for another moment.

My stomach felt queasy and I dug for my car keys. "Let's go."

I dusted the grime off the seat of my pants and climbed in my SUV. Irene hurried in beside me, and the moment she slammed the passenger door she burst into tears.

"Are you alright?" I asked, my hand frozen partway to the ignition.

She nodded miserably. "I'll be alright as long as I never have to see this godforsaken place again."

"You don't mean that," I said.

She turned on me. "The hell if I don't. I know things, Marley. Things about this place . . ."

Her eyes shifted out of focus into some distant memory. She stared at the house with a glazed, haunted look. "Just drive us out of here."

There was nothing I could do to ease the pain of the situation for her, and it made me feel helpless. A feeling I hated more than just about anything.

And I also hated feeling like everyone around me was not telling the whole story.

The door looks and obvious lack of sadness from Peter's brothers were more than a little disturbing. And what about Butch? His anger and abrupt command that Peter's things get disposed of so quickly were not the actions of a grieving father. More like someone who wanted to have the whole event behind him as quickly as possible.

I didn't even want to think about the sapphires.

The entire affair was a twisted spider's web of grief and half-truths. I knew instinctively that no investigation Loy conducted into Peter's death would receive anything close to cooperation from the remaining Houston men. It was plain they were already building a wall of hostile silence.

Even though it wasn't any of my business, my mind was already searching for an answer. What had really happened to Peter Houston? It seemed unlikely that Peter had died as a result of a simple fall from a horse when the feud between the three brothers was taken into consideration.

There were too many unresolved questions. There was a deeper mystery surrounding this death, and my mind was already trying to pull the tangled threads apart to see the truth.

A smart woman would leave it alone. A careful woman would have nothing to do with such a hotbed of trouble.

Maybe, for once in my life, I would do the smart thing, the careful thing, and stay out of the situation.

But that would mean leaving Irene to cope with the loss of her cousin with no clear answer as to why he had died. It was easy to convince myself I needed to uncover the truth about Peter's death for the sake of my best friend.

Getting to the truth, considering the character of all those who were involved, was going to be like hunting a wounded bear in the darkness. But for Irene, that's exactly what I was prepared to do.

CHAPTER 5

I couldn't sleep. The moon, nearly full, drifted in and out from behind the clouds and I lay in bed staring up at the ceiling. My brain was on full alert and the likelihood of even feeling drowsy was slim. There was no help for it, so I climbed out of bed and shambled downstairs to the kitchen to make tea.

The box said "Bedtime Tea" on the outside and had a picture of a peacefully snoozing kitten.

"If only that were true," I mumbled.

The clock was creeping towards 10:30 when lights from a vehicle splashed across the window. Frowning, I gripped my hot tea tightly and went outside onto the front porch to see who was coming to see me at such a late hour.

All I could make out were headlights and my hand clenched on the mug with apprehension. But when the outline of Loy Shucraft stepped out of his truck into the glow, I relaxed.

"You and Wendy have a fight and you need someplace to crash?" I asked.

He reached inside his truck with one hand and killed the engine. The lights died and he shut the door with a weary gesture.

"Marley, we need to talk."

I stepped aside and waved him into the living room.

He climbed the stairs like they were the Swiss Alps and when we settled into chairs he took off his brown baseball cap and set it on his knee, rubbed his eyes and yawned.

"So," I began cautiously, "what happened?"

"Someone broke into Irene's place tonight."

I let that sink in for a moment and took a deep breath. "Okay."

"She's alright. As far as she could tell they didn't take anything. She wasn't at home. The café was getting a shipment from the restaurant supply company and she went in at seven to sign for it and get things stowed in the cooler. She was gone about an hour and when she got home the back door of her house had been smashed open. Your dad's trailer was parked in the driveway. It was torn apart."

"What do you mean torn apart?" I asked, still breathing slow and deep.

"Thoroughly searched," he said. "Like they were looking for something."

"But Irene said they didn't take anything?"

He grimaced. "From her house, at least. It will be a while before she can go through the horse trailer and make an accounting. If they were after something small it won't be missed until she goes through every box. I'm sure she won't remember everything that was packed away in there in the first place. After I got her to quit yelling, I took a look myself and it seems there could have been something valuable stashed in with all that junk."

"I'll go over tomorrow before work and give her a hand putting things back together," I said.

"No, you won't. I locked the trailer inside the sheriff's impound garage. Finn and I are the only ones who have keys. I told her to go over there sometime with him and do an inventory of Pete's stuff, but in the meantime, we won't have to worry about anyone pawing through it again."

"What if they already found what they were looking for?" I asked. "There were quite a few arrowheads and clay pots that are small and would be easy to miss."

"I guess we just have to hope that Irene can recall the majority of what the two of you handled, but it's a long shot. By the way, you didn't take anything from Pete's cabin did you?" he asked.

"Nothing that someone would break into a house for."

"Are you are sure about that?" Loy asked. "Is there anything you can think of that stood out while you two were cleaning? I don't know, like a folder stuffed with savings bonds or a picture of the mayor in bed with a goat or something?"

I shot him a pained look and leaned back in my chair, my heart sinking.

He searched my expression. "Alright, spill it."

"I think I know what they were looking for."

Loy's face shifted through a series of emotions. Finally, he settled on irritated. "That would be helpful information for me to have right now."

I set my tea on the coffee table and rubbed my eyes. "When Irene and I were almost finished with the job, she found a bag of sapphires hidden inside a package of Legerski sausages in the freezer."

"Irene already told me," he said. "I'm just comparing stories here. What did Irene do with them?"

I shrugged. "She gave them to Felicia."

He tried to cross his long legs, bumped the corner of the coffee table with his boot and set his foot back on the floor gingerly. "Did anyone see her give them to Felicia, other than you?"

"Jackie, the man who works for Butch. He was the only other person there."

"So, only you and Jackie, Irene and Felicia know where they are," he said.

"Not exactly. Felicia did something with them but I didn't see what. Unless she told one of her brothers or her father she had them she's probably the only one who knows what happened to the bag. But I can't see her confiding anything in her family."

"Neither can I," he said. "So it could be either of the boys, or Butch, or those felons they've got working for them out at the Lazy Ox Yoke, who went looking for them over at Irene's."

"And it might not be any of them," I pointed out helpfully.

He gave me a sour look. "I think in this case it's safe to make the assumption that it was someone from the ranch."

"You always told me never to assume anything," I said.

"Marley, the youngest Houston brother just had his head bashed in, you and Irene found a bag full of precious stones hidden in his freezer, and now someone is tearing through his stuff looking for something. I think it's a short walk between cause and effect."

I lowered my eyes, thinking about the event that had prompted all of this. "Butch told us you were there when Peter's horse came in."

The sheriff clamped his mouth shut and stood up. He propped one hand on his gun belt and worked his lips back and forth. "We can't discuss this."

"Could you at least tell me what you saw?" I asked.

He shook his head and looked at the floor. "Dammit, Marley."

"Please?"

His pale blue eyes lifted. "There isn't that much to tell. I was asking Butch where Ned and Vern had got to, he was being his usual cooperative self, and here comes Pete's horse around the edge of the cabin, dragging a body."

"Did you know right away that he was dead?" I asked carefully.

Loy gave a single nod. "It was pretty obvious."

"Did it look like an accident to you?"

Loy studied me. "If I was a smart man, I would order you not to snoop around and ask your silly little questions concerning this case. Then you would rush right out, defy my request, and flush the killer so I could bag him like a fall pheasant."

My eyebrows popped up. "Flush the killer? So . . . not an accident then?"

He shook his head. "It looked like a clumsy effort to cover up a homicide. In my opinion. We'll wait to see what the medical examiner has to say first, but if this was an accident it was one for the record books."

"Why do you say that?" I asked.

"Pete's head wasn't just smashed on one side. The back of his head was caved in and so was the left side of his face. If he fell off a horse and hit the back of his head, then it appears he managed to climb back into the saddle, bearing a fatal injury, and then fall off again only to land on the left side of his face onto a rock the exact same size and shape as the original rock that killed him the first time."

"Oh."

Loy let out an exasperated sigh. "And he managed to accomplish that feat not twice, but six times."

"That sounds like an argument to me. Or a fight over a bag of sapphires," I said.

"Definitely heat of the moment," Loy said.

"Six times?" I asked. "That's not just heat of the moment, Loy. That's rage."

The sheriff crammed his baseball cap firmly in place and pulled the brim down. "And that is why I want you to lock your doors from now on. Got it?"

I lifted a hand. "I promise. But it might not be a bad idea to go talk to Felicia about the stones. She needs to know someone is looking for them."

Loy walked to the front door. He paused long enough to answer me over his shoulder. "I already did."

"What did she say when you asked her about them?"

He pushed open the door. "She pretended like she didn't know what I was talking about."

I watched him wade through the darkness to his truck, his broad shoulders lit faintly with moonlight. As he drove away I stood on the porch, thinking.

Cool mist drifted through the treetops. It was two days till the full moon, and a bright glow illuminated the forest around the house with eerie shadows. The night air smelled faintly of damp leaves and decomposing vegetation. The cold winter months had frozen Killdeer Valley mercilessly. Now that spring had managed to struggle back, things held in an icy suspended state for months were beginning to thaw and come alive again.

I was grateful Irene hadn't come home early from checking in her café shipment and surprised the burglar in the act of searching her house. Having your things rummaged through was one thing, walking in on the guy doing the rummaging was another altogether.

Loy was making a safe assumption when he concluded the burglary and Peter's death were probably connected. It was too much of a coincidence. Especially now that I knew that Peter had probably been murdered, and hadn't died as the result of an accident.

Loy was probably right about another thing as well. Most likely it was someone from the ranch. Someone who knew Peter, and was close enough to take a disagreement personally.

What had the person who searched Irene's house been looking for? It had to be the sapphires. What else could it be?

The fact that Felicia lied about the sapphires didn't surprise me much. She lived under such hostile conditions she had probably developed a habit of being evasive simply as a survival mechanism.

So, who could have broken into Irene's house? It could have been anyone from the Lazy Ox Yoke. And it was probable that the person who had killed Peter was the same person who had searched Irene's place and the horse trailer.

Was it one of the Houstons, or someone who worked for them?

I had no idea what to make of Jackie Miller. He seemed genuinely concerned for Felicia, but it was a mistake to come to conclusions based on a single first impression. He had reacted when he'd seen the stones, after all. I had the feeling he knew they were there and was surprised when Irene discovered them. It didn't mean he had killed Peter, though. Honestly, I wasn't sure what it meant.

And what about Peter's brothers? Would Ned or Vern be capable of killing a sibling for profit? I couldn't answer that. I didn't know them well enough to make a judgment that harsh. That thought was best filed under the category of "possible" for the time being.

I didn't want to think about Butch Houston. Or the two lumps, Barry and Eric, who worked for him. But fleetingly I had to admit there wasn't much doubt in my mind that any of them might be capable of violence. Maybe it was faulty thinking to paint Butch with such a broad brush simply because I didn't like the man. But something told me if he considered an action justified, there wasn't much that would stop Butch from doing it.

CHAPTER 6

"The cell tower will be up in four weeks."

I gaped at my father across the fence. "That's fast."

He looked happy, and for some reason it irritated me.

"They are starting work on the gravel road this afternoon, and they need to run an electrical line up the slope. But after that? We won't be waiting very long."

A couple workers in bright yellow vests were straddling the irrigation ditch at the bottom of the pasture, doing what they could to get proper measurements. Their orange tripod and surveyor equipment gleamed garishly against the bright green buffalo grass of the field. Birds fluttered in the trees at the edge of the pasture and the sky was pale blue and perfect. The air smelled like sagebrush and Russian olive trees.

I scanned the rolling pastureland with a heavy heart. Tall pine trees and aspens to the west, the valley stretching out below. It was an idyllic area. Unspoiled.

Well, it had been until now.

My shift at the branch library was over. I had driven by the pasture on my way home and seen him pulling up fence posts. There was plenty of time to argue with him about the need for progress and now was my chance.

"Dad, are you sure about this?"

He grinned at me. "You one of those wackos who thinks cell towers are the government's way of using microwave mind control on the populace?"

"They're ugly," I said.

He laughed. "So are shopping malls. I never heard you complain about those."

"I complain about them all the time."

My father shoved his leather gloves in his back pocket and squinted into the afternoon sun. "Marley, you and I never did cope very well with change. It's a Dearcorn trait I ain't too proud of. But dammit, we have got to think about the future, and what's best for the valley."

"Did the cell phone company send a representative who sold you on the idea that you would be making the world a better place for our neighbors?" I asked.

He glanced away. "Something like that. But mostly I was interested in the eight hundred bucks a month."

"You don't need the money," I pointed out.

"No. But I want it."

I let my eyes drift up the hillside. "I thought the tower was going on the hill above the caretaker's cottage."

He shook his head. "That was never the plan. This area has a straighter shot towards town, and I got to tell you Kiddo, the local law enforcement folks are giddy about this new tower."

I felt my stomach do a small flip-flop. "I'll bet they are."

He must have picked up on the cold edge in my voice. Cautiously, my father leaned in and propped an elbow on top of the fence post. "You alright about Finn renting the cottage from me and living so close by?"

My lips tightened. "It's fine."

He watched me for a moment. "I can tell him no."

"Dad, he's already living there. I can see the Killdeer County deputy's truck parked in the driveway from here."

He glanced over his shoulder across the dirt road. "No you can't."

"It's fine," I repeated.

He was wise enough not to push a topic when it was still a bit sore. It wasn't that I was unhappy about Finn taking over the cottage, but the truth was I wasn't sure how to feel. Since losing my husband, I felt too emotionally battered to even consider romantic interests. But honestly, Finn's presence on our property was more of a comfort than a burden.

As long as I didn't think about it too hard.

My father scrutinized the damp soil beneath his feet and dug a toe of his boot into the ground. "It's nearly dry enough to start bringing in the big gear. I'd expect them to get the gravel down in the next few hours and in a week or so we should see the flatbed come in with the tower. It has to be stable enough for the crane, so I would bet they wait until it's been dry for a week before they roll that in."

"I never thought I'd see the day when you would let someone build a road across the old alfalfa field," I said.

He pulled a pair of fencing pliers from his tool belt and began yanking out the staples holding the barbwire to the wooden fence posts. "Got to modernize sometime."

"You're taking down the whole fence?"

"Got to. If I don't, they will, and I want to salvage this wire so I can put it back up when they are done."

"You could buy more barbwire," I said.

He looked at me aghast. "Why would I want to go and do a thing like that for?"

"Alright, I'll leave you to it, then." I turned to head back to my black SUV but stopped. "Hey, Dad? Is Irene okay? I heard about the break-in."

His face clouded instantly. "She's staying with me for a few days. Just till Loy can get it all sorted out. Probably kids, I'd imagine. But, just in case, right?"

"That's most likely it," I said, not believing it for a second. "Kids making mischief."

He bent to his task and I drove away, a pang of regret settling over me unexpectedly. Why was I so sore about a cell phone tower? It wasn't as if we were selling the land or giving it over to be used as a nuclear waste dump. But it still chafed.

By the time I pulled into my driveway it was pushing two in the afternoon and I still hadn't had any lunch. I'd managed to get back up to a normal weight again after losing more than ten pounds after Leif had died. Eating was still a chore but at least I managed it with more regularity these days.

I pulled myself up the front steps and the moment I stepped through the front door all of my senses went on high alert.

I felt the chill instantly and knew that something wasn't right.

The house was freezing inside. As I walked further into the house my jaw fell open. The living room was a shambles. Books, papers and sofa cushions were scattered across the floor haphazardly like they had been thrown aside. As I headed down the hallway, I saw the back door hanging wide open, the lock smashed apart, and splinters of wood littered the tiles inside the kitchen.

My heart hammered in my chest. Drawers were half open, and cupboards stood ajar, linens were strewn on the floor and a dish lay shattered on the tiles.

All of my senses sharpened and I listened to the house intently. There was no movement that I could discern, but that didn't mean I was alone.

Standing there doing nothing was not a very good plan.

As softly as possible, I lifted the receiver from the phone on the countertop and dialed 911. Not uttering a word, I set the receiver down and backed out of the kitchen as fast as my feet would carry me, turned into the living room and bolted for the front door. I didn't look back. My keys were still in my hand and I sprinted for my SUV.

The screen door banged shut behind me as I grabbed the driver's side handle, and I glanced in the backseat to make sure the vehicle was empty before climbing in. I gunned the engine and backed down the driveway in a spray of gravel and flipped a hard turn at the end of the lane.

By the time I reached my father's pasture my heartbeat was twice normal speed and my skin felt clammy. I drove straight to the bottom of the pasture and slammed the brakes so hard the entire vehicle slid for six feet before stopping. I jumped out, leaving the door hanging open.

My father was watching me with a quizzical look. "You get another bear in your back yard?"

"Someone broke into my house," I said.

His face shifted from curious to flaming angry in the space of a single breath. He carefully set the fencing pliers on top of the post and stepped across the remaining wires. Without a word he

73

walked past me to my SUV and put a hand on the door.

"Dad—"

"Stay put."

Before I could stop him he climbed inside, spun the wheels and was gone.

All I could do was pace the road and twist my hands together. I listened intently. Not a single sound drifted down the valley, but it wasn't any comfort.

After several minutes I noticed the two surveyors looking down at me with curious expressions on their faces. They had moved to the top of the hillside and were standing there, watching. From their new position on the hill the road was clearly visible, and it gave them a good view of the redneck fire drill that had just occurred. I was too worried to wonder what they were thinking.

It couldn't have been more than ten minutes when I heard the siren, but it felt like two days.

Finn's truck roared down the road and when he saw me standing in the ditch like an idiot he rolled to a halt and flipped off his lights. "Someone called the emergency number from your house. What are you doing here?"

Before answering I clambered inside his truck and slammed the door. "My father's up there. We need to go. Now."

Finn didn't waste any time jabbering, and to his credit he drove in utter silence, totally focused on the task at hand.

"Someone broke into my house," I explained.

"Nathan is there now?" he asked.

"Yes. Hurry, Finn. The place was torn apart."

When we rolled up the driveway Finn was already unsnapping his pistol. He spared me a glance. "Put your head down below the window."

"It's not—"

"Now."

There was no arguing with him and I ducked down until I was out of sight.

Finn slowed until he was side by side with my SUV in the driveway and he studied the porch, the trees and the roadway intently before killing the engine. He lifted the mike of his radio and contacted the dispatcher.

"Valerie, this is Unit 2 and I am on scene at a possible 459 at Marley's residence. Request backup."

Her voice came back, laced with static. "Copy, Finn. Loy is on his way. It will be a while. He was at the dump on a call and it should take at least fifteen."

He left the keys in the ignition and shoved his blond hair out of his eyes. "If you hear shots I want you to drive out immediately. Do you understand me?"

I nodded. He wasn't looking at me. I swallowed and answered. "I will."

He looked directly at me then. "You give me your word."

"Alright, I promise. Just go!"

He stepped from the truck and locked the doors before cautiously moving towards the house.

As he approached the porch my father stepped from the front door and waved to signal him. Finn kept his pistol ready and the two of them disappeared inside.

I watched the porch from my crouch on the floorboards, feeling utterly foolish. If there was anyone hiding in the bushes, no doubt they would have seen my head poking up over the dashboard.

Minutes dragged by, but finally my father came down the steps and stood beside the truck. "It's alright."

My heart had started hammering all over again, but I managed to step out and make it up the stairs without tripping on my own feet. Finn stood at attention on the top step.

"Dammit," I muttered. "What the hell is going on around this valley? First Peter gets killed, then Irene gets robbed. What next?"

"I need you to look around carefully and see if there is anything that is missing," Finn told me. "But please do not touch anything. If you notice something that looks out of place bring it to my attention."

"Something that looks out of place?" I asked. "Are you kidding me?"

Finn sighed and rested his eyes on me. "If you see something that doesn't belong, or you notice personal property has been taken."

My gut told me it was a complete waste of time, but I did what he asked and walked through each room in turn. Nothing stood out. Where I could, I checked items a burglar would normally take and took a mental inventory. I had a very small collection of jewelry in a velvet box in my bedroom, but it looked unmolested. The office was mostly intact, and nothing small seemed to have been touched. The larger drawers had been rummaged through but nothing appeared to be missing.

By the time I was finished checking the bathrooms, as silly as that seemed, Loy had arrived and he and Finn were standing on the front porch, their heads bent in quiet conversation.

Loy's face was bright red with anger. When he saw me his expression shifted instantly from concern to relief. "Are you alright?"

"I will be as soon as you catch the bastard."

I felt my father put a palm on my shoulder. "The place was empty when I got here, Loy. It had to have been hours ago. The door was open long enough that even the upstairs was cold."

Loy gave Finn a pointed look and jerked his chin towards the trees. "Check it out."

Finn was gone in a flash, but he slipped out the back door and I assumed Loy had sent him to search the surrounding forest for traces of my trespasser.

"There was nothing taken," I said. "My jewelry box is still here and so is the television and the DVD player."

The sheriff's jaw muscle worked back and forth. "You got a wall safe in this place?"

"Just a file cabinet. But I never lock it."

Loy was not really listening to me. He had already made up his mind about something and his face was rigid.

"You want to tell me what's really going on?" I asked.

"I need you to think about this before you answer," he said.

My shoulders shrugged of their own accord. "Alright."

"Marley, did you lock your SUV last night? It's important. Think about it carefully."

"I don't have to think about it," I said. "Of course I locked it."

His eyes snapped to my face. "And the SUV wasn't broken into? The doors were alright and the windows weren't broken when you went to work this morning?"

"Don't you think I may have mentioned it by now if someone had smashed my car windows?" I asked.

He grimaced and looked at his boots. "Well, shoot."

I waved a hand towards my disheveled home. "Loy, is there some reason that should upset me more than this?"

He rubbed his jaw with one big hand and propped a palm on the butt of his pistol. "That means whoever broke into your house might come back, because he didn't get a chance at your vehicle yet."

I felt my shoulders slump. "Oh."

The sheriff fixed me with a hard look. "Finn is going to be staying with you for a while."

"Loy, that's not necessary."

My father nudged me with his elbow. "You need to listen to him."

I glanced between them. The sheriff wore a tired expression. Tired and furious.

It went against my wishes, but I could see that Loy had plenty to worry about and the last thing he needed was to have me argue with him over my safety.

I nodded reluctantly. "Alright, then."

He blinked surprise that I caved in to his suggestion so easily, and before I could change my mind he went down the stairs and waited by his truck, his eyes searching the trees.

Finn appeared from nowhere, stopped beside Loy and shook his head. "Nothing. He may have driven up. There are a number of tracks in the drive but they are indiscernible, and there was no sign in the trees that I am able to see. The back door was obviously kicked in, so he was able-bodied and not concerned about making noise. Was anything taken?"

The sheriff chewed the inside of his cheek. "No, Marley thinks she accounted for everything."

"I will finish my threat assessment of the property and retrieve an overnight bag in a few hours. There is a high likelihood that he hasn't found what he was looking for, and in all probability he will return to search again."

"That's what I'm afraid of," Loy said.

"I can hear you," I said from the porch.

They both ignored me.

"Maybe you should take her to the caretaker's cottage?" Loy suggested.

Finn shook his head once. "The doors are inferior there. This building has a more sound construction and I can use the upstairs to my advantage. The master bedroom is ideal as a safe room. Worst case."

The sheriff nodded. "This may take awhile. You prepared to stay here for a few days?"

"Of course. It's sensible," Finn told him.

They shared a look that told me they had more information than they were willing to tell mere civilians.

Loy climbed inside his truck and my chest tightened up as he drove away.

"Dad, what's going on?" I asked. "This can't have anything to do with Peter, can it?"

My father stood beside me, but his eyes were locked on Finn and his face was troubled. He put an arm around my shoulder protectively. "It don't do us a bit of good to think it doesn't."

CHAPTER 7

"Hugo decided he wanted to start getting in shape, because someday he wants to be a famous explorer, and he says explorers are always hiking places," said Wendy.

I smiled. "If there is anyone on the planet who should be a famous explorer, it's your nephew."

Wendy Martinez beamed. Her perfect blonde French braid hung over one shoulder attractively, swaying as she unpacked a box of yarn from a shipment she had just received.

I sat in an old comfy chair across from the counter in Wee Wooly's Yarn Shop, taking turns between staring out the window and staring at my toes. Finn had told me to wait for him in a public place until his shift with the sheriff's department had ended for the day. I'd come to Wendy's yarn shop on Main Street, thinking it couldn't get much more public than downtown Killdeer, but for the last two hours it had only been Wendy and me.

I'd gotten to be close friends with her nephew, Hugo, and we were catching up on the eleven-year-old and his exploits since I'd last seen him. Since Hugo came to stay with his Aunt Wendy in Killdeer for a few weeks each summer, I'd probably be seeing him in less than a month and I was truly looking forward to his visit.

"So he wanted to get in shape," I prompted, encouraging her to continue with the story.

She laughed out loud and rested her palms on the edge of the box. "He lives close to a park in Pennsylvania, but not a big park, one of the more quiet neighborhoods, and he convinced my sister to take him there in the afternoons so he can hike up one of its steep trails."

"I can see him coercing her into it," I said.

"Well, one afternoon he is really hoofing it up this hill, totally focused on the trail, and he doesn't even see this skunk coming at him until it's only a few yards away."

"He ran into a skunk?"

Wendy laughed again and pinched the bridge of her nose with two fingers. "So he freezes, right? And the skunk, it totally freezes too and they are both just standing there looking at each other."

"Oh my gosh."

"And Hugo tells me, there's this awful moment when they are both waiting for something to happen but nothing's happening."

"What did he do?" I asked, thinking that a city kid coming face-to-face with wildlife unexpectedly couldn't end well.

"He told me that he wanted to seem as nonthreatening as possible. So he holds out his hands, and he says to the skunk, I'm a vegetarian!"

I laughed. "Did it work?"

"The skunk turned, Hugo turned, and they both ran the opposite direction as fast as they could. That was the end of his fitness kick."

I leaned back against the chair, picturing the scene. "He's not a vegetarian."

Wendy resumed unpacking the box. Skeins of purple and red yarn tumbled onto her sorting table. "He may as well be. Try as I might, the kid seems to live on cheese and sugar when he comes to stay with me."

A shadow moved across the floor and the front door bell tinkled, announcing the arrival of another person.

Finn stepped inside the yarn shop, looking around him with an expression of discomfort. He kept both hands firmly at his sides as though the yarn might contaminate him and suddenly induce a desire to take up needlepoint.

Wendy gave him a sympathetic look. Most of the men in Killdeer seemed terrified of spontaneously combusting if they touched something innately feminine. That irrational fear had always amused me.

"I am here," Finn said, stating the obvious while keeping a safe distance from the display of knitting needles.

I got to my feet. "Thanks for letting me hang out here, Wendy. Tell Hugo I said hello and if he wants to come stay with me a few nights this summer when he comes to visit, I'd love to have him."

She gave us a wave and Finn relaxed noticeably as we left. His shoulders eased back from their crouch and his face returned to his normal, flat expression that was so irritatingly impossible to read.

"I would have arrived sooner, but there was an altercation at the Broken Spoke Saloon."

"This early in the afternoon?"

Finn shrugged a shoulder. "Apparently, five p.m. is the customary time to begin the Thursday night shuffleboard tournament. Barry Wayland, the hired hand from the Lazy Ox Yoke, became insulted when his opponent suggested that he'd enjoyed the company of Barry's sister the previous evening."

I sucked in my breath. "I'll bet that didn't go very well."

"When I walked inside Barry had been pulled off of the man by two other patrons, and he was yelling."

We came to a stop beside my SUV and I rummaged for my car keys. "What was he yelling?"

"Something like, 'I've walked over better men than you just to see a fight.' The other man was no longer able to stand."

"Was he still conscious?" I asked.

"Yes. And shouting obscenities. I sorted it out."

For the first time I noticed the knuckles on Finn's left hand were slightly red. I decided I didn't want to know the rest of the story.

The two of us stood awkwardly on the sidewalk. The whole situation felt contrived and I struggled to gather my thoughts.

"So, how does this work?" I asked, fiddling with my keys.

His law enforcement truck was parked behind my black SUV, inches from my back bumper. He scanned the street and put on his mirrored sunglasses.

"How does what work?"

"I've never had a protection detail assigned to me, Finn. I don't know what you expect me to do."

He studied me for a moment. "I expect you to follow whatever instructions I give you, without hesitation."

It took a great deal of strength not to roll my eyes. "Listen. The only reason I agreed to let you come stay with me was to keep Loy's head from exploding. I'm not going to be a pain in the ass, and I'll do what I can to make this as easy on you as possible. But the fact is, nothing bad is going to happen and mostly this is an arrangement that I'm willing to put up with so that our local sheriff can have one less worry weighing him down."

He tilted his head to the side a millimeter. "I see."

"It's not like there is some crazed killer out there stalking people and chopping their heads off," I said.

"Just a crazed killer caving in people's skulls," he said evenly.

I looked at my hands. "Alright, look. Peter's death was terrible. But I can't imagine that it has anything to do with me. Obviously somebody from the Lazy Ox Yoke thinks that Irene or I have those damn sapphires that we found in Peter's freezer."

Finn waited for a moment before responding. "The trouble with you, Marley, is that you do not know what it is that you don't know."

"Could you say that again, in English this time?" I asked.

He rubbed his jaw. "My first suggestion is that you cease jumping to conclusions."

"When do I ever jump without a damn good reason?" I asked.

He lowered his head for a moment. When he looked back up his mouth was set in a serious frown. "What I expect, is that if I instruct you to do something for me, you will comply and you will do it instantly without asking any questions or arguing. What I expect, is that if we find ourselves in a situation where you are in danger, you participate actively in your own self-preservation. The best way to accomplish that goal is by compliance."

I actually felt my face grow hot. "Compliance."

He sensed my anger and held up a hand. "Between the two of us, who is the more qualified to identify and deal with a credible threat?"

"I'd say you suck at it, because if you tell me I need to be compliant one more time there will be a serious threat standing right in front of you, Finn."

He sighed. "This isn't going very well."

"Maybe if you bothered to tell me why you and Loy are so sure there is more to worry about than a cat burglar, I could see my way clear towards following your instructions."

"Marley," he began.

"And another thing," I said. "Why isn't Irene in protective custody like me?"

"Because they managed to search her vehicle and we don't believe they will target her again."

"And how did you come up with that brilliant deduction?" I asked.

"Based on the fact that they moved on to target you."

I had the sense to close my mouth and managed to keep it closed while I thought about that. As much as I hated to admit it, I wasn't angry with Finn. I was angry that someone had trespassed in my home, pawed through my things, made a mess of my late husband's office and generally caused me to feel violated. I wasn't angry with Finn, but I sure was managing to make him the target of my irritation in spite of that.

My chest felt tight as I took in a deep breath. "Sorry. I'm not sure why I am yelling at you."

His tone softened. "I understand. You are upset. It isn't easy to think clearly when you are in an unbalanced emotional state."

"You think I'm unbalanced?" I asked defensively.

"It's nothing to be ashamed of. I wish I could tell you more about why Loy and I are being so cautious, but it would be better if we don't discuss the case. It will only worry you and could compromise your ability to focus on what's important."

"And what is important?" I asked.

He looked at me quizzically. "Your safety, of course."

I felt a little of the heat drain from my face. "There is something I need to be worried about, isn't there?"

"More than likely we are being overly cautious. But it is better to take greater steps than necessary if there is any doubt."

My anger deflated and I shoved my hands inside my jacket pockets. "Okay, what do I really need to do?"

"I already gave you instructions," he said.

My irritation threatened to bubble to the surface again, but I managed to tamp it down. "Right now. Here at this moment. What's our next step?" I asked.

He nodded towards the road that led out of town. "You drive home, and I will follow you. I want you to park your vehicle at the front of your house as usual, but I want you to leave it unlocked. The idea is that if the perpetrator comes tonight, he will be able to search it without making any noise and perhaps he will be satisfied that what he is looking for is no longer in your possession, or never was."

"And then hopefully give up bothering me," I said.

"That's what we are trying to accomplish. I will leave my truck parked in front, next to yours, to deter him from coming inside the house. I don't anticipate a problem."

My heart sank at those words and I dropped my chin to my chest. When I looked back up I shook my head with exasperation.

Finn stared at my expression, frowning. "What's wrong? I told you I don't anticipate trouble."

"Nobody ever does, Finn. Nobody ever does."

CHAPTER 8

As we drove out of Killdeer in tandem the bright sun glinted through my passenger-side window at an annoying angle, just below the right side visor, and just above the lip of the door. It made my eyes water but there wasn't a thing I could do about it. Once more I was thankful I knew the rutted dirt road by heart and could probably drive it in total darkness, or half-blind, like I was at the moment. As we drew nearer to the turnoff that led towards the little caretaker's cottage I kept my eyes focused on the tree line to avoid the glare.

When I turned at the fork leading towards my house, some inexplicable impulse hit me with an overpowering surge of alarm and my foot hit the brake.

Finn's truck nearly crashed into my back bumper. He managed to stop a yard from my SUV and I could see him in my rearview mirror. Needless to say, he looked unhappy.

I sat in the middle of the road unmoving, gripped by the feeling that there was something very important I needed to pay attention to at the moment, but I wasn't entirely certain what it was.

Finn sat in his truck for a full minute, staring at me. Finally, he carefully put his truck in park, stepped out and came to my open window.

He took of his sunglasses and looked at me. "Why are you stopped?"

I pointed towards my father's caretaker cottage where it sat to the left of the fork. It was visible from where we were, but not clearly. Something had snagged my attention, and I stared at the little cottage intently. "When was the last time you were home?"

He glanced over his shoulder. "Three and a half hours ago."

Something felt off to me. I couldn't place it, but instinctively my senses told me that there was something wrong.

I watched the cottage for a moment, thinking.

It looked exactly as it always did. The deck was partially hidden by the branches of a tall cottonwood tree. The driveway, such as it was, had taken a beating from the winter months and it occurred to me that my father would need to bring in a truckload of fresh gravel soon.

There wasn't a car parked anywhere near the place. Our end of Killdeer Valley was deserted aside from my father's ranch house, my home, and the caretaker's cottage. Seeing another vehicle drive down our road was an event, and for the moment it appeared that Finn and I were the only two people within a dozen miles.

The cottage had recently received a fresh coat of paint. White trim sparkled against the new shade of terra-cotta that my father had carefully applied before winter. The trees behind the house had sprouted a fresh crop of leaves and a cottontail rabbit hopped across the front yard. I looked hard at the trees behind the house and couldn't see anything out of place. A flash of movement drew my gaze, but as I stared at it, the outline of a clump of leaves was all I could make out. There was nothing there but a bush.

What had caught my eye?

Finn sighed and put his sunglasses back on and gave the cottage a long look. "Would it make you feel better if I went to see if everything is alright?"

"I need to feed the horses anyway. It will only take a minute. Do you mind?"

He stalked back to his truck without uttering a word and pulled away, veering towards the little cottage abruptly.

I drove the short distance up the road and parked in front of the barn. Lil Nipper and Peanut nickered a friendly greeting when I crawled between the strands of barbed wire. Their water barrel was full. Obviously my father had been here. Hay had already been put out and I spent a moment scratching Peanut behind his left ear. He leaned into it like a giant dog, relishing the attention. His eyes closed and he heaved a happy sigh.

Lil Nipper took the opportunity to bite Peanut on the flank, and as the mustang shuffled sideways, the pony muscled his way to the front and demanded his equal share of attention.

I scratched them both, keeping one eye on the road.

The air smelled like last year's hay and juniper. A breeze carried the taste of warming pine resin from the stand of tall trees the lined the pasture off in the distance.

I went inside the barn and saw that my father had nailed a couple heavy hooks on the wall above the old wooden toolbox. He'd hung the pony's saddle and bridle up on the wall, out of reach of pesky mice, and I stood back to admire them. The saddle was hand-tooled artfully and it made an attractive display.

"Cute," I said, grinning.

What had happened to the old horse blanket I'd brought here after leaving the Lazy Ox Yoke? I recalled I'd tossed it on top of the saddle after coming back from helping Irene, but now it was gone. I searched the barn halfheartedly. It was full of hay, a few tools and supplies that my father kept handy for repairing fence, and two huge barrels with the word "oats" written on the side in white paint. The oat barrels were sealed tight with heavy lids that snapped shut to keep the rodents from discovering the bonanza of free food. I scanned the floor of the barn, and I even looked up in the rafters in case my father had tossed the blanket across a beam so it wasn't under foot.

No horse blanket.

Well, it would turn up.

I headed back outside and watched the road.

Finn should have been able to check the cottage in a couple of minutes and would be back soon.

I felt a little embarrassed now. More than likely I'd reacted for no reason and everything was fine at the cottage. But recent events had made me jumpy and I told myself sometimes a little too much caution was a good thing.

Finn's truck finally pulled out of the driveway of the cottage, turned, and headed towards me.

Peanut and Lil Nipper had settled down into a contented snooze, their heads bent and tails swishing at spring flies. They looked happy, so I left them to their afternoon nap and climbed between the wires to wait. Finn stopped his truck beside me and rolled down his window.

"The house was unmolested," he said.

"Well that's good news. Thanks for checking. It's a relief to know it wasn't broken into."

"I didn't say it wasn't broken into, just that it was unmolested."

I blinked in surprise. "Someone broke in?"

He let his eyes drift over the pasture. "I left the house unlocked so that he could go through it systematically without causing any damage."

"Finn, that's crazy. Why would you do something like that?"

He spared me a look over the top of his mirrored shades. "I would think the answer to that question is obvious. Now, let's go."

He left me standing on the side of the road and drove off.

I cast a final glance back at the cottage, and a shiver jolted through my bones at the thought of someone digging through the drawers and tossing the mattress off the bed to see what was underneath.

My gaze lingered on the cottage for another moment, but nothing unusual stood out, and I couldn't determine what it was that had caused me to think something was wrong.

Finn's truck was already a couple hundred yards away and I scrambled to catch up.

He parked in front of my house and I pulled in beside his truck with a feeling of nervous dread.

I was nervous about the burglar, although probably not as much as I should have been. But the thought of spending a night alone with Angus Finn was truly unsettling.

Which was ridiculous.

There was nothing whatsoever to be nervous about. It wasn't as if he had designs on me.

Our past blundered attempt at a relationship had sealed the deal on that possibility.

So why were my palms leaving little puddles of sweat all over the steering wheel?

Annoyed, I climbed out and trudged up the front steps, glaring at my keys and feeling foolish.

I unlocked the door and Finn put a hand on my arm. "Wait here."

His touch sent an unexpected shock of electricity through me.

I did my best to ignore it.

He went inside and after a minute he came back to the porch.

"Alright. You can come in."

My patience was thinning. "Do we have to go through this ritual every time I come home? It's going to make unloading groceries a huge pain in the neck."

"Did you remember to leave your vehicle unlocked?" he asked.

I made a face, lifted my key fob and pushed the button with a wave of my wrist.

The SUV chirped obediently as it unlocked and I tossed the keys in the glass bowl by the front door.

Finn carefully locked the front door behind us and I went into the kitchen while he proceeded to check the house for Viet Cong tunnel traps, or whatever it was bodyguards did.

I was doing my best not to get snippy, because Finn's previous jobs had been as a professional bodyguard and security chief, and his behavior was a product of habit and training. I tried to imagine how the President and the First Lady felt living with a dozen guys just like Finn crawling all over the house talking into their wrists and checking the cereal bowls for listening devices, and I shuddered. What a horrible way to put in time.

The refrigerator was depressingly empty, so I made sandwiches and chocolate milk for us both, and opened a box of crackers. We ate standing up beside the kitchen counter.

"What do you wear to bed?" Finn asked.

I choked on a crust of bread and took a quick drink of milk. "Excuse me?"

He stared at me. "What sort of clothing do you wear when you go to sleep at night?" he asked again.

My face blushed hot. Finn had seen me naked plenty of times, but oddly enough he had never seen me prepare for bed like a normal person. When we had been a couple, Finn and I typically fell into bed after ripping our clothes off, but we'd never spent the night together. Whenever I'd awoken the next morning he was always gone.

He had never seen me in a pair of pajamas before. "Why in the world do you need to know that?"

Finn rolled his shoulders like he was loosening up for a boxing match. "If we are forced to leave the house in a hurry, you might want to wear something that is suitable for the weather. Sweatpants? And you might want to have a pair of shoes beside the bed that you can slip on quickly."

"How long am I going to have to deal with this babysitting detail?" I asked.

He stared at me. "Marley, we need to talk about your attitude."

My lips pinched together. "What about my attitude?"

He leaned on the counter and a lock of blond hair fell across his eyes. He shoved it aside and drummed the fingers of his right hand on the countertop. "I don't think your heart is in this."

"I can't argue with you there," I said.

"What if I told you that your reluctance to cooperate isn't only putting you at risk, but me as well?" he asked.

I tossed the bread back inside the refrigerator a little harder than I'd intended. "Enlighten me."

He stood up and brushed a crumb off the front of his black shirt. "Let's assume that someone does break into the house while you are home."

The lunch meat sailed into the refrigerator like a fastball. "Okay, let's assume that."

"What if I instruct you to move as quietly down the stairs as possible and you stop to argue with me about which side of the steps you prefer?"

The cheese rocketed inside the fridge as fast as the lunch meat. "Let's be serious. I would never do that."

"Wouldn't you? I can see from your stance and hear in the tone of your voice that you are not taking this seriously at all," he told me.

"And why does that put you at risk?" I asked.

"Because while I am telling you, for the second time, to move to the left side of the staircase, our attacker uses that moment of hesitation on my part to put a bullet into the back of my skull."

I closed the refrigerator door softly and gave him an apologetic look. "Do you and Loy really believe we are looking at someone who is capable of killing another person over a lousy bag of uncut sapphires?"

"People have killed for less," Finn said evenly.

"They can't be worth that much money," I said.

Finn drained the rest of his chocolate milk. "Irene estimated there were sixty stones or so. The bag could be worth as much as ten thousand dollars if that number is accurate."

"Ten grand?" I asked.

"Even so," Finn said quickly, "no, we don't believe he is willing to kill for the stones alone. Even for Killdeer, as impoverished as it is, that seems desperate and petty. We think it is something else."

"Do you think that Peter discovered a deposit of precious stones on the Lazy Ox Yoke, and then one of his brothers bashed his head in so they could take the quarry for themselves?"

Finn grimaced. "At this point, we need to stay open to that possibility."

"So he might not be concerned about the monetary value of the stones we found in Peter's freezer," I said. "He might want them back so he can keep the discovery a secret."

"Or maybe it has nothing to do with the stones at all," Finn pointed out. "Not every evil that occurs has greed at the root."

I rubbed my tired eyes. "I can't understand what else could motivate a person to commit murder."

"Revenge. Jealously. Greed isn't the only thing that drives an individual's desires."

"So, what you are saying is, that you and Loy really don't know why this guy is breaking into houses and why he killed Peter?"

"I do not assume that the same person is responsible for both crimes, even though that is what the sheriff believes," Finn said.

I digested that little tidbit for a moment. "No wonder you are being so paranoid."

"This would be much easier if Felicia Houston would simply tell us what she did with the stones after Irene gave them to her," Finn said.

"She's lived her entire life being terrorized by her jerk father," I said, coming to Felicia's defense. "Her brothers are one step away from committing a felony every other day and the one person she trusted and relied on just got killed in a spectacularly brutal fashion. I can forgive Felicia if she is confused and not thinking all that clearly right now."

Finn nodded. "Fair enough. Eventually, though, she will have to tell us what she did with the sapphires. Loy is in the process of getting a search warrant, and when it is granted he will tear the Lazy Ox Yoke Ranch apart until he finds them. He is particularly determined on that front."

"Maybe you should ask Irene to go talk to her? She might see reason if her cousin explains it carefully."

"And put Felicia at risk? That's not acceptable. Whoever has been searching for the stones probably believes they have left the Lazy Ox Yoke. If Irene, or Sheriff Shucraft for that matter, were to discuss it with Felicia openly the focus of the search might shift to her and that would be undesirable."

I washed the two plates and the single knife, dried them off and stuck them back where they belonged. The dishes felt like they weighed as much as a cinder block. Every bone in my body was fatigued from stress. "My brain can't think about it anymore tonight, Finn. I know it's early, but I'm going to go get ready for bed and read until I fall asleep."

He stood up straight and pierced me with his sharp gaze. "I want you to spend as little time as possible concerning yourself with the thought of an intruder breaking into your house. If there is any reason to be concerned I will wake you. Don't waste your time and energy worrying."

"Thanks," I said halfheartedly. "I'll do my best."

I went upstairs, feeling like my arms and legs could drop off at any moment. As I pulled on a pair of sweatpants and set my sneakers at the foot of the bed, every groan and creak emitted by the big log home made my skin crawl.

Fleetingly, I wondered how much I could get if I sold the huge house. It was beautiful, but not for the first time I wondered what a single woman was doing living alone in a home big enough for a family of six.

Pushing the thought aside, I concentrated on getting prepared for bed and tried to do as Finn had instructed, and put my worry away for the evening.

It was not an easy thing to accomplish.

Since it was spring, the air was full of new moisture and the wood beams high overhead were swelling with humidity. Every ninety seconds another log popped and creaked as the wood expanded. It sounded exactly like someone creeping across the floor trying to be quiet while they snuck up on me.

It was going to be a very long night.

CHAPTER 9

The telephone jangled and I sat up like I'd been hit with a cattle prod. The bedroom was pitch-black.

Halfway through the second ring I snatched the receiver and fumbled with the button. Somehow I managed to press the phone to my head.

"This had better be good."

My father's voice hummed in my ear. "Kiddo? Are you alright over there?"

I stared at the clock, willing it to come into focus.

"I'm alright. Dad, it's not even five in the morning."

He talked fast. "I just got home. Is your deputy there? I need to talk to him. Put him on, would you?"

I ignored the "your deputy" line and let the phone drop into my lap.

"Finn!"

Footsteps thudded somewhere outside my bedroom and the door flew open.

He stopped in the doorway and scanned the room. "What's wrong?"

I lifted the receiver, irritated. "It's for you."

Finn averted his eyes as he approached the bed and groped for the phone without looking directly at me, which was ridiculous because I was fully dressed.

He turned his back. "Yes?"

I could hear my father's excited voice.

Finn nodded, staring at the carpet. "This morning, would you say?"

My jaw popped as I yawned and struggled out of bed. I padded barefoot to the bathroom and when I came out Finn was still standing with his back to me.

"Someone searched your father's ranch house last night," he said.

"Was he home at the time?"

"He was with Irene at her house in town. It was the same pattern. Someone kicked in the back door and obviously looked through the entire home, discarding items as they went through them. He's unharmed."

"I have had just about enough of this jerk," I said. My heart hammered like a piston. "It's like the Dearcorns and all known close associates are being stalked."

He turned around then and faced me. His normally sharp blue eyes looked a little tired. "Nothing was taken. Not even your father's Springfield rifle. This is obviously the same person who searched your home."

"You think?" I asked sarcastically.

"Becoming angry isn't going to help the situation," he said.

"It might make me feel better if I got angry. It's better than being afraid."

"I can assure you, your safety is not an issue."

I waved my hands with frustration. "How long will it be until this guy climbs in my bedroom window and clocks me over the head?"

He looked mortified at my comment and clamped his mouth shut.

His expression was so pained I took in a big breath before speaking again. "I'm sorry. You didn't deserve that. I know that's not going to happen. I'm just really angry right now."

He swallowed hard and his eyes roamed over my face. "Understandable."

He handed the phone receiver back to me.

I absently set it in the cradle and slumped back on the bed. "It will be a huge relief when this is all over."

"Hopefully I will be able to let you return to your normal routine in a few weeks."

I sat up. "A few weeks? Please don't tell me you are being optimistic here."

"I'm being realistic," he said.

"So what does that mean for today?" I asked.

"You do not have to cover a shift at the library in Fable, so I suggest you go spend the afternoon with your father at his home and avoid situations that might make you vulnerable."

"Like walking around socializing with other people and generally living my life in a normal fashion," I said.

"Let's call it preventative situational awareness," he told me.

"Whatever that means."

"It means we take steps to anticipate events that—"

"Finn, it was rhetorical." I looked him over carefully. "How much sleep did you get last night?"

His brow furrowed slightly. "I didn't sleep, of course."

"How can you not sleep for more than twenty-four hours and then go to work the next day and expect to function?" I asked.

The corner of his mouth tilted up. "I have worked under far worse conditions."

"This isn't a foxhole on the front lines. Why didn't you lie down on the couch for a while last night?" I asked.

"I was watching your vehicle to see if he came back to search it," he replied.

"All night? Didn't you take a potty break?"

"Marley, I need to go shower and head to the station. Please lock the door when you leave. Can you do that for me?"

I suppressed a smirk. "Yes, I can do that."

He backed out of my bedroom and I flopped back on the mattress for a few moments, thinking.

I had spent my entire adult life tackling challenging situations head-on. Slinking around went against my nature. The last thing I wanted to do was sit around and wait for some greedy coward to sneak into my house again and paw through my underwear drawer.

It seemed incredible to me that someone would be willing to kill, and risk being shot breaking into people's houses, all for the sake of one lousy bag of gemstones.

There had to be more to the story than that.

After mulling it over before falling asleep the night before, I'd made up my mind someone from the Lazy Ox Yoke Ranch was responsible for Peter's murder, and for the burglaries. I agreed with Loy more than Finn, and to me it seemed likely that the same person was behind both crimes. But to prove it, I needed to know more about the Houston family.

The problem wasn't going to solve itself. It was time for me to actually do something about it.

I showered and clambered into jeans and a long-sleeve gray T-shirt, made coffee in the kitchen and filled a to-go cup full of steaming French roast before snatching my car keys from the bowl by the front door.

My car looked unmolested, but before opening the door I checked the backseat, just in case. As I scanned the interior of my SUV something on the bottom of the door caught my eye and I knelt down for a closer look.

A thin piece of invisible tape had been pressed over the seam between the door and the frame. If someone had opened the door, the tape would have been broken.

I stood up and checked the other doors, and they all had similar pieces of tape pressed over the seam as well.

Finn had obviously set it up so that if someone had rummaged around in my vehicle, he would have known about it.

I climbed inside my SUV and slammed the door. That Finn felt it was necessary to take such precautions only served to make me more determined to end this.

I drove to Lil's café, even though I knew it was a possibility Irene wouldn't be at work yet. It was still ridiculously early.

When I parked in the dirt lot behind the café her little red pickup truck was nowhere in sight and I knew she hadn't arrived.

No matter. I could wait.

I sat in the seat, sipping coffee, and thinking.

This had not been my choice. I hadn't wanted to get involved, but complaining about it wasn't going to do any good. Even though I hadn't started it, I was bloody well prepared to end it.

Eventually Irene's red truck trundled into the lot. She stared at me for a moment before getting out and walking to my car.

She leaned a hand on the door and I rolled down the window.

"I know my hash browns and biscuits are good, but really? Waiting for me to open is sort of silly," she said.

"I want you to tell me everything you know about the Houstons."

She pulled her hand away from the door. "I'm not sure what you mean."

"Irene," I said, my voice dark.

Her hands shook as she rummaged in her cheap purse for keys to the café. "I already told you what was important."

"You left some things out," I said.

Her mouth twisted into a grimace and her eyes looked pained but she didn't reply.

"Irene, last night Finn put a tiny piece of invisible tape on the bottom of all four of my car doors, so if our sapphire burglar came in the night and searched my car he would know about it."

She glanced up with a worried look. "Did he search it?"

I shook my head. "Finn didn't think I would notice the tape so he didn't say anything. But when I got in my car this morning I could see the tape hadn't been broken. So that means he still needs to come back and search my car, if he's going to be thorough."

Irene rubbed a hand across her forehead. "I can't believe this is really happening."

"You need to tell me everything," I said again. "Even if it doesn't seem important."

"Why do you think there is anything to tell?"

"You said that you knew things, Irene. On the day we went to the Lazy Ox Yoke to clean out Peter's cabin, you said that you knew things about the Houstons. And the way you said it made me think that those things were . . . bad."

Her lips worked back and forth. "I don't see how the past can be important to what is going on today."

"It might have everything to do with what is going on today," I pointed out. "What if there is a personal reason why all of this is happening and it doesn't have anything to do with greed? You might be the only one who can shed light on it."

It was a rotten thing to say, and it was manipulative. But I didn't know how else to convince her.

Her face pinched with pain and she gave a slight nod. "You have got to swear to me that you won't ever, ever, repeat any of this."

I lifted one hand like I was taking an oath. "I swear. If you don't want me to ever talk about it, I won't. But it would really help me to figure out this mess if you would tell me everything you know about your family."

She pointed to the back door. "Let's go inside first. It's too cold to be out here."

After she poured a glass of orange juice and took a long drink, we settled into a booth. She closed her eyes for a moment and didn't seem inclined to say anything.

I didn't push her, and waited quietly while she gathered her thoughts.

Perhaps in anticipation of her story, Irene snatched a couple of napkins from the holder on the table and wadded them in her palm. Whatever story she was holding back, it was obviously painful for her to revisit.

"Take your time," I said.

She stared out the window and I could see her expression shift as the past came flooding back. Irene's eyes welled suddenly as some snapshot of pain that she had buried long ago rose to the surface once more.

She dabbed her face with the napkins and finally managed to look at me.

"I was just a kid, really," she said. "But being a kid doesn't mean you never have to deal with grown-up problems."

Her lower lip trembled and she looked away, staring outside at nothing. Her voice sounded like it was coming from far off.

She turned back and finally managed to look up at my eyes.

"It all started with the fire lookout tower."

CHAPTER 10

"I was fourteen when it happened," Irene said, taking her time.

"Felicia was a baby then?" I asked.

Irene nodded. "She wasn't even six months old. Aunt Barbara asked me to watch her so often I started to think that Felicia was mine."

My lips curved up a little, thinking about Irene changing diapers and cleaning spit-up off of bibs.

"The older boys were ten and eight. Anyway, Ned was almost big enough to reach the pedals on the truck and he wanted to learn how to drive so bad I had to hide the keys so he wouldn't start the thing up and crash into something."

"You had your hands full," I said.

She chuckled. "Peter was only three. He was into everything, climbing up on the dressers and trying to jump off. I couldn't believe that one little kid could have so much energy."

I gave her an encouraging nod.

"Vern and Ned were too big to stay in the house all day, but too small to help with work on the ranch, and so they just ran wild in the hills until they wore themselves out and fell into bed at night. I can't tell you the number of times I had to doctor cuts and scrapes on those two. They never left each other's side."

"So tell me about the fire lookout tower," I prompted.

Her eyes glazed for a moment, drawing on an old hurt to bring the memory to life.

"Vern was the one who found it in the spring that year," she said with a bitter tone. "It was a long time before I figured out what they were doing out in the hills all day long. When I made them take me to see it, it seemed like the thing was mostly safe, even though it was so high off the ground. I figured that it was better they spent the days playing in the fire lookout tower than down at the river where they could drown each other."

"Boys don't seem to have much fear at that age," I said.

"Or common sense. Anyway, by late August it was hotter than hell. Too hot to play outside so the boys lived in that fire lookout tower."

"Was the tower on Lazy Ox Yoke land?" I asked.

"On the west slope, going towards Wilson's ranch, sort of hidden in the rocks at the top of the granite peak overlooking the valley," she said. "Right at the edge of Butch's property. Forest Service jurisdiction. Not technically on the ranch, but a stone's throw away from it, so as far as I was concerned, as long as nobody ever said anything, they could camp up there all they wanted."

"I've never seen it," I said, frowning.

"It's impossible to see from the road. The Forest Service built it on the top of the hill due west from the ranch. You have to hike to it. Maybe a mile and a half? There used to be an old Jeep trail leading up to the base but it's been abandoned so long it's overgrown and you can't even see it anymore. The tower is hidden in the trees, too. Back when it was built the trees were small up there, but now they stand as tall as the tower, so unless you are standing right underneath it you can't even tell it's there."

She soldiered on. "Aunt Barbara was gone that day. Again. I had no idea where she went to all the time but I assumed it was something to do with the ranch. It seemed to happen every August. Uncle Butch and two of the Larson brothers were working down at the alfalfa field putting up hay."

"Sheriff Larson?" I asked.

She nodded. "But the summer before he got elected. He was working at the hardware store and just getting extra cash from Butch that season so he could buy a new Buick. They worked fourteen-hour days."

"Sounds about right for haying season," I said.

"Well, like I said. It was hot, melt-the-asphalt hot, and Ned and Vern got it into their heads they wanted to act like real Forest Service fire watchers up in the tower that day. They packed all their gear, took sandwiches, a .22 varmint rifle and canteens. But they didn't fill the canteens up with water, they filled them with their daddy's whiskey instead."

My mouth gaped. "Oh, boy."

"I had no idea what they were up to. I was so busy with Felicia and Peter those two could have started a cattle rustling business and I wouldn't have figured it out. Anyway, they took off and I told them to be home by supper. Hours dragged by with nothing happening. It was quiet. Too quiet, you know?"

"Where was your Aunt Barbara all this time?" I asked.

Irene flashed me a hard look. "That's where this whole story is headed."

Her sharp tone took me off guard. I had a feeling I was about to get the version of the day's events that hadn't been spoken of for more than thirty years.

She heaved a sigh. "Vern and Ned took one of the cutting horses up to the lookout tower and I suppose they set up their binoculars like they were forest rangers. They tied the horse below the steps and settled in for the afternoon. And then they started drinking."

I was astonished. "Did the Forest Service know the boys were using their property for a jungle gym?"

"The thing was brand-new back then, but they never used it. Not once. Government spent all that money to build that monstrosity—it's huge by the way—and they never put a man in it at all. I guess they decided that if the mountain around the Lazy Ox Yoke burned it wasn't worth the money or the manpower to put it out, so they let the whole thing go."

"Wow."

She shook her head. "Then that day Vern and Ned get next to smashed. Can you imagine two young boys drinking straight whiskey? Things must have gotten boring while they were in the lookout tower scanning the foothills for trouble, and when some of the fresh heifers and calves wandered close to the base, they both got the idea to go try out that cutting horse."

"Was there something special about the horse?"

"Yup," Irene grimaced. "Butch is mean as a snake, but the man knows how to train horses. That gelding was so well trained Butch could practically use him to round up cattle like a stock dog. Verbal commands would work just as good as reins on that horse. The boys thought he was the best thing in the world. They both climbed in the saddle, and took a lasso, and rode out to run the cows."

I didn't say anything, but the look on my face must have been enough.

Irene raised her eyebrows. "Butch would have beaten them both to within an inch of death if he had seen them chasing those heifers. Turns out, he didn't have to."

"What happened?" I asked.

"Ned was in front, holding the reins, and he had Vern behind him in the saddle riding at full tilt. They went running up on those cows and spooked the whole herd. Well, those heifers started running back towards the ranch as hard as they could, and the boys panicked."

I echoed her grim tone. "They knew if Butch saw a herd of heifers running and them behind, it would mean trouble."

She nodded. "Ned spurs that cutting horse so he can get in front of them and cut them off before they crest the hill. He was whipping that horse with all he had and Vern was hanging on the back like a rag doll when they hit the gopher hole."

My stomach clenched at the image. "How bad?"

"Broke that cutting horse's leg instantly. That big gelding pitched to the side and Ned went flying over his head. But Vern didn't have the sense to let go and that horse rolled over him."

"Oh, Irene," I said.

"I think the only thing that saved Vern's life was the saddle horn. It was just tall enough that when the horse rolled over his body it didn't crush the boy, but it did break his arm."

"Jesus."

"Ned knew he was in trouble up to his neck, and he knew if he let his brother die Butch would kill him. So he picks up Vern in a fireman's carry like he'd seen on television and started walking. That kid carried his brother over a mile back to the ranch."

I felt guilty, but I had to ask the question. "What about the horse?"

"Ned couldn't shoot it with a .22 varmint rifle, so he left the poor animal there, screaming and lying in the dirt. He knew he'd have to go get a bigger gun, either that or tell his dad and have Butch put it down."

"So you were there alone with Peter and Felicia when the boys got back to the house?" I asked.

"Ned was yelling for help and I came running down the steps with Felicia on my hip and Peter in tow when I saw them. Christ almighty, can you imagine?"

"What did you do?" I asked.

"Ned collapsed in the yard, he didn't have the strength to make it up the steps. I saw right away Vern was hurt bad enough he needed a doctor."

"Not something they teach you about in home economics class, is it?" I asked.

"Maybe they should if you live in Montana," she said. "We were all lying in the dirt in front of the house and Vern is on his side throwing up so hard from the pain and the whiskey I thought his socks would come up. Ned is flat on his back sobbing that he killed his father's cutting horse. Felicia is crying and I'm crying too, because it's so damn horrible. I tried to get my legs working so I could run inside the house and call the ambulance."

"Oh, Irene," I said.

"And then, finally, Aunt Barbara pulls up in her car."

"About time," I said.

"She figures out what happened, carries Vern to the backseat of her car and yells at me to take care of Ned, see to Peter and Felicia, and off she goes to the hospital."

"She left you there alone?" I asked.

"Not only that, but after I get Ned inside and tried to clean him up best I can, he tells me about the cutting horse still out in the field. I didn't know what else to do, so I got the rifle and went out and shot the poor thing myself. I knew Uncle Butch wouldn't be back till dark and it was too far for me to walk out to the alfalfa fields to get him."

"What did you do with the kids?" I asked.

She turned red from shame. "I left them with Ned, who was hardly able to stand up, much less see to a toddler and a baby. But when I got back they were all still in one piece."

"Did your Aunt Barbara make it home before dark?" I asked.

"She got back to the house less than ten minutes before Uncle Butch."

I shook my head. "What about Vern?"

"She left him at the hospital because he was too hurt to move. She came back to the ranch so she could do damage control."

"It was a little late for that," I said.

She paused and her eyes narrowed to slits. "Then I found out where she had been all that time."

"Did she tell you?"

Irene laughed bitterly. "I figured it out."

"So what had she been doing?"

Irene scoffed. "Well, I was steamed by then. And I'm shouting at Aunt Barbara and carrying on.

I wanted to know where she had been all day long that was so damn important she'd leave me alone with four kids to look after all on my own. She was throwing dirty clothes into the washing machine and hosing off the driveway when I finally lost it. I think I actually shoved her. All I remember about that moment was saying she needed to have a really damn good reason why she was gone, and she looks over at me and slaps me across the face."

"Did she say anything?" I asked.

"Oh yeah, she did."

A long pause filled the air with tension. When she met my eyes Irene was clearly livid.

"Aunt Barbara said to me, 'Irene, you can't ever tell Butch I was gone. Ever. If you do, he'll kill us both.'"

I digested that for a moment. "Kill you both. Did she mean you?"

"Not me. She meant Butch would kill her and someone else."

I shook my head. "But what was she talking about?"

"Think about it, Marley. Her . . . and someone else."

In an instant it was clear. "Barbara wasn't gone doing ranch business, was she? She was having an affair."

"For years," Irene said. "She was carrying on with some man for years. She told me every August during haying season was the only time in her life she felt really happy and alive. And then, as if that wasn't bad enough, she tells me the real bombshell."

"What could top that?" I asked.

"When she said that Uncle Butch would kill them both, she wasn't talking about her and her man-friend."

That puzzled me. "If she wasn't talking about the man, who did she mean?"

"Who do you think?" Irene asked.

My eyes darted around the room while I tried to piece it together. Then a thought occurred to me. "You think she meant one of the kids?"

She slumped. "That's exactly what I think she meant."

"One of Butch's kids isn't his at all?"

"And she was certain if he ever found out, Butch would kill her, and he would kill the child."

"Irene, this might be really important," I said. "Do you know which one of the kids it is?"

She rocked her head from side to side. "Not a single clue. I never did know. Aunt Barbara grabbed me by my shoulders and shook me so hard my teeth rattled. She made me swear on my mother's life that I would never tell a soul."

"And you never did," I said.

"Until this moment. Aunt Barbara never gave me one hint about which of the kids it was. I am absolutely certain that Uncle Butch never even suspected there was an interloper in his brood."

"Do you think that any of them knew?" I asked.

"The boys or Felicia?" she said. Her jaw worked as she thought about it. "I don't think so. But, despite how they might look to the outside world, the Houston kids aren't exactly stupid. I suppose it's possible that over the years one of them might have put two and two together. But I have no way of knowing."

"Could your Aunt Barbara have gotten a guilty conscience and told the child at some point?" I asked.

"I doubt she did," Irene said firmly. "I don't think she would want to risk it ever coming out and getting back to Butch. If for no other reason than to protect the child from him. He was mean as a snake, after all."

"He still is," I pointed out.

Irene rested her eyes on me with a plaintive look. "You can't say anything, Marley. Promise me."

"Don't worry," I said. "This isn't my story to tell. If it ever comes out, you can be sure it didn't come from me."

She relaxed noticeably. "I wish I knew which one of the kids it is. Don't think I didn't start wondering if it was Peter, and Butch found out somehow after all these years, when I heard what had happened."

I patted her hand. "It might have something to do with what's happening today. But then again, it might have nothing to do with it."

"I've tried to catch some clue about which one of them isn't Butch's, you know, looking at the color of their eyes, the hair, that sort of thing. But I can't make anything other than a random guess. and don't think anyone will ever know for certain. I doubt very much the man who fathered the child even knows which one it is."

"Your Aunt Barbara didn't ever tell you who the man was she was seeing?" I asked.

A look of utter certainty crossed her face. "She never told anyone. I can promise you that. When she died five years ago, there was no tearful deathbed confession from Barbara Houston. It was literally a secret she took to her grave.

CHAPTER 11

The Killdeer Community Hall was filled with folks from all over the valley. The sun was still shining, but hanging low in the spring sky like it was a guest at the funeral. The air was warm for spring, and more than one person in the hall waved a makeshift fan to stave off the heat from so many bodies pressed into one space.

Peter had been killed five days ago, and since it was a Sunday, everyone who had a connection to the Houstons, and a great many who didn't but were just curious, were in attendance.

The coffin stood at the front of the room. It was basically a pine box, nothing special. For obvious reasons the lid was closed.

I marveled at the crowd. Easily two hundred people crammed themselves in chairs and lined the back wall of the community hall.

It reminded me of when my father would shoot and butcher a steer on our ranch. The carcass was endlessly fascinating to the other steers, and predictably they would crowd around the remains, sniffing and shoving each other to get a good look at their fallen comrade.

It seemed that people and cows weren't that different after all.

Ned, Vern and Felicia sat in the front row of the hall wearing expressions of angry grief. Ned had combed his hair, put on decent clothes and hardly looked like himself, except his face was still red from sun and wind. Vern was disheveled, looking like he hadn't shaved for days, and his dark hair appeared less like it had been combed and more like it had been greased. His suit was wrinkled.

Butch Houston sat one seat apart from his three remaining children, which seemed odd to me, but maybe it was his way of showing that he was still in charge of the clan in spite of tragedy.

Or maybe he wanted to set himself apart so he could give himself the illusion of being above the whole thing.

Peter's service was coming to a close and Irene sat beside me while her shoulders heaved up and down from grief. My father sat next to her with one arm draped over her protectively.

I handed her another tissue.

"The café is closed for the day," she said, wiping both eyes for the hundredth time in the last hour.

My father shot me a worried look. If she wasn't opening her café it was serious.

"I think it's a good idea for you to take some time away from work," I said.

"Just today," she said quickly. "I'll be back at it tomorrow. I really can't face people today."

I scanned the crowd, hoping that folks would start moving outside, but they all seemed hesitant to leave and nobody was heading for the door, in spite of the service having ended ten minutes ago. Butch seemed reluctant to rise and so the entire hall remained sitting, not wanting to be disrespectful and depart before the Houston family. My eyes lingered longingly on the door and I tried to muster the courage to be the first one brazen enough to bolt.

Loy stood at the back of the hall with his brown baseball cap in hand. When he caught my eye he waved me towards him.

"I'll be right back." I got to my feet, grateful for an excuse, and went to stand beside the sheriff.

He nodded towards Irene with a worried look. "How's she doing?"

"Terrible. But we won't leave her alone today and she's keeping Lil's closed until tomorrow."

Loy looked down at his hat. "Can I have a word in the parking lot?"

I followed him outside and we stood underneath a giant elm tree that had been in front of the hall for more than forty years. The sheriff propped his back against it and cocked one knee.

"Marley, you've got to let my deputy get some sleep at night."

"He's the one who chooses to stay awake. I don't have a thing to do with it. Why don't you tell him to go back to his own place and let things get back to normal?"

"Because things aren't normal," he said, an edge to his voice.

I studied him for a moment. "You must have gotten word from the medical examiner."

He nodded grimly. "Homicide. Pure and simple. Clumsy attempt to make it look like an accident, and when I say clumsy I mean it."

I thought about that for a moment. "Didn't you say that Peter's head was hit six times?"

Loy ran a hand over his jaw. "It was nasty. Someone beat him to death with a hard object about the size of a big stick or a small rock. The damage was so bad the medical examiner wasn't sure what sort of weapon was used."

"And then they tried to cover it up in a hurry," I said.

"I think what you mentioned earlier about it being an act of rage was accurate. I don't get the impression from the damage that it was a simple case of stealing a couple dollars out of his wallet. It was motivated by something a lot stronger than that."

For one moment I actually considered telling Loy about Irene's revelations concerning the paternity of Butch's four kids, but I'd made her a promise and decided to keep my mouth shut about it for the time being.

"You can tell Finn to sleep at his own place. I'm pretty sure our bandit isn't going to break in while I'm home," I said.

"That's not going to happen," Loy said. "Finn is staying right where he is. I'm not going to argue about it."

A gust of warm wind tossed my hair into my eyes and I pushed it aside. "If you still think it's necessary."

"I imagine Finn already told you there are a few bits and pieces that you are not aware of concerning this case. It would make me feel better, until we can get it all sorted out, if you weren't by yourself. At least at night, anyway."

"Maybe if you tell me what those bits and pieces are, I could help you make sense out of this."

He gave me a stern look. "I know I've been loose-lipped in the past and shared all sorts of information with you that was privileged, but this time, I can't."

The sound of approaching footsteps drew our attention and Loy closed his mouth instantly. He stepped away from the tree and turned to see who was walking towards us.

Vern and Ned Houston strode across the yard, side by side, their shoulders set with determination.

Ned positioned himself a couple steps in front of his younger brother, taking the lead. He looked stiff with anger as he stepped before Loy. "Sheriff, we need a word."

Loy put on his public service expression. "Alright."

"We want to know what's happening to Pete's things. Are they going to a museum? Are they being sold? We got a right to know."

Vern crossed his arms, his jaw jutting out in solidarity with his brother.

The sheriff cleared his throat. "I was told that Butch released all of your brother's possessions to Irene."

"What if that's not what we wanted?" Vern asked.

"Take it up with Butch," Loy told him.

"We are taking it up with you," Ned said, his tone hostile.

"It's not my decision, boys," the sheriff replied.

The two men shuffled their feet awkwardly.

Finally Ned turned his gaze on me. "You tell Irene we want Pete's things back. You understand me?"

The sheriff took a long step and got between us. "She can't do that, Ned."

"She can," Vern said. "Everyone knows that little Marley Dearcorn is the only one Irene will listen to."

A vein began to bulge on Loy's forehead. "I've locked Pete's things in the sheriff's evidence building. Irene is planning to have them looked at by a local artifact dealer to see if anything is worth selling. If she finds something of value, she's assured me that she will come to you-all with a price. If you agree to sell it, she will divide the proceeds between you three siblings equally. Does that sound fair to you?"

Vern glanced at his older brother with uncertainty. "But Pete told us years ago there weren't nothing in that collection worth more than a couple hundred bucks."

"Then you'll get your share of a couple hundred bucks," Loy said. "Irene was given verbal permission by Butch to take care of it. Now, if you boys want to go hire an attorney and pay him a couple thousand bucks to win you the right to total ownership of items worth a lot less than a Maytag washing machine, you knock yourselves out."

More shuffling.

Ned crammed both hands inside his pants pockets. "Loy, you know our daddy ain't in his right mind. He's been doing things lately that no sane person would ever dream of. This whole deal's not fair, not one little bit. He wasn't thinkin' straight when he told our sister to clean out Pete's cabin and get rid of everything."

"I'm not in the 'fair' business," Loy told them. "I'm in the 'uphold the law' business, so you two need to sort it out with Butch if you've got an issue."

"Felicia always gets a cut off the prime and we always get left with the flank," Ned said. "Can't you side with us on this?"

Loy laughed out loud. "How do you figure? She's not the one who stands to inherit a third of one of the most valuable pieces of land in Killdeer Valley. If I recall, your sister won't get one square foot of land and you boys stand to gain several thousand acres apiece."

"There's more to the Lazy Ox Yoke than what's above the ground," Vern blurted out.

Ned gave his younger brother a withering glare.

Vern dropped his eyes, but he looked like he wasn't very happy about being chastised in front of others.

The brothers exchanged unhappy expressions and their bluster seemed to evaporate.

"Well, then," Ned said. "I guess there's no help for it. You never gave us a break on anything else, why I thought you might start being a decent man now just goes to show what a fool I am."

The two of them backed away, bitter expressions firmly in place.

"Thanks for nothing, Sheriff," Vern said as they turned to leave.

We watched them until they shuffled out of sight.

"Think they will vote for you next election?" I asked.

Loy snorted. "Hopefully I'll be running unopposed."

The sheriff watched the two brothers until they were well out of sight before turning his attention back to me. His mood had started out dark and had turned positively black.

He put a hand on my shoulder reassuringly. "Tell Finn he can sleep at night, will you? He's no good to me stumbling around all day shooting coffee into his eyelids just to stay awake."

"I'll tell him."

He dropped his hand and started to turn away.

"Hey, what did he mean?" I asked.

Loy stopped and studied my face. "What did who mean?"

"About Felicia getting her share out of a prime cut and them getting flank? That doesn't make a bit of sense to me."

For a moment I thought he wasn't going to answer. It was obvious he was trying to determine what to say, and what not to say, if the gymnastics on his face were any indication.

Finally he gave up and leaned close to me. "Felicia will get all the mineral rights to the Lazy Ox Yoke. Butch doesn't want anyone to know, because he's convinced that someday she will be ridiculously wealthy as a result and he wants to protect her from gold-digging gigolos, as he put it."

"No wonder the boys are so crabby," I said.

Loy gave me a puzzled look. "The land is probably worth a lot more than the mineral rights."

"For now," I said. "But what if someone found a big sapphire mine on the property and Felicia decided to develop it?"

He stared off into the distance. "I thought of that too, but I've not been able to get my warrant yet so I'm stuck until that comes through. I can't even determine if there are gemstones on the property, or if they were leftover stones from some other source and I'm on a snipe hunt."

"Why can't you get a warrant? It's a crime scene, after all," I said.

"The house and the cabin are not crime scenes. The place Peter fell off his horse is the crime scene and it's a half-mile away from his cabin. Butch got an attorney and he's making things extremely unpleasant for me at the moment."

"And the boys are about as cooperative as wounded bobcats," I said.

"At least nobody else has had their place broken into," he told me with a growl.

I was surprised by that. "Really? So the burglaries have all stopped?"

He looked supremely unhappy. "It's not necessarily a good thing. No one has called to report a break-in since your father's house was tossed. Either he found what he wanted, or he is trying to decide what his next move will be."

"You still think the same person is responsible for Peter's death and the break-ins?" I asked.

"I am leaning in that direction, but Finn is trying to talk me out of it. If I could get Felicia to open up about those damn rocks my job would be a whole lot easier. It might give me a better idea of what's motivating this creep."

"It might give you a better idea, but then again it might not," I pointed out.

Loy nodded. "Depressing thought, but that could be true. Why would someone want to kill Peter if there is a sapphire mine on the ranch? It wasn't like he had any rights to it or could make any legal decisions concerning development."

"Unless he made a deal with his sister?"

"That could be. Maybe he was protecting Felicia," Loy speculated.

"From what?" I asked. "Butch? Her brothers?"

"I don't have a clue. Pete and his sister were close. Just as close and Vern and Ned used to be, until they tried to irrigate off of the same water rights. Then things got personal."

"Maybe Felicia didn't know a thing about the sapphires, and her brothers wanted to keep it that way," I suggested.

"Brotherly love takes on a whole new meaning when you talk about the Houston boys."

I laughed bitterly. "You got that right. It might be worth it to Ned or Vern, either one, to keep their sister in the dark concerning any precious minerals on the ranch. Maybe Peter knew about the possibility of a quarry on the property and one of them wanted him to keep his mouth shut."

Loy sighed, deep and long. "You and I need to quit discussing this now. And anyway, I've got to get back to the station. Valerie has a stack of paperwork lined up for me and I can't put it off any longer."

He pivoted on one foot but then stopped himself. "Keep what I said about Felicia and her mineral rights to yourself, would you? Butch already has it in for Jackie Miller because he knows the guy fancies his daughter. He doesn't want any other greedy bastards trying to take advantage of the girl."

I nodded. "Sure, Loy. No problem."

As he ambled towards his truck, the community hall was finally starting to empty out and people funneled through the front door solemnly.

I watched the crowd disperse and saw Felicia walking beside her father with her head bent low. It was plain to see she was weary and emotionally drained.

As the pair made their way to Butch's old truck, I could see his arm straining from the effort of holding himself up with his cane while accepting the handshakes of a couple acquaintances offering condolences. Butch was obviously in pain, physical and otherwise. The old man's knees shook so hard they looked like they were about to give out. His elbow visibly trembled as he gripped his heavy cane for support, and Felicia stood stoically at his side with one arm outstretched in case he needed help.

Felicia's face was blotchy from crying. She didn't seem to understand what was being said around her—that or she simply didn't care. Aside from standing close to her frail father, which was probably done strictly from habit, she looked as if she had no idea the rest of the world even existed at the moment.

It would have been nice for her if Jackie Miller had been close by, to offer moral support if nothing else. It seemed a bit strange to me that he wasn't there to pay his respects. Maybe he had attended the service and I had missed him somehow?

As I searched the crowd of people moving back to their cars, I couldn't locate Jackie.

I felt a stab of sympathy for Felicia. On the one day she probably needed him the most, Jackie was not there. For her sake I dearly hoped that the man truly was her advocate, and not another vulture trying to take advantage.

My stomach felt sour, and before I had to face the inevitable invitation to join the family at the Episcopal church for a quiet potluck dinner, I decided crowds were not what I needed at the moment.

Funerals were still a bit too emotionally draining for me. The sun would set in a couple more hours and I planned to be in bed by 9:30 so I could shake off the melancholy with a good book and, if I was lucky, not have any terrible dreams.

I drove towards home, weighing the revelation that Felicia stood to inherit the mineral rights to the Lazy Ox Yoke someday. Did it have any bearing on Peter's death? Possibly, but there was no way to know for sure.

One thing did irritate me greatly, though.

Their brother was lying in a coffin and all Ned and Vern seemed to be able to think about was how unfair it was they didn't have any claim on his possessions. It wasn't uncommon, in my experience, to see families tear each other apart over who got to take Grandma's color television after her death. I wanted to believe fighting over Peter's belongings was the only way his two brothers could express their grief in a way that didn't make them look as though they were succumbing to the emotional pain.

But the longer I thought about it, the more I had to face the fact that the truth of it was a lot uglier.

Honestly, I wasn't entirely certain that Ned and Vern felt any grief at all.

CHAPTER 12

Former Deputy Sheriff Nick Wilcox stood beside the gate leading to my father's pasture, his usual look of utter disdain firmly in place.

His slight frame looked a bit bulkier, and I could tell that since he'd given up law enforcement he'd taken up weight training. Which was a good thing because Nick had always struggled to have enough flesh on his bones to keep his pants up.

I pulled up behind his black Jeep and stopped, but for one rebellious moment I considered ignoring him and driving away.

His smug face tilted up and he pointed at me with two fingers. Then he motioned for me to come towards him.

I suppressed a sigh, doing my best to maintain my composure.

Nick always managed to be irritating no matter what he did.

He turned his hand over and coaxed me towards him with his two fingers like he was summoning a fourth grader.

"You really are a jerk," I said under my breath.

I slammed my SUV into park, killed the engine and climbed out.

By the time I'd reached the fence I was feeling uncooperative. "What can I do for you, Nick?"

He curled a lip with irritation. "Dearcorn. I want a word."

Since I'd first met him nearly three years ago, Nick had taken great pains to remind me every chance he could get that he was a deputy sheriff and that I should address him as such. But he wasn't a deputy anymore. Now he worked for the weather station above Killdeer as the security chief and I knew that no longer being a member of law enforcement bothered him. I'd put as much emphasis on his first name as I could because in the past it had always bothered him.

He propped a hand on the top strand of barbwire fence and looked everywhere but at me directly. "The two squints that worked at the weather station wanted me to tell you goodbye."

"Squints?" I asked.

"You know, the rocket jockeys, the guys who sit around all day squinting at astronomy charts?"

"Will and Seth?" I asked. "Are they gone?"

"Course they are gone." He stared at me. "Why else would they tell me to come and say goodbye to you?"

"Well, thanks," I said. "That was nice of you."

The briefest flicker of regret crossed his face and he turned his back to me. "They both moved back to California, or Massachusetts, or some other damn place. I'm leaving too. Just so you know."

That surprised me. "I take it the data storage facility taking over the station doesn't need a security guard?"

"Course they need a security guard, but I happen to have better things to do than sit around all day watching some pasty-faced guy with a pocket protector play with hard drives all day."

"So you got a new job someplace in Killdeer?" I asked.

He snorted. "Hardly. I'm getting the hell out of this Hick-topia."

"Well, good for you," I said.

"Every spring the windshield on my car turns into a giant bug pizza. Every time it rains the roads get so bad you can crash just driving to the grocery store. I almost hit an elk yesterday coming back from town."

"One man's paradise is another man's purgatory," I said.

"It's a big world and I intend to see it all," he said with a sweep of one arm.

"Where are you moving?" I asked.

He paused for emphasis. "Australia."

"Wow. That's . . . nice."

"Nice?" he asked. "I'm going to be the new chief of security at the Murchison Radio Astronomy Observatory."

"Is that anywhere near Sydney?" I asked.

"Of course it's not anywhere near Sydney. It's in western Australia."

I didn't exactly know what to say. "Congratulations?"

"You're damn right, congratulations. This is my chance to make a name for myself in the international scene. After putting in a year at a world-renowned facility like the Murchison, I can write my ticket anywhere."

"Good for you, Nick," I told him. "Really. I think that's great. When are you leaving?"

"Can't wait to get rid of me?"

"That's not what I meant."

"Dearcorn, you and I have squared off against each other since day one. Don't pretend we haven't."

I sighed. "I think it's great that you finally seem to have found a job you will really like, and one that might take you places."

He studied me for a moment, his jaw muscle working hard. "Thanks, I guess."

An awkward few seconds dragged by.

"So, good luck, I suppose," I said.

"Technically, I'm still an employee of the weather station," he said.

"It's not really a weather station," I pointed out.

"Nope. It ain't. And I'm still legally bound to keep any and all information gathered at the station strictly confidential."

Another few seconds plodded by. He dropped his chin to his chest and I could see he was struggling with what he wanted to say.

I grimaced. "Ah, okay?"

Nick reached into his back pocket and withdrew a crumpled piece of printer paper. It was folded over four times, and I could see it had been sat on for a few hours.

He handed me the paper and glanced away quickly.

I wasn't wild about holding onto anything that had been in contact with Nick's backside for any length of time, but his odd demeanor prompted me to take it.

"What's this?"

He spat on the ground. "This here is a photograph that you are not supposed to be seeing, now, or ever. Got it?"

"Sure. I got it."

Reluctantly, I unfolded the paper and looked at it. There was nothing on the page but a photograph of a stand of trees and thick bushes.

"What am I supposed to be looking at here?" I asked.

"You don't see it?" he asked.

"See what?"

Nick snatched the paper from my hand and spun it around. "Right here. See this?"

He pointed at a particular portion of the photograph and shook the page at me.

I stared at it obediently. "It's a bush. Okay? I'm looking at a bush. Is there something special about it?"

"You see the arm? The leg? It's a man, Dearcorn. Not a bush. This is a photograph of the guy who has been breaking into your house and your dad's place."

I gaped at him for a moment. "Where did you get this?"

He let his head roll backwards. "Oh for the love of . . . Finn told me you are smart. After all the damn clandestine meetings you and Finn had on the road between Killdeer and your father's ranch, by now you've had to have figured out we've got motion detectors and cameras all over the perimeter of the station's property."

My eyes drifted up the slope of the green mountain. My father's ranch sat snugly on the valley floor between two tall outcrops of granite, one to the east, and one to the west. The weather station had been built atop the eastern peak, and it looked down over the valley from a lofty height.

In the past, when Finn had held the job of security chief at the weather station, I'd always been able to get in touch with him by parking my car on the roadside at the base of the mountain. I'd never understood exactly how the whole system had worked, but Finn would always arrive after a short period of time. I hadn't put a great deal of thought into how he had always known I was there, I'd just taken for granted that the weather station had some sort of alarm system or that Finn had a permanent telescope set up that allowed him to survey the valley floor.

So they had a system of cameras set up in the forest? That made a lot more sense.

"Show me the guy again?" I asked. "I can't make him out."

"There, he's right there," Nick said insistently.

"It still looks like a bush."

"If it was in black and white you could see him plain as day," he said.

"I don't understand."

"He is dressed in camouflage," Nick told me impatiently. "You know? Pants and jacket painted like leaves? You can't see him because of the colors. It's fooling your eye. Pretend it's in black and white and you will see what I'm talking about."

"You don't have a black-and-white photo, do you?" I asked.

"Look again."

"I am looking."

He traced his finger over the page. "See? That's his leg."

My eyes adjusted to the colors and finally managed to tune them out. The man in the photograph appeared suddenly. "I see him now. Good God, he's really decked out in the war paint, isn't he? If he stood still you could walk right by him in the woods and you wouldn't even know it."

"That's sort of the idea with camo," Nick said sarcastically.

"Where was this taken?" I asked.

"I zoomed it in to hide the landmarks. The location of the camera is confidential and I can't divulge that information."

"Confidential? This creep broke into my house."

"And I'm sorry about that," he said with a bit more whine in his voice than was necessary. "But that's not my problem."

"Can you at least give me a general idea of where he is standing?" I asked.

"It's not very far from the caretaker's cottage," he said reluctantly. "But that's all I can tell you."

My eyes wandered over the figure in the photograph, looking for anything helpful. The man was dressed head to toe with spring-colored camouflage that perfectly matched the foliage around him. His head was masked with a tight stocking cap that hid his entire face, except for the eyes. He was in profile, but with the mask and what appeared to be paint discoloring the area around his eyes, it was impossible to tell whc he was.

"It could be anyone," I said.

Nick tore the paper from my hands and shoved it back inside his pants pocket. "I was afraid of that. There's nothing about him that you recognize?"

"Maybe if you let me take another look," I said.

"Not a chance. I'm not even supposed to be here. Did he look like anyone you know?"

"He looks like about ten guys I know," I said.

"All I can tell you, is that based on the proportion of the trees in the background, and some careful measuring on my part, I can estimate that he is about six feet tall."

"Give or take what? An inch?"

"More like three inches," Nick told me. "Margin of error."

"Great. So he's either five foot nine or six foot three. But you can't be sure."

"Hey, I didn't have to show this to you. The least you could be is grateful," he snapped.

I gave him an apologetic look. "You're right. Thanks for letting me see it. You don't know when the picture was taken, do you?"

"About six Thursday evening."

My memory tumbled backwards until I could recall where I had been at that time.

"Oh my gosh. Finn was following me home then. I made him stop and go check out the caretaker's cottage because I thought I'd seen something there," I said.

"Nice going, Marley. You made him walk right into an ambush."

"I had no idea there was actually someone at the cottage. I thought I'd seen something, but if I had thought it was this creep I would never have told Finn to go over there."

"Too bad Finn didn't catch him in the act."

My heart thudded faster at the thought. "Nick, do you think I could have gotten Finn killed?"

"I doubt it," he said. "This guy obviously doesn't like confrontation. I couldn't make out a weapon anywhere, unless he has a concealed pistol or a knife, and he always waits until the houses are unoccupied before going inside."

I glanced at Nick appreciatively. "Once a cop, always a cop, right?"

"It's common sense. Loy filled me in on his pattern after I showed him the photograph. Your burglar doesn't want to get hurt, right? So he watches a place until he's sure it's empty, then he goes in. He has a goal in mind and it doesn't involve tossing a place when anybody is home. Seems to me he's looking for something specific. Do you have any idea what he's after?"

My cheeks colored slightly. "I have an idea. But I don't want to make any assumptions because what if I'm wrong?"

"That's the first smart thing I think I've ever heard you say," he told me.

"Thanks. I think."

Nick studied the hillside with hooded eyes. "I read the papers and I know about Peter Houston. Someone associated with the Lazy Ox Yoke has a motive to commit murder. Now, it may or may not be Mr. Camo-pants who is the killer, but it's obvious the two crimes are related. It's too much of a coincidence that the break-ins started right after the homicide."

"I thought so too. And so does Finn," I said.

"But the method is all wrong," Nick said.

"What do you mean?"

He absentmindedly patted his shirt pocket where he used to keep his little notebook. "It's not the same style. I have to think it's two guys. One of them, a hothead, vicious, takes matters into his own hands. The other, timid. Likes to get what he wants by being careful and cautious."

"Could it have been one man driven to do something desperate?" I asked.

He dropped his hand after noticing the pocket was empty. "Maybe. But I'm not law enforcement anymore, am I? It doesn't matter what I think. It's Loy's case."

"It matters to me. Nick, I never met anyone who was as good at forensics as you are. I know you aren't a deputy anymore, but it would be nice to get your opinion."

A shadow of pride flickered across his face for half a moment before it was instantly replaced with smug certitude. "Okay, you want to know what I think?"

"It might help me if I had some insight," I said.

"I'll give you some insight. Keep your busybody nosy little self out of it."

I stared at him.

"And let the sheriff handle it," he added.

"Gee, thanks, Nick."

"Anytime." He turned to walk back to his Jeep without a second glance in my direction.

As he drove down the washboard dirt road I watched him until he was out of sight.

A plume of dust lingered in the air after he was gone, and I watched it dissipate.

In spite of his brusque departure, I smiled a bit as I headed for home. Nick was like a toothache, but I knew I'd miss him after he was gone.

CHAPTER 13

Dusk settled over the valley as I drove to the barn to feed the horses. A hard wind blew down from the north, tossing up old leaves and chilling the air with a bite reminiscent of winter. The air rolling down from Canada was heavy with moisture, and clouds rode in on the crest of a low-pressure wave that promised rain. It would be miserable and cold all night. And the wind would howl until sunrise.

Both horses plodded towards the fence as I parked. Peanut tossed his head happily and blew a loud snort as I approached.

"You two are like a couple of dogs."

The air smelled sour, and somewhere off in the distant trees a pair of magpies squabbled over something that hadn't made it through winter alive.

Peanut and Lil Nipper stood at the gate, noses hanging over the wire. My funeral clothes were about to get hay all over them, and I grumbled as I unlatched the post and started to step through.

Lil Nipper tossed his head with irritation and shoved Peanut aside. When the mustang turned away and I saw his flank, I almost dropped the gate.

A garish swath of color marred the mustang's hair.

A bright blue circle the size of a truck tire had been spray-painted over Peanut's shoulder. The dots and slashes left no doubt at all as to what the paint symbolized. It represented the crosshairs of a telescopic rifle sight.

Peanut had been painted with a bull's-eye. He was a walking target.

I closed the gate and hurried to his side.

"You okay, boy?"

He nuzzled me impatiently, seemingly more interested in whether or not I was planning on putting out hay than the vandalism that had been done to him. I searched him front to back, looking for any injuries or signs of trauma, but aside from the blue paint, he seemed perfectly healthy.

I tugged Lil Nipper close to me and ran my hands over him too, just to be safe. Nothing.

At least the Icelandic pony had managed to dodge the graffiti.

I was so angry it didn't occur to me that I should be worried. Someone was obviously trying to tell me something and the most important thing at the moment was figuring out what.

I stomped into the barn and squinted into the dim interior. Everything looked exactly as I'd left it, except for the wall.

Painted with the same bright blue color that he'd used on Peanut, my burglar had left me an unmistakable message written across the wall above the hay.

Give It Back.

I stood there, staring at the wall, fury making the blood run so fast in my ears the only sound I heard was the rhythmic pounding of my pulse.

"I think I've had just about enough of you."

It was getting dark. There wasn't anything I could do about the paint marring Peanut's side until I changed clothes and got a bucket with soap, so I pitched hay for the two horses and closed the gate behind me.

My foot was too heavy on the gas pedal and I nearly lost control as I sped around the bend leading to my house.

I went through the front door, slammed it shut, and lifted the phone receiver before stopping to check the back door. A quick glance told me it was still locked. The repair job my father had done after the door had been kicked open was holding strong. That fact gave me little comfort at the moment.

My fingers trembled as I punched the number to the sheriff's station. The phone rang and the dispatcher answered.

"Valerie, it's Marley. I need you to radio Loy and tell him someone spray-painted my mustang."

"The kind with four legs, or four wheels?" she asked.

"Legs. Tell him my burglar painted a bull's-eye on Peanut. He'll understand."

I slammed the phone down hard.

My legs shook with adrenaline. I glanced out the window and saw long shadows taking away the remaining light.

Cleaning the paint off of Peanut now would mean using a couple of flashlights, or a lantern. I wasn't sure soap and water would be enough. The paint looked like it had been sprayed, and so that probably meant it was oil-based and had come from a can. Soap was probably not the best thing for it. Maybe a bottle of vegetable oil was better. At least it wouldn't do any more harm to Peanut's skin.

Frustrated, I stomped upstairs and stripped off my good clothes and pulled my black high heels off, leaving them in front of the closet. By the time my feet were in sneakers again and I'd pulled on a sweatshirt, the last fingers of sunlight had left the valley and darkness pooled in all the low places like water.

The image of the paint inside the barn flashed into my mind and made my blood race.

Give It Back.

Whoever he was, that bag of sapphires meant more to him than just about anything.

My hands vibrated with anger as I threaded my funeral dress onto a hanger.

Before hanging the dress up where it belonged, I stopped long enough to check that the zipper was up and that I hadn't left any unwanted damp tissues crammed in the sleeves.

Then something occurred to me.

Why had he said it instead of them?

Was he talking about the bag itself? Why hadn't he referred to the sapphires as them instead?

I shoved the dress inside the closet.

"Don't overthink it, Marley," I told myself.

After all, this man was obviously more physically inclined than intellectually gifted. Maybe he'd just gotten his number agreement wrong when he'd written the sentence.

It bothered me. Not enough that I wasn't still angry, but there was something odd about the wording of the warning.

I smoothed the fabric of the dress to be sure it wasn't twisted before kicking my black heels inside the bottom of the closet with irritation. Just as I was about to grab a jacket I heard a noise.

The front door slammed shut downstairs.

All of my anger evaporated instantly and I sucked in a breath.

Had I left the door open? Had a strong gust from the windstorm caught it and blown in backwards?

Straining, I closed my eyes and forced myself to recall exactly what I'd done the moment I'd walked through the door.

I clearly remembered slamming it shut.

Had it blown open somehow?

That was impossible. Someone had just come inside and shut the door with a bang to let me know he was there. Valerie had probably called Loy after I'd hung up the phone, and Sheriff Shucraft was most likely stalking through my living room at that very moment.

I glanced at the clock beside the bed, confused.

Loy must have been very close by to make it to my house so fast. It hadn't taken him five minutes.

I was about to call out to him that I was upstairs, but something stopped me.

Loy would have shouted out to me, identifying himself. But whoever had just come through my front door hadn't said a word.

Frowning, I stepped into the hallway and strained to listen.

Someone was moving around in the kitchen. I could hear the sounds of heavy footfalls heading to the back door. Whoever it was, he obviously didn't care whether or not he was quiet.

When the door leading to the back yard opened and didn't close again, my heart started pounding.

That wasn't Loy in my kitchen.

That was the sound of someone looking for something inside the house.

Another second passed and realization hit.

It was the sound of someone looking for me.

I was positive it wasn't the sheriff. And I was fairly certain it wasn't Finn or my father.

That meant I was in serious trouble. The man who'd just come through my front door wasn't wasting his time trying to find the sapphires any longer. He didn't need to search for them if he could get me to show him where they were.

And that was exactly what he had come to do.

I swallowed hard and tried to think. It wasn't going to take him very long to figure out where I was.

My feet seemed to move by themselves as I backed into my bedroom, quiet as a cat.

I didn't dare close the door or he would hear it.

Loy could be anywhere in Killdeer. It might take him half an hour to reach me. If the man in my kitchen got to me first, it might be half an hour too late.

I had to get out of the house, and I had to do it fast.

Footfalls moved across the kitchen floor and I heard the burglar head for the hallway. It would only take him seconds to search the office and the living room, and then he would undoubtedly come upstairs.

It was impossible for me to make it down the stairs and out the door before he got to the living room and I abandoned that plan instantly.

There was nothing left to do.

I had to find a place to hide.

For one horrible moment I pictured myself pressed to the floor underneath the big bed, shaking with fear, until he came into the bedroom, lifted the dust ruffle and found me.

Getting pulled out from underneath a four-post bed by the hair was not going to end well for me. I had to put as much distance between us as possible.

The roof of the back porch rested a mere three feet below the bedroom window. It would be easy for me to step out onto the porch roof and use it to climb up to the main roof.

It was a lousy idea, but it was the best one I had.

The window was unlocked. I'd cracked it open that morning to let in a bit of fresh air, so I would be able to slide it without making much noise.

The bedroom windows, thankfully, were the type that slid back and forth instead of turning open with a crank. Since the house was relatively new the window eased open with hardly a sound. I popped out the screen, wincing as the metal frame made a soft twang in my hands.

For a moment I froze to see if anyone was dashing up the stairs, alerted to my presence, but, hearing no sound, I laid the screen on the roof outside and climbed out the window.

I used the precious seconds I had left to slide the window shut and put the screen back in place. There was no way I could lock it from the outside, but hopefully when he came into the bedroom and saw the window closed he wouldn't think to check that.

I turned and started climbing up.

The roof was steep. Terrifyingly steep.

I managed to shimmy over the gutter and pull myself up to the main roof without falling off the porch, which I counted as a small victory.

I scooted away from the edge on my knees and half-walked, half-crawled to the crest of the roof as quietly as possible.

When I reached the top, the only shelter available was the brick chimney that vented the big gas fireplace in the living room. I eased myself next to it and propped my back against the cold bricks.

If the burglar somehow suspected I was up here, when he poked his head over the gutter all he would see was the chimney.

I hugged my knees to my chest and tried to make myself as small as possible.

The only thing I could do now was wait. And hope.

Wind blew my hair into my eyes. I didn't want to risk raising my arm to brush it aside and display an elbow or a shoulder carelessly, so I squeezed my eyes shut and kept my hands wrapped around my knees.

Seconds passed. Then minutes. There wasn't a sound from below, but the stiff wind prevented me from hearing anything softer than a shout.

My teeth chattered and I clenched my jaw shut to stop them.

Something scraped on the shingles behind me.

My eyes popped open and I strained to listen. Even over the wind I clearly made out the sound of booted feet slipping on the shingles. I held my breath, not making a sound.

The man was coming to check the chimney to see if I'd managed to hide up here. What the hell was I going to do when he found me?

If he grabbed me all I could do was try to push him off the edge. What if he dragged me down with him?

My heartbeat was so loud I was sure he could hear it.

The sound of footsteps drew closer.

As a last resort I could jump off the roof and hope the fall didn't kill me.

The roof vibrated slightly and I could feel him getting closer. There wasn't any other way out of this. I had to jump.

My legs shook when I tried to move them, and just as I was about to make a run for the edge I saw headlights splash across my driveway.

He must have seen them too, and the movement behind me stopped.

A vehicle pulled to a stop below.

The burglar didn't waste any time trying to be quiet now. The roof shook as he sprinted back to the edge.

A loud thump told me he'd jumped onto the porch, and another let me know he hadn't bothered to climb back inside the bedroom window; he'd just jumped off the porch into the back yard.

I stayed still, not wanting to take any chances.

Finn's truck sat below and I heaved a thankful sigh.

Before he shut off the engine the high beams flicked on, then off. The truck engine fell silent.

I clenched my teeth, wanting to shout a warning to Finn, but not sure if that would be helpful to him or a distraction.

If I asked him that question, Finn would have said unequivocally that I should stay put and stay quiet, not draw attention to myself and let him handle things.

How was he going to handle this if he didn't even know there was something wrong?

I peered around the chimney and tried to see if I could spot anyone running through the woods. If the burglar wasn't lying in wait inside the house, surely he was getting as far away from here as possible.

But it was too dark to see anything clearly.

How long should I wait?

As cold as it was, I'd die of hypothermia before Finn managed to find me.

I peered around the chimney again and gasped when I saw a figure standing behind it.

"Marley?"

I stood up instantly. "Finn?"

His shadowy form was by my side in a flash and he put a hand on my shoulder.

"I want you to follow me back to the window, then we will go to my truck and I will get you out of here. Can you do that?"

My voice sounded like a little girl's. "You're damn right I can do that."

He led me to the window and held up a hand. "I go in first. I'll tell you when to follow," he said.

He eased through the window like a panther and after a moment I felt a hand on my arm.

"Quietly," he said.

I slithered through as best I could, and when my feet hit carpet Finn took my left hand and squeezed it.

"Put your hand in the middle of my back. Walk behind me, but don't remove your hand. I need to know where you are at all times."

I didn't argue. I didn't ask any questions. I pressed my palm between his shoulders and that was where it would stay until he told me to move it.

For the first time I noticed Finn was holding a pistol. He raised it shooter's-stance with both arms and led us to the bedroom door.

When Finn moved, I moved. When he turned the corner towards the stairs, I stayed behind him in lockstep and kept my palm on his back like it was welded there.

We went down the stairs at a near sprint and I marveled at how quickly Finn could move without making a sound. He stopped at the bottom of the stairs and swiveled the pistol from living room, to hallway, and back to the front door.

His voice was barely audible. "I'm going to open the front door. You need to stand on the left side until I tell you to move into the yard."

I didn't have time to reply. Finn darted forward and had one hand on the knob before I even managed to dash towards the wall.

As if I'd been trained to do it for years, the moment I reached his side again my left hand went right back between his shoulders. I tried to keep from gasping air. Cold sweat stuck to my clothes and I couldn't stop shivering.

Finn pulled the door open and stood motionless for nearly a minute while he scanned the porch, the trees, and the vehicles.

"Now."

He moved so fast I had to sprint to keep up. We were down the stairs and racing for his truck before I had time to catch my breath, and when Finn shoved me facedown on the front seat of his truck and practically landed on top of me, what little air I had left was crushed out my lungs.

He whispered in my ear. "Keep your head down."

"I can't breathe," I said.

He slithered over me and climbed into the driver's seat. In one fluid motion he started the truck and threw it into gear.

We careened backwards down the driveway and didn't stop moving until we reached the road.

Finn shifted gears, spun the wheels, and I rolled back into the seat as the truck shot forward.

"Marley, put your seat belt on."

"I have to sit up to put my seat belt on," I said.

"Keep your head below the neck rest," he told me.

I struggled to snap on my belt while keeping my head down. Not an easy thing to do.

"Valerie must have gotten you on the radio?" I asked.

He spared a quick look in my direction. "No."

Finally the belt snapped into place and I managed to get my legs straightened out. "Then how did you know he was in my house?"

Finn paused noticeably. "I didn't know until I arrived."

"Did you see him?" I asked.

"I saw you sitting on the roof in front of the chimney. It seemed unlikely you were up there because you thought it was a good time to clean out the flue."

I actually laughed out loud with pure relief. "Finn, remember when I said it was a stupid idea to have you come stay with me?"

His eyes were fixed on the road. "Yes."

"I take it back."

CHAPTER 14

Loy sat across from me at his desk, his muddy boots propped up on top of a pile of important-looking files. He was sipping coffee and looking at me over the rim of his mug.

"It's eight-thirty in the evening," I said, giving his coffee cup a pointed look. "Don't you plan on sleeping tonight?"

"And miss out on all this fun?" he asked.

A crash emanated from the tiny kitchen down the hallway. It was the third such sound to come from there since Finn had stalked out of Loy's office after he'd deposited me in front of the sheriff.

I glanced towards the kitchen. "That's the second time he's dropped something."

"Not dropped, thrown," he said.

"Why is he throwing things?"

Loy looked at me like I was stupid. "He's not being clumsy, if that's what you are thinking. He's being pissed off."

I wrapped my hands around my cup of hot chocolate. They had finally stopped shaking. "So he takes out his frustrations by doing angry housework?"

"The station's never been cleaner," Loy said.

"Why is he so upset? I'm the one who had a prowler."

The sheriff rocked back and forth in his chair, staring at me. "A prowler who chased you up on your roof."

"It isn't his fault," I pointed out.

"But he thinks it's his fault the guy managed to get so close to you."

My mouth was working up to a frown. "He shouldn't blame himself for anything. If he hadn't come along when he did—"

Loy held up a hand abruptly. "I don't even want to think about it."

"It's one of the Houstons," I said. "Got to be."

He barked out a bitter laugh. "Well, I know it ain't Butch."

I gave him a smirk. "Not unless Butch had a pair of bionic knees installed and didn't tell anyone about it. I think he'd have a hard time climbing a flight of stairs, even more jumping off a roof."

The sheriff continued to watch me with a look I couldn't quite make out. Concern? Consternation?

"They have got to know we suspect them," I said.

"Suspect and prove are two very different things," he said quietly.

"How is your murder investigation going?" I asked.

Loy took a long drink from his cup. "None of your damn business."

Another crash came from the small kitchen.

I winced. "Are you going to have any dishes left after he is done washing them?"

"He's just worried."

"Well, I'm not sleeping at the house alone, so what does he have to worry about?"

"You are like a cross between an orchid and a tumbleweed," Loy said.

He lifted his boots from the desk and let them fall to the floor with a thud. Crumbs of mud remained. "You know, don't you, that Finn could work on any continent, in any country he wanted to, right?"

I shrugged. "Okay."

"He didn't have to come back to Killdeer. With his résumé and past experience he could be protecting the President of France or make a bazillion dollars working as a private bodyguard for some Saudi Arabian prince."

I blinked at him. "So?"

"So why do you think he came back here after he finished dealing with his problems back in Africa?" Loy asked.

"He likes the slow pace?"

"He came back for you. You are the reason he is here."

I didn't say anything for a moment and let that sink in. "Okay."

Loy set his cup on the table and coal black liquid sloshed onto the very important-looking papers, mingling with the mud. "Christ almighty. He never told you that he's in love with you. Did he?"

My face burned crimson. "Not that I recall."

"And how he reacted when you decided to marry Leif? Not that Leif was a bad guy or anything, far from it. But when Finn's head twisted all the way around and he went barking mad after your engagement got to be common knowledge, that didn't at least give you a hint?"

"He never said the words."

"I'm not sure they are in his working vocabulary. But right after Finn took the job as my deputy, I got him falling-down drunk on Old Man Barbula's homemade vajunka and he spilled his guts."

"That's disgusting."

"Not like that," Loy said impatiently. "He told me how he feels."

I didn't say anything. But my expression must have said it all for me.

The sheriff leaned in. "If you even took one step in his direction, Finn would run a thousand miles to meet you."

"Loy, I'm not anywhere close to being ready for that again. I know Leif and I were only married for a short time, but dammit, I still miss him."

"I'm not telling you that you need to stop missing Leif Gable," he said.

"So what are you trying to tell me?" I asked.

"Just . . . keep an open mind. Alright? I know you aren't ready for anything now. But someday you will be again. And trust me, if you asked him to stay around even on the possibility that you might want him, Finn would never leave Killdeer again."

"That's not exactly fair for him, now is it?" I asked.

"Fair don't enter into it, darlin'. He doesn't need a promise, just the chance. Even if that's all you can give him, I think it would be a smart move on your part to do it."

"Why are you telling me this?" I asked suspiciously.

Loy's face pinked a shade and he let a smile slip to his lips. "Wendy and I are probably going to get married."

"Hey, that's fantastic. Good for you. Anytime soon?"

He shook his head. "Next summer sometime. We don't know yet for certain. But it will happen. And when I'm married, things will change."

"Well I should hope so," I told him with a wicked smile.

He rolled his eyes. "No, that's not what I mean. Things will change between me and you."

I studied him for a moment, not sure I understood what he was trying to tell me.

"Marley," he said slowly, "we have had a pretty unconventional relationship since we were kids. I still feel like I've got a stake in your life, to some degree. I'm a lot more protective of you than I am of anyone else who lives in my jurisdiction. But after Wendy and I get married I'm not going to be around like I am now. I'll have other responsibilities."

"Of course," I said.

He looked down at his hands. "And I would feel a lot better if you were not out there fending for yourself."

"Loy, I've taken care of myself just fine."

"Except for getting shot. And falling off a cliff. Oh, and chasing a murderer into the woods by yourself."

"I got out of those situations alive," I pointed out.

"Not without help, you didn't. Help and a great deal of good timing and luck. Do you have any idea how much that makes me go crazy when I have to watch you put yourself at risk all the time?"

"You don't need to worry. I really can take care of myself," I said.

"But a lot of the time, you choose not to," he said darkly.

It was my turn to stare at my hands.

"What I'm trying to say is that I need you to do something for me."

I glanced up. "Anything."

His eyes looked sad. "Whenever you call me, I will always come. Always. I love you like family, and probably more than that. But after Wendy and I get married I need you to let me go so I can be there for her. Do you understand?"

My lower lip quivered in spite of my best efforts to prevent it. "I think so."

"You and I, our friendship, we will always have that. But you need to call someone who can be there for you one hundred percent. I can't do that anymore."

"But Finn can?" I asked quickly. "Loy, after I met him, he didn't even tell me his real first name for a year. How can I rely on a man like that?"

"I know, he's a weirdo. But just tell me one thing. Do you feel anything for him? Anything at all?"

The question stung. The truth of it was that I did have feelings for Finn, but they were impossible for me to fathom. Finn wasn't the only one trying to have a normal life.

And now, if what Loy said was true, it seemed that Finn's definition of a normal life included sharing it with another person.

"I don't have anything to give right now," I said.

"He's not interested in what he can get from you," Loy said. "He's interested in what he can provide. There's a difference."

"Am I invited to the wedding?" I asked abruptly. "You and Wendy, I mean. Am I invited?"

"Only if you promise to think about what I said."

The phone on Loy's desk jangled to life and he snatched the receiver. "Sheriff Shucraft."

He put a hand over the mouthpiece. "It's your dad."

I nodded and held out my hand to take the phone, but Loy shook his head and leaned back.

"No, Nathan. She's sitting right here in front of me. She's fine."

The sheriff reassured my father about six times and I finally got the gist of the conversation. Apparently my father had just driven by my house and found it deserted, with my vehicle parked out front, and he'd assumed the worst.

I stood up to let him play the role of Chief of the Reassurance Committee. I couldn't face Finn at the moment, so I wandered to the door and went outside down the front steps. I'd seen a brown deputy's jacket in Finn's truck, and with the evening chill settling in I was starting to need it.

When I looked up, the glow of a cigarette caught my eye and I stopped.

Someone was leaning against the back bumper of Finn's truck, smoking in the darkness.

I stood there trying to determine who it was, watching him like a fool for a full minute before he noticed me.

He eased around the bumper and rubbed the cigarette under his boot. "Miss Dearcorn. Sorry to surprise you."

His voice was familiar and I relaxed slightly. "Jackie. How are you? We missed you at Peter's service."

Jackie Miller ambled to my side and tilted his head down, looking ashamed. "I wasn't allowed to go. Mr. Houston said it was for family only, so I stayed away."

"That's too bad," I said. "Felicia could have used your support."

His eyes snapped to my face. "Was she alright? I was worried, but what could I do?"

"She was holding up," I said evasively. "I think it would go a lot easier for her if she came down here and told Loy what she did with those damn sapphires."

"Miss Dearcorn," he said. "It's not what the sheriff thinks."

I cut him off before he could finish. "Then maybe Felicia should tell him how it really is."

Jackie took a step away, looking shocked. "She . . . she gave them back to me. After I told her why Pete had them."

"She gave them back to you? Those sapphires were yours?"

He nodded miserably. "I've been going to the day-dig over in Philipsburg for two years. Every weekend I could manage it. Mr. Houston told me I couldn't ever take a second job working for another ranch, even on my own time, or he'd fire me. But how am I supposed to afford the down payment on a house if I can't get any extra money?"

"Peter was hiding the sapphires in his freezer for you? But why would he do that?"

"Because he loved his sister. Pete was the only one of his family who was happy I wanted to be with her. But how can a man who lives in a bunkhouse and chases cattle for a living ever expect to be anything more than a boyfriend to someone like Felicia? She comes from money. I'm just a vaquero. But if I had my own house. A good job. Maybe she would accept me."

"Jackie, I don't think she cares about money," I said.

He looked up, hopeful. "That's what she said when I explained about the sapphires. They were supposed to help me build a new life. She said she didn't care about all of that."

"But Butch would care about it," I said.

"That's right," he said intently. "I couldn't go to him, ask him for his blessing, unless I was able to prove myself."

"Why didn't you tell Butch about the stones belonging to you that day we found them in the freezer?" I asked.

"And have to explain what I was planning to do with them? It's not the time to tell Mr. Houston about my feelings for Felicia. He would fire me, send me away."

It was clear from the anguish in his voice that lying had caused him great stress. But I was certainly sympathetic to his plight. Butch could frighten a charging bull with his meanness. As much as I disagreed with evasiveness, in this case, I could certainly understand it.

"Jackie, you need to tell all of this to the sheriff," I said. "Do you have the sapphires with you now?"

"Yes, of course."

He pulled out the small leather pouch and held it where I could see it.

I nodded towards the station. "Loy is at his desk now. Go talk to him. Explain what you were planning and tell him everything you just told me. He will understand."

Jackie shifted back and forth. "The sheriff and I are not very good friends."

"Why not?" I asked.

"He thinks all the hands working for Mr. Houston are crooks. I don't think he will believe what I tell him."

"He will believe you," I said.

We stood looking at each other, neither one moving. Finally Jackie nodded with obvious reluctance. "Alright. But I won't be able to make him trust me."

"It's Loy's job to be suspicious," I said.

He shook his head ruefully. "But that day, I told him everything I saw. There was nothing I could say about what happened to Peter. I know the sheriff thinks I am not telling the whole story about what happened but I am."

I turned my head to the side. "Did you see something on the morning Peter died?"

"No, I didn't. That's why the sheriff doesn't believe me. There was nothing to see. I was out with Eric and we wanted to shoot soup cans with my .223, but when we saw Mr. Houston come back to the house in the truck we had to quit. Mr. Houston doesn't like us shooting cans on his time."

I frowned, thinking. "What time were you shooting your rifle?"

"In the morning. Before the sheriff came out."

I recalled hearing shots fired while I was waiting for Loy to meet me out at the deserted Wilson ranch, and Jackie's story matched with the time frame that I remembered.

Then something occurred to me. "You said Butch was coming back in the truck? Where was he coming back from?"

"He was towing the horse trailer, so I thought maybe he went into town to get feed. But Mr. Houston can't carry feed alone because of his knees. Then I thought maybe he was coming back from getting gasoline, but why would he take a trailer to do that? So he must have been moving one of the horses, but when Eric and I came back down off the hill, there wasn't a horse in the trailer. It was empty."

"Mr. Houston was driving an empty horse trailer around?" I asked.

"This is why I don't want to talk to the sheriff again," he said, exasperated. "He thinks that I saw something more and I am not saying. But there was nothing to see."

My skin tingled from the chill air and I rubbed my arms. I wasn't sure why it was significant that Butch was out moving around on the morning of Peter's murder, but I was certain it was.

"Thanks for listening to me about my crazy ideas," Jackie said. "I never had ambition before I met Felicia. All I've ever known how to do was ranching. I want to be something more for her. Not very many people would understand that. Her brother understood. I wish we could find who did this to him."

He tipped his hat and turned towards the sheriff's station, resolute.

As Jackie walked up the steps I turned to Finn's truck and tried to open the door.

It was locked.

Of course.

And I was freezing.

A hand came out of the darkness and I jumped nearly a foot in the air.

Finn inserted a key in the door and opened it. He reached inside his truck and pulled out the jacket, placed it over my shoulders and closed the door.

"How long have you been standing out here?" I asked.

"Since you came outside," he said.

"Did you hear our conversation?"

Finn nodded. "I did."

I stuck my arms through the sleeves and zipped up the coat, even though it was four sizes too big. "Do you believe him?"

Finn returned his keys to his pocket. "What he says is possible."

"Is he telling the truth about Butch hauling an empty horse trailer back to the ranch that morning?" I asked.

Finn examined some imaginary point off in the darkness. "Perhaps."

"What else are you and Loy not telling me about Peter's death?"

"You know I cannot discuss it."

"So, there is something else you are not telling me," I said.

He let his eyes rest on me. "One thing."

"What if I promise not to share it with anyone?"

Finn chuckled. "You have a way of convincing people around you to share things they normally would not."

"I was sort of thinking of myself here," I admitted. "If there is some crucial piece of information that might help me figure out who has been breaking into my house, I'd sort of like to know about it."

"We did not have this conversation," Finn said firmly.

"Alright." I waited.

He dropped his eyes to the ground and swallowed. "Peter Houston was probably already dead when you drove out to the Wilson ranch that morning. He most likely died an hour or so before you encountered Ned and Vern during their altercation. Anyone who was at the Lazy Ox Yoke that morning is still a possible suspect. Including both brothers."

I let that sink in for a minute. "That changes everything."

He scanned my face. "You need to keep that to yourself."

"Don't worry," I said quickly. "I will."

Finn wasn't even wearing a long-sleeve shirt, but he looked perfectly comfortable. I was freezing, standing there in his huge jacket. Not for the first time I marveled over Finn's ability to defy the elements.

I looked through the station's window and saw Jackie Miller standing in front of Loy's desk holding out the bag of sapphires, his face filled with reluctant shame.

Even though I wanted to go back inside, I knew it wasn't a good time. Jackie needed some privacy to get his story out and I was determined to let him have it. He struck me as a bit slow, but earnest and determined. His straw-colored hair stuck out at odd angles and he looked more like an Iowa farm boy than a ranch hand.

"I know Jackie should have told you and Loy about the sapphires sooner," I said. "But I think I can understand why he didn't."

"You are right. He should have come forward sooner," Finn said.

"How he feels about Felicia was clouding his judgment," I said defensively. "In a sad way, I think it's kind of sweet."

"It's obstruction," Finn said.

"Not really a 'love conquers all' sort of man, are you?" I asked with a chuckle.

He turned slowly and looked at me. His expression was unreadable. "Conquer is not the word I would use."

"What word would you use, then?"

He gave just a hint of a smile. "Endure."

CHAPTER 15

At sunrise the next morning the doorbell rang.

Before I even had a chance to pull on a bathrobe, Finn had already opened the door and was conversing with whoever stood on the porch. I hurried downstairs and saw Irene coming inside from the cold with her heavy parka and a fuzzy white hat pulled down over her ears. It was spring, but that didn't stop Montana from blasting us with a cold snap now and then just to remind us who was boss.

Irene clutched an old file box with both hands. Her eyes looked wild.

"Is everything alright?" I asked.

She headed for the kitchen without saying a word and I followed her. Finn locked the door silently and went back inside the office, where a single lamp burned. More than likely he had spent the night sitting on the little couch in the office, listening for trouble.

Irene was already brewing coffee when I sat at the kitchen table. She banged cups on the counter and rummaged in the refrigerator for milk.

The file box sat in the center of the table ominously. I watched her work, wondering what could possibly be inside it.

"Good morning," I said.

She stopped what she was doing and really looked at me. "Marley, it's time we got this mess sorted out."

My stomach clenched. "It's not even six."

She plunked the milk jug on the counter. "I think I figured out a way to tell which one of the Houston kids is the bastard."

I sat up straighter. "That would be incredibly helpful."

The coffeepot started its busy burbling and she fell into a chair across from me. She rubbed her eyes and I could see they were red from crying, or lack of sleep, or both.

She leaned back in the chair. "Mom."

"Your mother?"

Irene nodded. "She had leukemia, you know. We tested the whole family looking for a suitable bone marrow donor."

I studied the file box. "As I recall, nobody was a match."

She put her hand over the tattered brown cardboard and rubbed the surface like it was a living thing. "This is all of the paperwork from Mom's cancer treatments, hospital documents, bills. All her records, everything. You know the goddamned hospital charged her twenty-six bucks for two aspirin? Anyway, it's all here."

Irene's mother, Rita Baker, had passed away while I was living in Helena, Montana, and working at the Fish and Wildlife branch office. I came home for the funeral, but most of the trauma had happened while I was out of the picture, and the details were fuzzy.

"You even tested Felicia?" I asked.

"We tested everyone we could get our hands on looking for a match," she said, her face weary.

165

"And you kept all the records?"

"This was before HIPAA and so record keeping was a bit loosey-goosey at Parkman General during that time. I kept stuff that got sent to the hospital from friends, cousins, women from the beauty parlor, no matter how big or small. Get well cards, receipts, you name it. There's stuff in here I haven't even looked at in a decade. But somewhere inside this box there are papers with the blood types from the possible donors."

"And that includes the Houstons," I said.

"Aunt Barbara, Butch, all the kids," she replied.

I thought about it for a long minute, trying to recall the distant biology classes I'd had. "It might not help us. There is a chance it won't mean anything at all. Blood type isn't always a clear indicator of lineage."

"It's the best thing I could come up with. And if we do find something that seems out of whack, at least it's a place to start," she said.

The coffeepot finished its song and I stood up. "Let me get a little caffeine into my system."

She nodded and held out a grateful hand as I passed her a steaming cup. "This might take awhile."

"I don't have to work today. And it's far better to actually have something to do with your hands than sit around letting your imagination take over."

Irene flipped the lid off the box and tossed it on the floor.

As I sat down she handed me a fat stack of file folders and I set them carefully at my elbow. A flicker of movement caught my eye and when I glanced towards the hallway leading out of the kitchen I saw Finn standing there, watching us with a stern expression.

Irene saw my hesitation and turned. She watched Finn for a moment without saying anything.

Finn could have inserted himself in our project. If it was pertinent to his and Loy's investigation he had every right.

We stared at each other for a moment without saying anything.

Finally he spoke. "Let us know if you find anything of value."

"We will keep you in the loop," I said.

Irene was holding her breath, but when Finn gave me a slight nod and turned to leave, she let it out with a whoosh. "I keep forgetting he is a deputy."

"I can't seem to ever forget it," I said.

I opened the first file on my stack and started reading.

Irene did the same, and we both glanced up when we heard the front door slam.

Finn's truck engine rumbled to life and he pulled away from the house. Apparently he had decided to leave us to our quest.

"At least this way he knows where we are and what we are up to," Irene said.

We shared a smile, then bent to our task.

The coffeepot eventually emptied, and at some point Irene made us scrambled eggs with cheese. I broke out a box of chocolate truffles from somewhere in the back of the refrigerator and set them on the table between us.

Irene sampled the truffles. She looked up with surprise. "Wow. You ever get on my bad side just get me a box of these and all will be forgiven."

"Good thing I'm a saint," I replied.

Hours drifted by, and we shared the content of old cards, letters, and the occasional ridiculous hospital bill as we searched. But the blood type file was well hidden.

Halfway through my tenth folder, the phone rang and I stood carefully, feeling a twinge in my neck.

The moment I lifted the receiver he was already speaking. "Hey, Kiddo."

I tucked the receiver under my chin and sat back down at the table. "Dad, do you remember what blood type I am?"

"A-positive," he said instantly. "Is Irene there with you? I lost track of her."

"She's here. We are working on something," I said evasively.

"Tell her I'm down here at the café and her head waitress is out back smoking a butt and ignoring the customers."

"Lil's is busy and Cynthia is failing to rise to the occasion," I said to Irene.

She rolled her eyes. "Tell your father I will be down in a few hours. We need to get through this."

"She'll be down later," I said into the phone. "Why don't you put a For Sale sign on the window and see if you get any takers?"

"Yeah?" my father asked. "How much does Irene want for the café?"

"He wants to know how much you want for Lil's," I said.

"Two hundred," Irene told me.

"Thousand?" I asked.

My father piped in. "What did she say?"

"She will take two hundred thousand," I relayed.

He laughed. "It's a bargain. Marley, you should buy the café and then she can retire. We can go to Barcelona and Madrid on a romantic getaway."

"I'll give you one-fifty," I told Irene.

She snorted. "Two. Firm."

"Are you recording this phone conversation?" I asked my father. "We can use it later to set a price."

"No, but I will just call the NSA and ask them to forward me the tape," he replied.

"You want to talk to Irene?" I asked.

He grumbled. "Not if she is in the middle of something. Why did you want to know what blood type you are?"

"It was just on my mind," I said. "I've got to go, Dad. Talk to you later."

As I replaced the receiver in the cradle, Irene was slowly getting to her feet. She held a piece of paper in her hand.

"I found it. This is it."

I was by her side in an instant. "Whose results?"

She set the paper on a clean spot in the center of the table and smoothed it out. The edges were tattered from being folded haphazardly.

"It's Butch's," she said.

I studied the page. It was a human leukocyte antigen results printout.

"This isn't what I expected," I said. "What's a leukocyte test?"

Irene ran her finger over the lines of data. "To get a match for a bone marrow transplant, you need to do an HLA test, but doctors use blood type as another factor when they try to figure out if someone will be a suitable donor. Blood type, and about twenty other variables."

She flipped the page over. "It's on the back."

Handwritten notes were scribbled in red ink haphazardly across the page. It was messy enough to be a doctor's handwriting.

"I can barely read it," I said.

"My hands were always shaking back then," Irene confessed.

"This is your handwriting? I hardly recognize it," I said.

"I don't think I was supposed to have this but I was persistent. The doctor fed me information so I would leave her alone."

I scanned the handwritten notes quickly. At the bottom of the page it said "unsuitable" in all capital letters.

The rest of the page was a basic printout for a questionnaire. Things like age, weight, history of diabetes, even whether or not the donor had a tattoo were taken into consideration. Finally I found the line we were looking for.

"Butch is type O," I read.

"That gets us started. We need Aunt Barbara's HLA results," Irene said. "I wrote down everything they said on each one of the results for all the possible donors. So all of this stuff is here somewhere."

I leapt for my stack of files and began searching for a paper that looked like the one Irene held in her hand.

Now that I knew the format and color of the page I could scan the papers much more quickly.

It didn't take long to find it. "Here is Ned's result, and Aunt Barbara's."

Irene snatched one of the pages from me and flipped it over. "Aunt Barb was type A. Okay, so if the parents are type A, or type O, what does that mean for the kids?"

"It means none of them can be AB," I told her.

"I've got Peter's results here," she said. "He was O. So that rules him out as the bastard."

"I wish you would stop saying that word," I said.

"Where is Ned's result?" she asked, irritated.

I still held it in my hand. I flipped it over and showed her the scribbles. "Ned was A. It's a match for Aunt Barbara so it probably isn't Ned either."

"We need Felicia and Vern," she said in a rush. "Keep looking."

Both of us raced through our pages. Almost simultaneously I discovered Vern's test and Irene lifted Felicia's triumphantly.

"Felicia is type A, like her mother," Irene said.

I flipped over the paper in my hand and my mouth went dry. "Vern is AB. Butch can't be his father."

We looked at each other, realization dawning.

"It's Vern," Irene said softly. "He's illegitimate."

"We don't know that for certain," I cautioned. "This isn't one hundred percent accurate."

She slumped into her chair and crossed her arms, looking at me with her jaw set. "Yeah, I think it is."

I sat down hard, the page growing damp in my sweating hand. I pictured Ned and Vern locked together in a vicious fight, Ned holding a pistol to his brother's face. Had they really been fighting over

Clear Creek water rights? Or had it been something else altogether?

"Does he know? Can he possibly know this about himself?" I asked.

"It would explain why he's been breaking into every house in the damn valley looking for those sapphires," Irene said.

My gut was telling me there was something we were both missing. "Irene, we need to think about this. Why would Vern Houston risk getting caught, or shot at, burglarizing homes just for the sake of a lousy bag of rocks worth about ten grand? It doesn't make any sense."

"He's afraid someone will find out he's not Butch's kid and then his inheritance goes away. He wanted something valuable to fall back on."

"I can see the logic of that," I said. "But his share of the ranch is worth, what? Just under a quarter of a million dollars? Why would he risk so much for such a small payout, relatively speaking?"

"I don't know," she said. "Why does anyone do something stupid like that? I think he is just desperate."

Something about the whole scenario felt off to me. Vern was risking so much, for so little, if the sapphires really were only worth ten thousand dollars. It didn't seem like a fair trade to me.

Then I recalled what Finn had let slip when we were talking in the parking lot at the sheriff's station. Peter had been killed sometime before Ned and Vern had gotten into their fight that morning. What if the two boys hadn't been arguing over water rights at all? What if they had actually been fighting over something else entirely?

And what about Butch Houston? What had prompted him to be out driving around with an empty horse trailer that same morning?

Too many things didn't add up. I needed more information before all the pieces would fall into place.

It was possible that Vern was responsible for the murder, and for the burglaries as well. But I was really starting to believe that it wasn't about a little bag of blue stones after all.

"There has got to be more to it," I said.

Irene began putting papers back inside the file box. "Well, I'm satisfied. I'll go talk to Loy this afternoon and let him know what we found out. I think he will be able to narrow his search a little. It's got to be Vern. He has to know that Butch isn't his real father, and he's looking for insurance. If this got out, he'd lose his share of the Lazy Ox Yoke and Butch would disown him forever."

I watched her repack the box and didn't say anything. It felt wrong to me, but I didn't want to argue with her. What if she was on the right trail? What if Vern was acting out of desperation and that was all there was to it?

My mind recalled the spray-painted warning on the inside of my father's barn.

Give It Back.

What had he meant by that? Did he mean that he wanted us to give the bag back? It seemed to me if Vern had been talking about the sapphires he would have used the word them instead. My intuition was warning me that Irene was coming to the wrong conclusions.

"I've got to go," Irene said. "Judy is probably shortchanging the customers at this very moment."

She finished cramming things back inside the file box and struggled to push the lid down.

I stood up. "Irene, wait. What if we've got this all wrong?"

Her sharp blue eyes pierced me like knives. "We don't. It's Vern. It's been him all along."

The venom in her voice was startling and I was surprised. "You think he killed Peter?"

She practically growled a response. "Damn right I do."

"Whoa, whoa. We need to slow down and think about this," I said.

"Marley, how many times have Loy, your father, Finn and everyone else always told you to slow down and think about something? I cannot believe that you would say I need to slow down."

"I'm just saying that we shouldn't jump to conclusions, and think it over. We might not know all the facts."

She hefted the box and snugged it under one arm. "You can stay here and think about it if you want to. I'm going to talk to the sheriff. We are right. I just know it. Vern knows he isn't Butch's kid, and I would bet you that Peter knew it too and he got his head smashed in because of it. Those sapphires are nothing less than Vern's compensation package if Butch cuts him out."

She spun out of the kitchen and headed for the door.

I sprinted after her. "Irene, wait."

"I'm not going to rush out to the Lazy Ox Yoke and confront Vern. I'll go see Loy and tell him what we figured out. He can decide what to do from there."

"You promise me?" I asked.

"Do you think I am that stupid?" she asked.

"It seems like we might be sending the sheriff off in the wrong direction, that's all," I pointed out.

"He's a smart man," she said. "I'll tell him what I know and he can take it from there."

174

I watched Irene jog down the stairs and toss the box in the back of her little red pickup truck. She gave me a quick wave before leaping inside and urging the engine to life. Her eyes fell on me where I stood on the porch. She frowned when she noticed I was wringing my hands and she rolled down her window.

"Don't look so worried!" she yelled. "It's not like Vern's a psychic or anything. How's he gonna know what I figured out?"

She waved once, confidently. I watched her drive away, the cold stone of worry settling in my stomach.

As the sound from her truck engine died away, I lingered on the porch for a moment, staring after her. My feet seemed locked in place and I felt such a sense of unease.

When I turned to go back inside, the forest surrounding the house was ominously still. It was almost as if the very trees were holding their breath.

As I shut the door and locked it behind me, I realized what was bothering me.

Not one bird had been singing from the trees. Not a chickadee, or a woodpecker, or even a magpie chirped or squawked from the branches.

It was almost like the birds were all holding still, watching, and listening to something that they could hear, but that I could not.

CHAPTER 16

Finn came through the door promptly at six with tired eyes and slack shoulders. His walk was more of a trudge.

"When was the last time you got any sleep?" I asked.

He grumbled something and went into the kitchen. I trailed after and watched him lean inside the refrigerator and rummage through the contents. After some fumbling and exploration of the drawers, he managed to build a sandwich and poured himself a tall glass of milk.

After several bites, he finally focused on me. "Sorry. Food replaces sleep when I'm on duty, and if I can't get enough to eat my brain quits working."

"My God, you are human after all," I said.

He shot me a curt look and tore into a bag of chocolate chip cookies he'd snagged from a cupboard.

"You have any trouble here today?" he asked.

"Nope."

"I thought Irene would be here all afternoon, or I would have taken you with me when I started my shift."

"She left around three to tell Loy what we found out," I explained.

He shoved an entire cookie into his mouth, tucking it into his cheek. "What did you find out?"

"That Vern Houston isn't a Houston."

Finn stopped chewing and tilted his head towards me. "Say that again?"

"Vern, the second oldest boy, isn't a Houston. Butch isn't his real father. Irene is convinced that it has something to do with Peter's murder and all the burglaries that have been going on since."

"Why hasn't she told this information to Loy?" he asked.

"I told you, she went there this afternoon to do just that. Didn't you see Loy today?"

He leaned back against the counter and rubbed his neck. "Yes. I saw Loy. Irene didn't come to the station, as far as I know. She might be considering whether or not she wishes to share this. I believe these people are her family?"

"They are related to her by blood, but I wouldn't necessarily call them family," I said.

He considered that for a moment. "I would think she still holds a measure of loyalty, in spite of the tension. I will pay her a visit at the café in the morning. Give her a chance to explain."

I took one of the cookies from the package, dipped it in Finn's glass of milk and took a bite. He didn't even blink.

"Former Deputy Nick Wilcox showed me a photograph of the man who has been sneaking around the valley leaving me love letters spray-painted inside my barn," I said.

Finn gulped. "He did what?"

"Nick showed me a photo of the guy who's been breaking into my house. Mr. Camouflage? I took a hard look at him, and I didn't recognize who it was."

Finn was clearly irritated. "He was not authorized to share that information."

"Well, if I had been able to make him out, that might have been helpful, don't you think?" I asked.

"No one can make him out, Doll. He's taken great steps to be well disguised. Obviously he is someone accustomed to hunting in blinds. His camouflage is very effective."

"So he could be sitting outside my front door right now and nobody would be able to see him. That's comforting," I said.

He took another cookie and crammed it in his cheek. "I would be able to see him."

"With your superpowers, or your heat-seeking goggles?"

Finn displayed a rare smile. "Camouflage doesn't work on everyone."

"Well, it works on me. So I plan to stay out of the bushes for the next decade or so."

"That would certainly make my job a lot easier," he told me.

"Listen. You don't have to stay here tonight," I began.

The look he gave me cut off my next sentence.

"Okay, if it will make you feel better," I said quickly. "But at the very least, you have got to get some sleep. Alright?"

"I concur. My performance is suffering. We can go over a protocol before you go to bed tonight."

"No, no protocol. Just take the guest bedroom next to mine and go get some rest, will you? If someone breaks in I'll bang Morse code on the wall or something."

"I was planning to sleep across the threshold of your bedroom door," he said.

"Oh for the love of Pete," I said.

Both of us glanced down, suddenly feeling the awkwardness of the phrase. After Peter's murder, I would never think of that expression the same way again.

"Marley, I will sleep in the guest bedroom with the door open. I want you to close your door and lock it."

"It doesn't have a lock," I said.

He grimaced. "You are right. I forgot. I am exhausted."

"Finn, go upstairs and go to bed."

He took one last cookie and drained the rest of his milk. "I am no good to you with my current level of fatigue. I will sleep for six hours and be up by one."

"Why don't you sleep until you are not tired anymore?" I asked.

"At this point, I may not have a choice."

He stumbled down the hallway and climbed the stairs, and I heard him go inside the guest bedroom. It took about fifteen seconds for his weight to collapse on the bed, and I imagined he would be asleep in a matter of minutes.

I cleaned up the mess, scraped bread crumbs into the garbage and scolded myself for having three more cookies while I worked.

The revelation that Vern Houston might not be Butch's son was doing nothing to relieve my concern that Irene and I were somehow chasing ghosts. There was definitely something that we hadn't seen yet. Some critical piece of information had escaped us, and until we figured it out, I didn't have a single doubt that the camouflaged burglar would continue his criminal activities.

At least I'd managed to avoid being hit over the head like Peter.

So far.

After things were put away in the kitchen I went into Leif's office and searched inside the big desk until I found my list with important phone numbers.

This phone call was a small chore I hadn't done yet, and it was time I did. I'd promised Irene to get in touch with someone who could identify and appraise artifacts for Felicia. It just so happened I knew the perfect person for the job.

My finger stopped when it came to the right name on the list and I picked up the phone.

It rang five times, and I was about to hang up when a familiar voice finally answered.

"Hello?"

"John Taylor," I said, smiling. "How are you?"

"Hello, Marley. I am well."

"Listen, I need you to look at some artifacts for me," I said.

The phone crackled with the sound of papers being shifted around. "Are you going to bring them to me? Or should I come up to Killdeer?"

"It's a large collection," I explained. "Could you come here?"

"Certainly. When?"

"What is the soonest you can make it?" I asked.

"Well, I'm looking at my schedule now, and I'm afraid I won't be able to travel until next week. It looks like Wednesday is my first free day."

It wasn't ideal, waiting more than a week for his arrival. But it would have to do.

John Taylor was a friend who knew more about arrowheads, ancient pots, trade beads and old Battle of the Little Bighorn memorabilia than any other person I knew. There was no guarantee that he could spot some treasure hidden in Peter's collection, but if anyone could determine if there was a valuable item stored in the midst of the junk, it would be John.

"Wednesday is fine," I said.

"What is it that I will be looking at?" he asked.

"Better question is what you won't be looking at," I told him. "My friend Irene Baker had a cousin pass away suddenly and she is trying to find a good home for his collection of artifacts. It's probably worthless, mostly. But I have a feeling there is something in the pile of stuff that might be worth serious cash. At least, I get that impression."

"I'll come early so we can spend several hours looking through it."

"That's probably what we should plan for," I said.

"How about I telephone when I get to town and we can arrange a place to meet?"

"That will be fine. See you then."

After I hung up the phone I felt a sense of satisfaction for the first time in days. It was better than sitting around in my house, trapped like a mouse down a drainpipe while the cat sat outside staring in.

If there was something worth stealing, or worth killing for, in the collection, then John should be able to spot it. And if the collection of Peter's artifacts didn't have anything of value, that would be helpful to know as well.

It was a long shot, but it was a place to start.

By now I was convinced that the sapphires were not what my burglar was after. Immediately after he'd broken into my house I'd been too upset to think about it clearly, but looking back on the incident, it occurred to me that none of the smaller drawers had been tampered with. None of the usual hiding places where you'd expect to stash something small had been searched. It made me realize that whatever Mr. Camouflage was after had to be larger than something that would fit in the palm of your hand.

I went into the living room and flopped on the sofa. I tried to recall exactly how my home had looked after I'd walked in the front door and seen things scattered about.

I closed my eyes and pictured the house in disarray. The cupboards had been left ajar. So had the upstairs closets and dressers.

But all of the places the thief concentrated on had one thing in common.

An old expression came to mind. Something my mother used to say when we were playing a game called twenty questions.

The first question we always asked each other was is it bigger than a bread box?

Whatever the thief wanted was definitely bigger than a bread box. It was clear he'd been looking for something that would not easily fit inside a silverware drawer, or the glove box of a vehicle.

A shiver ran between my shoulders at the thought.

No wonder the burglar hadn't bothered to break into my SUV. He hadn't needed to. Whatever he was searching for was too big to fit inside the glove box, or underneath the seat. And my SUV had a hatchback, not a trunk. To see the back all he would have had to do was shine a flashlight inside.

I ran my hands through my hair and squeezed my eyes shut so I could concentrate. But no matter how hard I tried to focus my thoughts they only scattered like startled crows.

My head was spinning and I was getting nowhere.

I stood up and went to the window. The wind was picking up again and branches swayed rhythmically outside. A drop of rain spattered against the glass. The sun was setting, and in the dying light it was plain the black clouds overhead would deliver rain soon.

A flash of lightning jolted me from my thoughts. Thunder rumbled far off in the distance, and it took several seconds for it to echo across the valley, but there was no mistaking it. A storm was rolling in.

By morning we would probably see crisp blues skies, but tonight promised to be a typical Killdeer spring, complete with hard rain and savage winds. If it didn't turn to snow we would be lucky. Either way, it would be cold and wet, a perfect night to sit inside by the fireplace reading a good book or watching mindless television.

Finn was sound asleep upstairs so I vowed to keep the television volume down so I didn't disturb him.

I pulled on a pair of slippers and tossed aside a couple of throw pillows where they sat on the sofa, looking for the remote.

The phone beside the sofa rang, jangling to life unexpectedly, and I snatched the receiver quickly so it wouldn't ring again and wake up Finn.

The caller ID displayed a number I didn't recognize so I answered formally.

"Dearcorn's."

Silence.

"Hello?"

A man's voice, muffled, came over the receiver. "Is there anyone else in the room with you?"

I frowned at the phone and tried to place the voice. "Who is this?"

"Are you alone or not?" he asked.

"Listen, creep—"

"If you say a word, she dies. If you call anyone, she dies. I want you to listen to me, and do exactly what I tell you. Do you understand?"

My throat closed up.

His rushed voice continued. "Look on your front steps. Do not go outside. Do not call attention to what you are doing. Do you understand me?"

I was already standing by the window and my eyes immediately scanned the porch madly.

Darkness was falling and it was difficult to see, but when the lightning flashed again, I finally saw it.

A coffee cup sat by the steps. It was an ordinary cup, aside from the logo.

The cup was custom-made. The logo was plain to see.

It said Lil's Café on the side in cheerful red letters.

"You see it?"

My breath came faster. "I see it."

"Not one word. You tell that deputy, the sheriff, anyone. She dies. Understand?"

I didn't say anything. I couldn't speak. I knew the she he was speaking of. Irene. He was talking about Irene.

"I asked you a question," he said.

"I understand."

"Bring it to the Wilson ranch. Leave it on the front porch. Then drive away and don't look back. If anyone follows you, she dies."

"Bring what?" I asked.

"The blanket you took. You come alone. If you don't you will never see her again."

"The blanket? But—"

"You've got one hour."

The line went dead.

My heart nearly went dead along with it.

CHAPTER 17

I stood there holding the receiver, listening to the dial tone. *You say a word, she dies.*

Irene.

He had taken Irene.

I set the phone down softly and tried to breathe.

One hour?

I didn't even know what he was talking about. What blanket?

Then I recalled the old horse blanket Irene had given to me at the Lazy Ox Yoke. What in the hell could he possibly want that for?

Vern. It had to be Vern Houston. For whatever reason, he was searching for that blanket and he wanted it back.

He wanted it back desperately.

I went as quietly as possible to the foot of the stairs. Finn hadn't stirred, as far as I could tell.

I crept to the top of the steps and peered around the doorway.

He was flat on his chest, and his breathing came in slow, even movements.

Finn was dead asleep.

The man had told me if I alerted Finn he would kill Irene. Could I take the chance? I had no way of knowing if he was watching my house at that

186

very moment. If he saw Finn suddenly leave in his truck it could cost Irene her life.

I backed down the hall and moved down the stairs quickly.

When I got to the front door I pulled on my boots and scooped my keys from the dish.

They rattled faintly. I cringed, hoping the sound hadn't been enough to wake Finn.

But there was no movement from upstairs and I took a split second to compose myself.

Blood pounded in my ears as I tried to keep calm.

What had happened to that damn blanket? I'd searched for it in the barn the afternoon I'd noticed it missing, but it wasn't there.

Where could it be?

I forced myself to stop and think.

She had been right after all. Irene had guessed it was Vern Houston who had been terrorizing us. She had also believed he'd killed his own brother.

But why would he do all of that for the sake of an old horse blanket?

That question didn't matter. What mattered was how to get it to him.

Vern had searched Irene's house, the horse trailer, my home and my father's ranch house. He'd even searched Finn's little cottage, probably as a last resort.

That meant if I went to any of those places looking for the horse blanket I wouldn't find it.

It was gone. It was simply, impossibly, gone.

And I had one hour to deliver it or he would kill her.

Standing there wasn't going to save Irene.
I had to move.

The front door opened smoothly and I closed it softly behind me. I went down the front steps and stopped.

How was I going to drive out of there without Finn hearing? There was only one way. I had to push my SUV down the driveway until it was far enough away from the house.

The driveway sloped down slightly, but was it enough of a drop?

I used the key to unlock the door so the remote control wouldn't chirp.

When I climbed inside and quietly closed the door, the reality of the situation hit me. Vern had already killed his own brother. It was unlikely he would hesitate to kill Irene.

I had one hour to save my best friend's life.

My legs started shaking as I lifted my foot and placed it on the brake pedal.

As I struggled to move the gearshift into neutral it wouldn't budge.

The car was too new. It wouldn't go into neutral, or reverse, without the engine running.

"Dammit, dammit."

There wasn't any choice. I had to start the car.

The lights were facing the front door and I turned them off quickly.

Bracing myself, I pushed the ignition button and the motor purred to life.

I watched the house for a moment.

Nothing.

The engine was quiet enough that it hadn't alerted him to the fact that I was leaving.

I eased the SUV into reverse and rolled backwards slowly, careful not to gun the engine.

Lightning flashed overhead, illuminating the trees all around.

The gravel crunched beneath the tires. A peal of thunder echoed across the valley and I pressed harder on the gas.

I backed all the way down the drive until the rear wheels hit the main road.

In one motion, I flipped on the headlights and threw the SUV into drive.

Fat drops of rain hit the windshield as I tore down the rutted dirt road.

In a matter of minutes the valley would be engulfed by the storm.

Vern expected me to deliver the horse blanket to the Wilson ranch in less than an hour. I didn't even know where the blanket was.

The nose of my SUV bounced sideways as I took a corner too fast and I nearly rolled the vehicle into the ditch.

Forcing myself to slow down, I struggled to think.

Where could it be?

There simply wasn't enough time for me to puzzle out what had happened to the old blanket. I would never be able to find it in less than an hour. Not without a great deal of luck and a lot of help.

What if I found an empty backpack or a box, and took that instead? Would he believe an empty box contained the blanket if I did a good enough job of selling it?

No. The moment he opened the box he would see right away that I'd fooled him and it might cost Irene her life.

I couldn't risk it.

There had to be another way.

I slammed on the brakes and sat there in the middle of the road thinking, staring straight ahead as raindrops flashed in the headlights.

If there wasn't a chance of locating the blanket what options did I have left?

There was only one that I could think of.

I had to find Irene.

If I could get to her, then it didn't matter where the goddamned horse blanket was.

"Okay, Marley. Think."

If Vern wanted me to take the blanket to the Wilson ranch and leave it there, that meant he was waiting close by. He'd want to be there to watch me put it on the porch.

So that meant he would need to have stashed Irene someplace out of the way. Someplace where no one would think to look for her so he could go to the Wilson ranch unencumbered by a hostage.

But where would he be able to hide her?

The stories she had told me about the ranch, the boys, her past and the experiences she'd endured raced through my head like a movie. Where could she be?

Would Vern risk hiding her in Peter's cabin?

Not likely.

There was too much activity on the ranch. Jackie Miller, Felicia, or even Butch could discover Irene tied to a chair inside the cabin, and then Vern would have too much explaining to do.

What about the Wilson ranch? Would he use the big empty property as a hostage site? Not likely. Certainly he wouldn't take her someplace he'd instructed me to drop off the ransom.

No. He would take her where she could make all the noise she wanted and nobody would be around to hear.

He would take her someplace no one would ever think to look for her. Someplace that he knew about, but that nobody else did.

Someplace familiar.

"The fire lookout tower."

My foot hit the gas pedal before the words were completely out of my mouth.

I didn't even consider the possibility that she was already dead. I couldn't.

I had to believe she was alive, and alright, and that I could get to her first.

My head spun as I tried to work out the logistics.

If Vern was waiting for me at the Wilson ranch, hiding in the trees in his camouflage gear, that would mean he wasn't anywhere near the fire lookout tower.

The road leading to the Wilson ranch went straight by the Lazy Ox Yoke. It would take me at least fifteen minutes, breaking every speed limit in the valley, to make it to that turnoff.

When I got there, how was I going to find the tower? I'd never seen it before and all I had was a vague description.

There wasn't any other way. I simply had to find it.

Irene said that it was due west from the ranch, about a mile or a mile and a half. She said it was on top of a hill, and so old now it was practically obscured by trees.

Would I be able to see it?

My hand tore open the console box and I rummaged for a flashlight.

A small steel tube fell into my hand and I pressed the button.

Light flooded the cab and I heaved a sigh. At least I would be able to see through the gloom.

Tiny flashes of reflected light gleamed as more raindrops padded on the windshield and on the road, and left trails of moisture down the side windows.

When I reached Main Street I was afraid to look at the speedometer. Luckily the chill night had kept most folks away and downtown was practically deserted.

Lil's café was a blur as I tore past. I didn't even register if any cars were parked in the lot.

Hardly a soul moved the length of town, and my wheels spun as I turned a hard left at the turnoff and headed for the Lazy Ox Yoke Ranch.

My teeth rattled on the washboard road and the flashlight bounced to the floor. I ignored it.

It took all of my concentration to drive.

By the time I reached the fork that veered towards the Wilson ranch, rain was washing down the ditches and pooling in the low spots on the road. Relying on instinct and memory, I cranked the wheel hard to the right and headed into the darkness.

The road was narrow and turning into a muddy quagmire quickly.

After driving for at least five minutes I slowed and pivoted the headlights to the west, facing the base of the ridge and the distant tree line. The headlights refused to shine that far and I couldn't see anything. Had I come far enough yet? Was the base of the ridge ahead?

I flipped on the high beams and squinted into the rain. It was impossible to see more than a few yards beyond the front bumper. Somewhere ahead, invisible, off in the distance, was the tree line and the slope of the hill leading to the ridge. At the top of that ridge, hidden in the darkness, was the fire lookout tower.

I closed my eyes and recalled the tense drive Irene and I had shared the day we'd come to clean the cabin. It had taken us more time to drive this far, because we had traveled much slower, but I guessed this was halfway between the bunkhouses and the turnoff. I knew that straight ahead, if I'd guessed correctly, this pasture would meet the base of the ridge.

It was as good a place as any.

My SUV was equipped with a sport suspension and I was about to put it to the ultimate test. I punched the button to lock the wheels into four-wheel drive, and slammed my foot on the gas.

The nose dropped sharply as I drove off the road and down the embankment. The wheels spun wildly in the mush and the back end slid sideways as the tires struggled to gain traction. Steam rose up from the tires as water splashed from the ground and hit the underside of the engine. The back end slid precariously and I shoved the pedal to the floor.

Finally the tires bit into something solid and the SUV bucked forward, bouncing up on three wheels over an unseen rock.

The front left tire soared into the air.

"Get back down!"

The weight from the engine dropped the front end like a brick and my teeth bit into my tongue. I tasted blood.

There was nothing I could do about it now and I clenched my jaw shut.

My hands struggled to keep control of the wheel as I drove across the prairie.

The minutes raced by.

Vern had called my home at exactly seven. The clock on the dashboard told me it was now nearly twenty after and at the top of the hour he would expect me to be driving into the compound at the Wilson ranch with the blanket.

Given that he might wait for ten minutes before coming to the realization that I wasn't showing up, I hoped that I'd have a least forty minutes before he came looking.

It would take him a lot less time than me to get to the top of the ridge. After all, this was his home. He knew the way.

Before he could make it back to the tower I would need to have Irene free and we would have to be as far away from the place as possible.

Every second counted.

A second rock appeared from nowhere and my right rear tire heaved off the ground. The SUV landed with a sharp crunch and the back end squealed with a sickening metallic grind.

I managed to make it to the edge of the tree line before the rear wheel seized up and the SUV pulled against the stationary tire like a limping beast. I wasn't making any forward progress now and had to stop.

Luckily I'd made it far enough.

The headlights illuminated a steep slope covered with row after row of lodgepole pine trees. My eyes drifted up, and up, and up.

The ridge was much higher than I recalled.

It wasn't just a ridge. It was a mountain.

My hands found the flashlight and I cut the engine. I didn't want Vern to see any strange lights sitting in the middle of the pasture and be warned that I was trying to get to Irene before him. I made sure the dome light was switched off.

I looked down at myself and cringed. Jeans. T-shirt. Hiking boots.

No jacket.

Not even a sweater.

This wasn't the best plan I had ever come up with.

Then I thought of Irene. I would let myself feel the cold and wet after I found her and made sure she was safe. Until then I didn't have time to worry about noticing the elements.

The moment I stepped outside my shirt became soaked. The rain came down in torrents, flooding the spring grass and turning the ground to muck.

The flashlight cut a dim path through the sheets of water and I struggled to keep heading towards the trees.

My entire body shook by the time I reached the stand of pine trees and I had to grip a branch to keep from falling down. The ground was slicker than ice.

Irene had said the fire lookout tower was at the crest of the hill, and if I tried to find it by walking from the west and hoping to run into it out of sheer luck, I'd probably fail. The only way I could be sure to find the tower was if I started climbing while I was still at the leading edge of the ridgeline, and followed the spine all the way up until I reached the base of the structure. At least I didn't need a compass. The only way to go was straight up.

I put my head down and started climbing.

The pine trees offered some shelter. The rain was still falling, but it was less suffocating now. The angle of ascent was so steep there was no chance I'd get turned around. If my feet started to carry me downhill I knew I was going the wrong way.

My meager flashlight managed to show me a couple yards ahead, but it wouldn't reveal more than that and I had to keep focused on the ground with every single step.

My skin puckered with goose bumps. Cold rainwater seeped through my hiking boots, and my toes were numb.

It hadn't occurred to me before, but there was some chance I might go into shock before I even made it to the lookout tower. The cold was painful.

I shoved the thought out of my head. Nothing would get in my way until Irene was safe.

There was no other choice than to keep going.

The area underneath the trees was blessedly free of mud, and a thick bed of old pine needles helped my feet keep moving. When I thought my lungs would burst I stopped, rested, then forced myself onward.

The climb was much harder than I'd anticipated. I was starting to wear out.

My lips were dripping water, and my words came out in a whisper.

"God, I know you and I don't talk much anymore, and I'm not asking this for me. But if you're listening, please give me what I need to get Irene out of this. I just need once chance here. That's all. Just one."

The muscles in my left leg spasmed and I had to rub them with my hand to make them stop. The pain was terrible but moving seemed to help, so I kept going.

I had to rest four times before I managed to make it to the summit. It was narrow at the top of the ridge, and it was easy to tell that I was going the right way. As long as I kept heading up and I managed not to veer down either side of the slope, likely I would be able to find the tower.

The summit flattened out and I had to keep shifting my position back and forth as I moved. The ridgeline was broader now, and not as easy to navigate. Was I still going up?

Once I had to stop and get my bearings to make sure I was still moving the right direction. The top of the hill had become too broad to use as a guide and I worried that the farther I went, the more off-course I would get.

The cold was slowing my reaction time. My legs didn't want to work, and my hands could barely hold on to the flashlight.

Stars swam in my vision and I shook my head to clear it.

Suddenly, the trees thinned noticeably. The summit was peaking at last. I hurried forward, and if I hadn't actually been looking up at that moment, I would have walked right into the main support beam of the tower.

My hands shot forward and I gripped the heavy wood gratefully. The beam was old, bleached gray, and rough from age. As I shone my light around the base of the tower I could see the entire area was almost completely surrounded by tall trees. No wonder it was invisible from the road. It was almost invisible from a few yards away.

Relief surged through my entire body and I felt a rush of hope.

I'd found it.

Now all I had to do was find the stairs and make it to the top.

And I had to do that before I lost consciousness and froze to death.

CHAPTER 18

The flashlight was still glowing strongly and I panned the ground. My sense of time was completely gone, and it had probably been longer than it seemed. I had to hurry.

The base of the lookout tower was huge. I shone my light up and the beam vanished in the heavy rain before it managed to reach the top of the structure.

Somewhere there had to be a staircase or a ladder.

I fervently searched for a staircase. My hands were so cold the idea of climbing a ladder gave me a stab of panic.

My soaked boots were slick as my tired legs fumbled across the ground, and I searched frantically for the way up while trying not to slip. Finally I managed to spot the first step of a steep staircase and relief flooded my chest.

Before starting the climb I took a hard look at the stairs. They were old and rotted. Some looked like they would snap if I put my full weight on them and I swore under my breath.

"Hurry, hurry," I told myself.

I started up and was careful to keep my feet close to the stringer on the side, hoping that the steps wouldn't be as prone to collapse at the edges.

Time was ticking away and checking each step before putting my full weight down was taking far too long. I had to pick up the pace. Once I got to the top we still had to come back down, and if I wasn't faster there was a good chance Vern would be coming up the steps as we were trying to escape.

I stopped scanning the individual boards and forced myself to move faster.

The steps wrapped around the base of the tower in a steep ascent that was similar to a spiral staircase and the going was hard. But at least it wasn't a ladder.

Should I call for Irene? A gust of wind blasted my face and rocked me sideways. If I called to her she probably wouldn't hear me.

The further I went, the more it seemed the top didn't exist and I was on a stairway to the moon. It seemed to go on and on endlessly.

Finally I saw the landing, and the prospect of finding Irene, getting out of the rain for a blessed few minutes and having this nightmare come to an end sent a surge of adrenaline through my whole body.

I started sprinting up the last few steps and when a board broke under my foot the world turned sideways.

The board buckled like it was made of paper and both my arms shot out. My weight pulled me down. The flashlight tumbled from my hands and the beam spiraled over and over as it fell.

My ribs crashed against the landing and pain stabbed through my gut like a knife. The impact knocked all the air from my lungs and I couldn't feel my legs. My hands clawed the landing trying to snag something to hold onto.

It was a miracle, but I wasn't falling.

For a moment I simply hovered with my right leg hanging precariously in midair before realizing what had happened.

My legs were numb from cold, but somehow I'd managed to stop my fall with my left leg. My knee was propped up on the step below the broken board and my ribs rested on the landing platform.

Gingerly, I took a shaky breath and pushed with my left leg.

The board creaked but it supported my weight and I shoved myself up and onto the landing with one kick.

I rolled to my side on the deck and lay there for a moment, heaving air back into my lungs.

The shock had nearly paralyzed my motor functions and it took a moment to get my hands working again.

Lightning flashed above, illuminating the roof of the shack for a split second, and it looked like the structure was old, but still sound. If Irene was inside, at least she would be dry.

Rain gushed over me and my skin stung with pain. I ran my hand over my ribs carefully, trying to determine if they were broken or just bruised, but my senses were so dull from cold and fear there was no way to tell how badly I'd been hurt.

At least nothing was sticking out through my chest and there didn't seem to be any warm blood oozing down my shirt, so I took that as a good sign.

Carefully, I eased up to my knees and sat still for a moment. Stars swam in my vision and I took a cautious breath. It hurt, but not so badly that it was incapacitating.

My feet seemed to move across the platform by themselves. My body knew it was dry inside the shack and it was going through that door with or without my consent.

Then a thought struck me, and panic set in.

Had I just made the worst mistake of my life and gambled Irene's safety on a hunch? Was she even here?

My icy fingers fumbled with the doorknob and it turned in my hand. The knob was old and resisted, but it still rotated and I felt the door surrender.

It opened a crack and I leaned my head in, listening.

"Irene?"

Nothing. For one horrible moment I believed all my effort had been a waste. She wasn't here!

Maybe she couldn't talk for some reason? Maybe she was unconscious?

That thought propelled me forward and I stepped inside the shack.

I called into the pitch-blackness. "Irene, it's Marley. I'm going to get you out of here."

The glorious sound of rhythmic thumping came from the back corner and I nearly cried with relief. She was inside the shack and pounding on something to let me know it.

I stumbled forward, heading towards the sound.

My hands waved in the air uselessly as I tried to move through the shack blindly.

A stab of fresh pain shot through my knee and my legs nearly buckled. Between my aching ribs and the cold, my body couldn't take much more of this.

I knelt down and used my hands to navigate. It was near total darkness and it wasn't until the lightning flashed again that I could make out the room.

The split second of light showed me the object I'd run into was a large woodstove. It was so old and rusted that I hardly recognized what it was.

Muffled words and more thumping propelled me forward again and I crawled across the floor, gripping the stove with one hand.

My fingers found a human leg and I jerked my hand back reflexively.

"Irene?"

I was rewarded with another muffled reply and I scrambled closer.

She wasn't tied to a chair the way I'd envisioned. I felt along her arms and they seemed anchored to the floor somehow. As I ran my fingers down to her wrists my heart sank.

Her wrists were bound together around the leg of the ancient woodstove. The thing had to weigh more than a couple hundred pounds. How the hell was I going to get her loose?

I knelt next to her as another flash of lightning illuminated her face and I could see duct tape covering her mouth. Fumbling along the sides of her head, my numb fingers moved agonizingly slow, but I managed to find the edge of the tape. It was stuck to her hair on both sides and I gripped one edge, cringing.

"Sorry."

She hammered on the floor with both feet frantically.

"This is going to hurt," I said.

I pulled hard and fast. Ripping tape and the sickening sound of tearing hair were followed by a sharp cry of pain.

Irene gasped for air. "Marley, what in the hell are you doing here?"

"Are you alright?"

"It's still on my face," she said.

"I can leave it if it hurts too much."

"No, just rip it off," she told me.

I felt along her cheek and located the tape still clinging to her ear. I grimaced with sympathy and tore it loose.

"Christ almighty! I take it back. You should have left it there."

"We don't have a lot of time," I told her.

"Marley, you need to get out of here. He's going to come back."

"It was Vern, wasn't it?"

"How the hell should I know? He never spoke, and never showed me his face. I thought it was, but I can't say for sure. It could have been Ned."

"Let me guess. He was dressed head to toe in camouflage and wore a mask."

"How did you know that?"

"That's not important right now," I said. "Did he leave a lantern or a flashlight up here?"

"How did you make it all the way up here without a flashlight?" she asked.

"I lost it. Are you going to help me out here, or what?"

"He used a flashlight to tie me up and took it with him when he left," she said.

I crouched next to her arms and felt along her wrists, trying to figure out what to do to free her. "Okay, what have we got here?"

"I'm tied to a stove," she said.

"Thanks. That's incredibly helpful," I said. "I don't suppose there is a hacksaw up here in a fully stocked toolbox?"

"Sure. It's next to the cappuccino machine."

Her voice trembled when she spoke and I knew her humor was an attempt to defuse her fear. I completely understood how she felt.

I eased along the floor on all fours, searching with my hands. "Do you remember if there is anything useful in this shack?"

"This place is older than you are. There isn't anything up here anymore."

She was right. The room was practically empty. As I felt along the floor it was apparent there wasn't going to be anything inside that would be helpful.

I scrambled back to Irene and felt along the stove leg again. The leg was stout and it would be impossible for me to bend it. I simply wasn't strong enough.

"You're dripping on me," Irene said.

"Could you be quiet while I think?"

"Listen! Did you hear that?"

I paused. "What?"

"What is that?"

I strained to listen. "I don't—"

"Shush! It sounds like a motor. I think he's back."

The wind howled outside and rain pounded against the windows. It was impossible to hear anything above the storm.

"He brought us up here on a four-wheeler. Do you see any headlights?"

I stumbled to my feet and managed to reach the door. It was too hazy outside to see clearly, but I couldn't see anything that looked like the headlight of an ATV. "I think you are hearing things."

My stomach felt sick from standing up so quickly. "He's supposed to be waiting for me over at the Wilson ranch. There is no way he could have gotten back here so fast."

Unless I had grossly miscalculated the amount of time I'd been wandering around on the mountain.

Irene struggled against the stove. "Will you hurry up and get me the hell loose already?"

I turned back and dropped to my knees beside her and examined the stove with my hands. "Okay, it's bolted to the floor."

"Don't you think I already know that?"

"What did he tie you with?"

"Nylon baling twine," she said.

"You couldn't have, I don't know, rubbed it against the stove leg and cut yourself loose or something?"

Her reply came through clenched teeth. "The stove legs are round. So it would take about thirty-seven years for that to work."

I tested my grip on the twine. "Will you be able to help pull? Maybe with both of us we can break it."

"Marley, it's baling twine. One strand can hold a hundred pounds and he looped it around six or seven times. You aren't going to be able to break it."

The twine was wrapped tight around her wrists and secured with a looped knot. I felt along the strands, looking for an end I could unravel, but it was no use.

Irene let out a long gasp. "Now what?"

I stood up and ran my hands over the top of the stove, looking for some sort of weakness we could exploit. The stovepipe was still intact. It sat atop the stove and was still attached to the ceiling of the shack.

I pushed the pipe with one hand. The metal was flexible and gave under pressure.

"Shut your eyes," I said.

"What are you doing?"

The pipe came free easily when I shoved. I pulled it from the stove and threw it to the side of the shack. The smell of old ashes wafted through the air.

"Could you please explain to me what you are doing?" Irene asked angrily.

I crouched down again and felt along the floorboards beneath the stove with both hands. My fingers were still cold as ice, but as I prodded the boards it was apparent the wood was partially rotten. Some of the planks felt crumbly.

"These boards under this side of the stove are pretty old," I said.

"Oh, good. If we only wait patiently it should decompose soon and then I'll be free at last."

I scooted closer to the feet of the stove and tapped the boards underneath with one knuckle until I found the one that seemed the most rotted. The wood had been eaten away from age and insects. It was weak and brittle.

"It's almost completely disintegrated."

I stood up and positioned my heel directly over the old board. Before she had a chance to ask, I brought my boot down hard and the wood shattered.

The board snapped beneath the two stove legs. They weren't bolted to the floor any longer.

"That's great," Irene said. "But I'm tied to this side."

"Move," I instructed.

"Where am I supposed to go?"

"Move out of the way," I told her. "I'm going to push it over."

I positioned myself with my back braced against the potbelly of the cold iron and dug in my heels.

Scrambling sounds told me she was moving, and then there was stillness.

"Ready?"

"I hope you know what you are doing."

My legs were still shaking from the hike, but adrenaline fueled my efforts and I heaved against the old iron.

For one agonizing moment, nothing happened at all. Then wood started to groan and creak, and as I strained against the stove I felt it start to shift.

Suddenly the rusted feet lifted off the floor and the entire thing rolled sideways.

Irene yelped. All resistance was suddenly gone and I landed hard on my hip as the stove toppled down.

Silence.

"I didn't crush you, did I?"

"No."

I swallowed and stood up. "Sorry. It wasn't as hard as I thought it would be."

"Good ol' reliable American steel," Irene said bitterly.

"Let's move it," I said. "We don't have a lot of time."

"What am I supposed to do with my arms still tied together?" she asked.

Out of sheer frustration, I felt along the floor until my hands found the stovepipe again. I picked it up and smashed it through the closest window. Shards of glass tinkled to the floor and I gingerly felt along the rough wood until I located a piece of glass big enough to use as a makeshift knife.

"Hold still."

She flinched when I started sawing at the twine. "Why didn't you just do that in the first place? We could have already been out of here by now!"

It was clumsy work, but after getting the knack for it I had her arms free.

I put a hand on her shoulder. "Can you remember how to get to the road from here?"

She lunged for the exit. "As long as we aren't in this crow's nest when he comes back, I don't care where we end up."

I stopped her before she reached the door. "It's cold outside. I mean really cold. We can't leave until we have a plan for a place to go."

"Right," she said, pulling open the door. "You stay here and make a plan. I'm getting the hell out of here."

She vanished outside and I had no choice but to follow.

Before she reached the stairs I shouted at her. "Watch that second step!"

When she didn't respond I hurried forward and groped blindly until I bumped into her from the back.

She wasn't moving.

"Irene, that second step down is busted. Be careful."

She stayed still. "It won't matter anyway."

I tugged her arm. "Why not?"

"Because there are headlights below and it's too late. He's back."

CHAPTER 19

I grabbed the railing on the deck and leaned over the side. I saw a single, faint light winking up through the falling rain. It wasn't moving. Luckily the downpour had slowed to a drizzle.

"That's not a headlight. It's a flashlight," I said. "Come on."

I grabbed her elbow, urging her forward.

Irene was still peering down at the ground. "How do you know it's not him coming up here?"

"Could you try to be a little more positive for a minute?"

"I've been kidnapped and tied to a stove and you want me to be a little more positive?"

"The steps are really fragile," I said. "We need to be careful. Take your time and keep your hands on the rail in case you break through."

She hesitated. "Are you sure that's a flashlight?"

I pushed her towards the stairs. "I'm the one who dropped it. So, yeah, I'm sure. Will you move it?"

We took great pains to step over the broken tread at the top and started our descent.

I herded Irene along in front of me like a lost sheep. She had taken my warning to heart and she tested every single step before putting her weight down. It would take us all night to reach the bottom if we didn't get moving.

"Okay, maybe we don't need to be quite this careful," I said.

"Do you want me to hurry or do you want me to make it off this damn tower alive?"

"Both! Can you go just a little faster?"

She grumbled and complained but our pace sped up.

The rain slowed even more, but it was still just as cold.

Now I was only soaked, as opposed to drenched.

Each step I took reminded me that my ribs were deeply bruised. Every breath was a challenge. But the pain wasn't so bad that it kept me from running for my life.

When we made it to the ground I fumbled along until I reached the glowing flashlight.

I lifted it and saw a dent in the side, but the beam was as reliable as before.

"Where did you park your car?" Irene asked.

"We can't go back that way."

"Why not? You don't think you can find it again?"

"Even if I could find it, we can't drive it. It's probably got a busted axle."

"That's just great. Does anyone know where we are?" she asked.

"Um . . ."

She threw up her hands. "Did you think this through at all before you came charging up here?"

"I was sort of focused on getting you out alive," I said.

"Then we don't have any choice. If nobody knows where we are but Vern, and we can't drive out, then we have to go to the Lazy Ox Yoke and get help."

"Are you out of your mind?" I asked.

"You have a better idea? It's more than eight miles to the main road. And even if we knew we wouldn't get lost and could actually find it, there's no guarantee that the first car we meet won't be Vern driving back here. It's less than two miles to the ranch."

I stared at her, cold rainwater tricking down between my shoulder blades. Worry and doubt had turned my stomach to ice.

"And after we get to the ranch, then what?" I asked.

"We get Felicia's attention and call for help."

"This is a terrible plan," I said.

"You are turning blue," she said.

Irene's face was illuminated from the glow of my light and her expression was determined. She grabbed my shoulder. "Don't argue with me. Start walking."

Irene snatched the flashlight and got moving. I stumbled after her, holding on to her back belt loop with two fingers as she led us through the gloom.

I didn't argue with her about who got to hold the light. She knew this territory better than I did. Our chances of finding the ranch with her leading the way were much higher.

Praying for help again just seemed ungrateful to me. After all, I'd asked that I could get Irene free from the lookout tower, but I hadn't specified anything after that. At this point, I figured we were on our own.

We trudged downhill for well over an hour. At least it felt like it. Probably it was more like half an hour and the pain in my ribs made it seem longer. The slope was so steep my legs nearly collapsed as we stumbled onward.

Each step I took caused tingles of pain in my feet and added to the misery. Every few yards I took a physical inventory and added up all the twinges and outright stabs of discomfort I was feeling. Luckily for me, at least I could still walk. I didn't even want to think about what we would have done if I'd broken a leg falling through that broken step.

"I found down," Irene announced at last. She fumbled with the flashlight as she squatted on her heels to rest.

"You found what?"

"Down. We are finally down off the hill and I know where we are again."

"You didn't know where we were when we started walking?" I asked.

"Not a clue. I figured as soon as we got to the pasture I'd recognize something."

My feet were crying with gratitude that we'd stopped moving. "You see something familiar?"

She pointed vaguely ahead. "I recognize the lights from the bunkhouse."

Instinctively I crouched beside her. "Turn off that flashlight."

She pulled it away from me. "Who's going to be looking out here anyway? The only people who will be in the bunkhouse are the hired hands and they don't know anything about this situation. Come on."

Irene shot to her feet and resumed her march. I trotted after her miserably. The bunkhouse lights glowed faintly ahead, and in spite of the underlying feeling of dread that was impossible to shake, knowing that we were only minutes away from someplace warm drove me ahead.

As we approached the rear of the bunkhouse I slowed my pace and hunkered down. I ducked underneath the window and pressed my back against the rough wood.

"What are you doing?" Irene asked.

"I'm being careful. I thought it might be a good idea, considering the circumstances."

I tried to peer inside the window, but a curtain obscured everything. Without actually going in, we couldn't determine who was inside.

"Nobody in the bunkhouse knows what just happened. You can sit out here and freeze to death. I'm going in."

"Irene wait, we don't know who knows about the blanket."

She stopped and turned the flashlight on me. "What blanket?"

"He called my house a couple hours ago and told me that if I didn't bring the blanket to the Wilson ranch and leave it on the porch, then you would die."

She didn't say anything for a moment and I put my hand over the flashlight so it wasn't giving us away. She seemed to be thinking.

"Did you hear me?" I asked.

"Was he talking about that crappy horse blanket that Felicia gave to us when we were cleaning out the cabin?"

"I don't know," I confessed. "Maybe. But the problem is, I don't know where it went. I put it in my father's barn and it vanished. I didn't have much choice but to figure out what happened to you."

"Because you couldn't deliver what he wanted," she said.

My teeth were chattering again but I manage to reply. "And I still can't."

She switched off the flashlight. A dim light shone around the curtain from the back window of the bunkhouse and illuminated the pasture around us faintly. I could see her shivering and realized she was trembling as much as me.

If we stayed outside much longer we'd both collapse.

"It still doesn't change anything," Irene said. "We need to get inside."

But her words were less confident than before, and when she headed for the bunkhouse door, it was clear she was not as determined.

We walked quickly and our teeth were chattering so hard the ranch hands could probably hear us.

"Are you sure about this?" I asked.

She nodded. "Let me go first."

Irene squared her shoulders and pushed open the door. It swung wide and she went through it without any hesitation.

Warm air enveloped me as I stumbled inside. My relief at escaping the cold was so great I didn't notice that Irene had stopped dead in front of me, frozen in place just inside the door. Her shivering had ceased completely and she stared straight ahead, unmoving.

I craned my neck to see around her and saw a man sitting in an old wooden chair.

He slowly raised himself up, his face a mask of disbelief and anger.

Butch Houston stared at us from inside the bunkhouse with his eyes blazing like torches. He looked at Irene and growled. "You."

"Now, Butch. We don't want any trouble," Irene said.

He lifted his cane and pointed it at her face. "Well, you got it anyway, didn't ya?"

CHAPTER 20

No one moved. An old wall clock ticked rhythmically, and the three of us stood where we were without uttering a sound.

A spark crackled inside the fireplace on the far wall and the dancing flames made every shadow in the room move together.

I was hardly aware of the warmth seeping into my skin. Seeing Butch Houston had me stunned.

"Well, shut the damn door," he said.

Irene stayed where she was, but Butch sneered and waved a hand.

"Shut it. I'm paying for all this heat."

The bunkhouse was empty. He was the only one there. Although his expression was hostile, he made no move toward us.

A cold gust blasted inside and I relented, closing the heavy wood door against the chill.

The old man sat back down in the wooden chair, his knees creaking.

I had no idea how much he knew about what Vern had been doing all this time. Did Butch know about the burglaries?

And more important, did he know what had just happened to Irene?

If he did, it might explain why he was here and both of his boys, and the workers, were gone.

It seemed possible that Butch had sent everyone away because he knew something of great magnitude was about to occur.

"What happened to your hired hands?" Irene asked, apparently reading my mind.

Butch smirked. "Gave them the night off."

A shiver of warning trickled down my spine.

A quick survey of the room told me that there wasn't a telephone we could use to call Loy, and for a moment I thought we would have to make a run for the house.

The air crackled with tension, but nobody moved or spoke. I waited to see what the old man would do next.

Another spark shot from the fireplace, causing me to jump.

"Felicia's over to the house," Butch said suddenly. "Why don't you head on over there, Irene? Phone up Nathan and have him come pick you two gals up."

I couldn't believe my own ears.

It seemed impossible, but he was helping us. How much did he know?

"I'll give Loy a call too, while I'm at it," Irene said bluntly. She stared right at Butch when she said it.

Butch gave a derisive snort. "You just do that, Little Miss."

It seemed inconceivable to me that he wasn't demanding to know what we were both doing in his bunkhouse, at night, in the middle of a rainstorm. He had to be more aware of the situation than he was letting on.

Irene looked over at me with a mixture of fear and hope battling for supremacy on her face.

"Marley should come with me. We don't want to be a bother."

"She stays," he said instantly. "There's questions need answering."

"Mr. Houston," I said. "I'm not sure I can give you any answers."

"I don't need you to talk," he said impatiently. "I need you to listen."

Irene's eyes darted between Butch and me frantically. She leaned towards me and whispered. "What should I do?"

"Go," I said. "Call Loy."

"What if Felicia isn't alone in the house?" she asked.

I knew she was afraid Vern might be waiting for her instead of Felicia. I glanced at Butch and whispered. "It's not like I can't outrun him."

She made an unhappy face. "That doesn't make me feel any better."

We stared at each other, undecided.

Butch slammed the tip of his cane down with a crack. "Goddammit, Irene. The sheriff is already coming out here tonight to arrest my boy. Think I'd do something to you two gals knowing the law's gonna be here in a couple hours?"

Irene and I exchanged a puzzled look.

"Loy is arresting your son?" I asked.

"So I've been told. But he's wrong," Butch replied. "It's all a mistake."

Irene pulled open the door. "I'm coming right back, Marley. And Loy is going to be here a lot sooner than a couple of hours "

Butch didn't protest as Irene walked out of the bunkhouse. She disappeared into the darkness and I closed the door behind her.

I was alone with Butch now, and although the warm fire filled the room with a comforting golden glow of heat and light, my insides still felt like ice.

Not a single light burned in the cramped living quarters other than the fireplace.

The space was filled up with old pieces of furniture, photographs, ancient and faded wooden hand tools that had once been useful, but were now nothing more than decoration.

The bunkhouse was a relic of the past. It was a monument for the old homesteaders who had lived, worked, and died trying to survive on this rugged landscape.

Looking around the room, I understood better where Peter had inherited his need to collect old things. Apparently Butch felt the same need. It was perhaps the one thing the two men had shared.

I went to the big fireplace and stretched my arms towards the warmth. The orange glow from the flickering flames cast eerie shadows over the old man.

His face was haggard.

His gnarled hands gripped the top of his heavy wooden cane and I could see the years had taken their toll.

"Not much to look at anymore, am I?" he asked.

"We all get there someday," I replied.

He grunted a response and watched me with hooded eyes.

"I figure it'll take that sheriff about an hour to get word and come out," he said.

"He might be here faster than that," I told him.

Butch laughed. "Not likely, I imagine. You and I still got a little time left."

I hadn't taken my eyes off him. "Time for what?"

Butch fingered the end of his cane thoughtfully. "You are part of a dying breed, Marley Dearcorn."

His voice sounded melancholy and I shook my head. "Excuse me?"

"Your family. Just like us. Our way of life is dying out. Fifty years from now this place won't exist anymore. Ranching will just be a memory. Like homesteading. Or war bonds."

"You've got a family," I said. "A legacy. They will stay here and work the land."

He scrutinized me. "Maybe. Them's that left might. But what happens when they are gone? This place'll get bought up by a corporation of some kind. Some football star will scoop it all up and turn it into a petting zoo. What the hell would I want to stick around and see that for? Dyin's better."

He sniffed and pulled a faded blue handkerchief from his pocket. He wiped his nose and I couldn't tell if he was cold or if he was suffering from a sudden attack of emotion.

"That's why I wanted to divvy this place up amongst them. A man will do anything for his sons," he said suddenly.

I managed my own snort of derision. "What about his daughter?"

Butch darted a glance in my direction. "Felicia? Ah, she'll be alright. She's got two brothers left to watch out for her. And that Miller? He ain't so bad. Might make a good husband to her."

His words shocked me. "You don't have a problem with Jackie and Felicia being a couple?"

"Do I have a problem with it? Course not. But I'll be damned if I'm gonna tell them that. What's the fun of having something, less it's forbidden?"

"It hasn't been very much fun for Felicia," I pointed out. "Worried all the time about getting your approval."

"I married Barb when I was nothin' but a worthless cowhand, and she was the rancher's daughter. Look what I managed to do with it. Made this place what it is today. You think I'm gonna hold it against Miller, considering that's how it all started for me?" he asked.

"But Felicia won't inherit the ranch," I said. "Only her brothers will own the land."

Butch rapped his cane against the wood floor. "You'd think that, wouldn't you? That I'd let my only daughter twist in the wind. Well, let me tell you something. Felicia's the one who will hold this place together."

"And how will she manage that?" I asked.

His crafty eyes twinkled. "'Cause I gave her the most valuable thing I could."

"The mineral rights?"

He blinked at me with confusion. "Where'd you get that idea? Course I didn't give her the mineral rights. What the hell good would that of done her?"

"What's left then?" I asked. "The boys get the land, what's left for Felicia?"

Butch's eyes gleamed and he gestured with his cane. "I gave her the water rights."

"For Clear Creek?" I asked.

"She's the sole shareholder, controls the whole thing."

The implications of that gesture were huge and I realized instantly what that would mean. Felicia was the peacemaker in the Houston clan, and Butch had given her the one thing she could use to control all of her brothers.

He had effectively given her the keys to the kingdom.

Now I understood what he had been trying to accomplish all along. His goal had been to hold his family together. He'd thought that by giving Felicia the water rights to the ranch, he could count on her to force her tempestuous brothers to cooperate with each other.

It had been a noble gesture meant to preserve his legacy. Unfortunately, it hadn't turned out that way.

My teeth had finally stopped chattering but I was still miserably cold. Butch seemed oblivious to my discomfort.

His admission of giving the water rights to Felicia wasn't the last thing he wanted to say, if his sad look was any indication. The regret was heavy on his face.

"You've told me what you were willing to do for your daughter," I prompted. "What would you be willing to do for your sons?"

He eyed me approvingly and gave a nod. Apparently I'd asked the right question.

His words were soft. "Question is, what wouldn't I be willing to do?"

A pattern was becoming clear. All I had to do was look closely enough, and I would be able to see it.

"What have you done for your sons?" I asked.

Butch's eyes misted over with a cloud of moisture. "The best I could. Brought 'em up right. Beat them when they misbehaved and taught all three of them not to be weak. Showed all my boys the world is mean, and to survive it, you've got to be just as mean."

"You really believe that?" I asked.

"The harder the wind, the greater the bend. The greater the bend, the stronger the wood," he said.

"You wanted to see how strong they really were, didn't you?" I asked.

"I wanted to see to it they survived. Can't be a man, not without facing a hardship and refusing to give in to it."

"You ever make any mistakes, Butch?"

He pierced me with such a sharp gaze I blinked.

"Maybe one."

"And what was that?"

"Forcing them to compete against each other. Thought I was making them tough. Building character. Giving them something to shoot for. Didn't think they'd ever turn on one another."

The old man cast his tired eyes away and the pain that marred his features was obvious.

"You didn't think that Vern would ever take it to the level he did," I said quietly. I wanted him to tell me which of his sons was responsible for all of the mayhem and tragedy. I wanted him to admit that he knew which of his two boys had become so obsessed with surviving that he would kill a sibling.

"Vern? Nah, I never worried about him," Butch said dismissively.

That surprised me a little and I pressed on. "Who did you worry about, then. Was it Ned?"

"Pete was always the outsider. He looked up to his older brothers but they didn't accept him."

It wasn't what I'd expected to hear. I was sure Butch would have implicated Vern or Ned, but he hadn't.

Why was it important to him that he explain Peter was the outsider?

Then it all snapped into focus. Peter had been the outsider to everyone in the family, except for one other person.

"Peter and Felicia were allies, weren't they?" I asked.

Butch stared at a spot in the old wood floor and didn't respond.

I pressed on, willing the jumbled story to come together. There had been a major flaw in Butch's plan to preserve his legacy by giving Felicia the water rights. And that flaw was underestimating the influence Peter had over his sister.

I spoke clearly. "You didn't take into account how much Felicia relied on Peter for counsel."

The old man gave such a faint nod I thought I'd imagined it. But his eyes told me I was correct.

"I'd hoped the girl would have had more gumption in her, like Barb. But things turned out different," he said.

"So one of your three sons did have the advantage over the others."

"It wasn't supposed to be like that," he snapped. "They was supposed to work together. Not turn on one another like wild dogs. Wasted. All that work and plannin' and tryin'. Wasted!"

Peter could easily have influenced Felicia, because of their connection. He could have effortlessly told her how to manage the water rights, and that gave him an enormous advantage over his two older brothers. For the first time in his life, Peter had become the sibling with the power.

He'd been killed because of his ability to influence his sister. At least, that was what Butch seemed to be implying.

223

Unless I had read the entire situation completely wrong, it was suddenly clear to me exactly what had happened to Peter.

Butch's tired eyes met mine and he seemed to be watching my expression.

He was confessing, in his own way.

He wasn't saying the words exactly, but he was confessing to me and I knew it.

His own sons had tried to destroy each other. And Butch had been forced to deal with the aftermath.

I imagined the old man had been shocked after he'd discovered Peter's body. He had probably guessed right away that Vern, or Ned, was responsible. But as a father, he had decided to try and fix it instead of reporting the murder.

If one son was gone from a ranch, it might still be able to survive.

If two sons were gone, one murdered, the other in jail, the Lazy Ox Yoke was doomed.

Butch had made the hard choice. The wrong choice.

He'd tried to cover it up.

"Not an easy thing," I said quietly. "Moving a body's not an easy thing. Hard work. Heavy work."

I cast a direct look at Butch's cane.

He rocked the heavy cane back and forth, his tone contemplative. "Oh, it's not so hard. Roll it onto a rug. Pull it into a trailer with a cutting horse and unload it again the same way."

Irene had told me Butch was a master horse trainer. She'd said the old man was so gifted he could make a horse obey verbal commands.

He wouldn't have even had to get into the saddle to prompt a well-trained animal to do his bidding.

"A cutting horse wearing Peter's saddle," I said. "He'd be used to pulling calves that way. Trained for it."

Butch turned his eyes back to me. "Not sayin' it did happen that way. Just sayin' it could have."

"Which one of your boys is the deer hunter?" I asked.

My question surprised him, and he had to stop and think it through. "Vern. He's the deer hunter. Uses a bow. Pours deer piss on his boots and paints himself up like Montezuma's revenge. Looks like a damn fool, but he brings in a lot of meat."

"And the blanket? I don't suppose you know anything about that, do you?"

He squinted through the firelight. "What blanket?"

"It's probably not important," I told him.

Headlights suddenly splashed across the window, framing the dim bunkhouse with ghostly shadows. Blue and red lights flickered, but there was no siren. The sheriff had just driven down the rutted road, passed by the bunkhouse and was pulling up in front of the family home.

He must have already been very close by when he'd gotten the call. It would only take a moment for Irene to point Loy in the right direction. He'd be parking outside the bunkhouse in a matter of minutes and that thought gave me great comfort.

Butch glanced towards the window and a mournful look twisted his face. "Looks like the sheriff got here quicker than I gave him credit for. Well, I suppose now's as good a time as any."

He started to rise and had to lean heavily on the cane.

I made a motion to help him up, but he waved me off belligerently.

"Leave it," he said. "Don't matter now anyway. I walked in here on my own two feet. I can walk out that way."

His words struck me with their finality. He sounded so bitter.

Butch was tired. He'd lived a hard life and now he had to walk outside in the rain to confess to the sheriff what he'd done.

I supposed that he was allowed to sound a little bitter.

The tragedy of the situation was heartbreaking. One way or the other, Loy would discover which of Butch's sons had murdered his brother. All of the old man's efforts had been wasted. No matter what he did now, the Lazy Ox Yoke was destined to lose two sons, and there was no other way for it to end.

In spite of the fact that what he had done was deplorable, I still felt sorry for him.

"Go on out there," Butch instructed. "Tell Loy I'll be along in a minute. Let me get my coat."

When I opened the door, a silver truck with low-profile light bars was pulling up in front of the bunkhouse.

It was the sheriff, as I'd hoped. I went outside and hurried to the truck through the rain.

He unlocked the passenger-side door and I climbed inside gratefully.

"Butch is alone in there, and he's coming out," I said.

"I'll go get him," Loy grumbled. "Irene called me and told me what happened."

I put a hand on his arm. "Butch is going to confess something to you."

The sheriff paused. "Well, that's a switch. Usually all I get's lies and half-truths."

We both looked up when the headlights caught movement in the doorway. Butch stood there in the bright gleam, motionless.

The old man held something in his hand, but he kept it away from the light and I couldn't make out what it was.

"Where's his cane?" I asked. "He'll fall over without it."

"I should go talk to him inside so he doesn't need to walk all the way over here to the truck," Loy said.

He pushed open his door and stepped out.

The old man stood with his head held high and his sharp eyes focused straight ahead.

"Sheriff? You on duty?" Butch called from the doorway.

Loy hesitated. His hand was suddenly on the butt of his pistol. "I'm on duty. Why don't we go back inside and we can chat, out of this weather?"

"You shouldn't complain about free water," Butch replied.

"Where are your two boys?" Loy asked cautiously.

The sheriff edged closer to the porch, and something about the way he moved made the hairs on my neck rise up.

"My two remaining boys?" Butch asked bitterly. "They'll be along directly, I imagine."

Loy stopped and his shoulders hunched up with tension. "I need you to come out of that doorway where I can see you."

The old man shook his head. "Can't be like that."

Butch raised his right hand and the silver gleam of an old pistol flashed in the light.

I'd seen Loy shoot his sidearm in the past, but I'd never seen him draw. It happened so quickly my eyes nearly didn't register the movement. One moment Loy was standing still, the next he was aiming his revolver.

"Hold it right there, Butch."

The old man sighed deeply.

He looked at Loy, his face filled with sorrow. "I killed Peter. I killed my son. Caught him with that bag of sapphires and I thought he had found some kind of quarry here on the ranch. I told him I didn't want all those damn day-diggers coming around, tearing the place to hell. Told him they had to go. He needed to get rid of them. He argued with me and I hit him with my cane. It's inside by the fireplace. It's got his blood on it."

"I need you to lower your weapon, Butch."

"Tell my boys—"

His words cut off as he choked back a sob. "Tell my boys, and Felicia, I did the best I could."

"Butch stop!"

The old man raised his arm higher and pulled back the hammer.

Loy shot him in the chest twice before he could fire.

Butch Houston wavered in the doorway as his eyes drained of life.

His body fell backwards and sprawled inside the door, motionless.

I was clambering out of the truck and racing to the bunkhouse door before Loy could shout for me to stop.

Off in the distance I heard someone screaming.

Felicia was running down the porch of the family house with Irene sprinting after her.

The headlights from Loy's truck illuminated the doorway and most likely she'd seen everything. The girl had probably watched as the sheriff had been forced to kill her father, and her wails of anguish pierced the air.

Before I could reach him Loy had already kicked Butch's pistol away and was checking him for a pulse. He shook his head, indicating that the old man was dead.

Then he retrieved the pistol and examined the cylinder. A low curse escaped his lips and he squeezed the pistol with one hand so hard his fingers turned white.

The sheriff slumped to his knees where he stood. "Goddammit, Houston. Goddammit to hell. It wasn't even loaded."

CHAPTER 21

Finn hardly uttered a single word to me for nearly two days.

His anger was so palpable it radiated off of him like heat lightning.

He was acting sheriff of Killdeer, while Loy was on administrative leave, and until the investigation was over he would be dealing with local calls alone, and relying on backup from the Parkman County sheriff's office for situations that required more than one man to handle.

Being acting sheriff was not helping his mood, or lessening his unadulterated fury towards me.

He was still staying at my house, and to say our interactions were tense was putting it mildly.

The shooting had occurred late Monday evening, but it wasn't until Tuesday afternoon that Finn finally had enough control over his anger to speak to me again.

The fact that I'd deliberately put myself at risk without going to him first had left him with a gaping hole of simmering hurt, and I could see that Finn was struggling to cope.

"You do not need to explain to me again," he said.

"It was the logical thing to do," I told him.

He held up a hand abruptly. "You've said that already. It doesn't mean it was the right thing to do."

We sat across from each other at the kitchen table with our empty plates pushed aside. All the ice had melted in my water glass. The dinner hour was long gone and we had circled the conversation around so many times my voice was wearing out.

I'd tried everything to convince him that my actions had been justified, and he was so close to losing his temper, more than once during our talk he'd simply walked out of the room and returned several minutes later, dripping sweat. The third time he'd fled I followed him and spied him doing push-ups on the porch.

Sometimes it looked as if his anger was so powerful the only thing that seemed to help was suffering an intense physical release.

I never worried for a second that Finn would unleash his fury on me, but my actions had already pushed him to the breaking point, and so while we talked I was careful to be as diplomatic as possible.

I was trying not to antagonize him, but somehow that seemed to be happening every time I opened my mouth.

"Marley, I understand why you felt compelled to act. Believe me, I do. But the fact remains. It was incredibly reckless and may have resulted in great harm coming to you. Can you understand how that makes me feel?"

I stared at the kitchen table and traced the grain of wood with my finger. Why did the most painful conversations in a person's life always seem to take place in the kitchen?

"I can't know how it makes you feel unless you tell me," I said.

My face must have betrayed that I was currently thinking about a far deeper, older resentment.

He rubbed his tired eyes. "Why do I get the impression you are not simply talking about the shooting?"

My tone was heavy with my own personal hurts and regrets. He'd obviously sensed it.

"Finn, you think it was easy for me? A voice on the phone tells me my best friend will die if I inform you or Loy that he's contacted me, and then he demands I exchange her life for some stupid blanket?"

He managed to give me a sympathetic look and his eyes softened. "You must have been very conflicted."

"Conflicted? More like I was scared out of my wits. You want to know what conflicted feels like, try dating a man for weeks who won't even tell you his real first name."

Finn's first name was Angus. I'd had to wheedle that information out of the two guys who worked with him, while we were still dating. The fact that he had kept that information from me for so long still stung when I thought about it.

He looked away from me and mumbled a reply I couldn't understand.

"What did you say?" I asked.

"I had to lie," he said forcefully. "You know that. Hiding my location and keeping my real name to myself were things I did to protect the people around me. What sort of life could you expect, living with a bloke who has a long list of enemies and no future? That's not what I wanted for you."

"Did you ever think to ask me if it was what I wanted?" I blurted out.

When had we veered off onto this topic?

Finn stood up and paced beside the kitchen table. "You needed something stable. You needed someone who could give you a normal life."

I thought about Leif and my painfully short marriage. "I guess that wasn't exactly meant to be, either."

Finn stopped and gave me another sympathetic look. "Marley, I'm sorry. I didn't mean to remind you."

"It's not as bad as it was," I said. "Remembering, I mean. I've gotten to the point now that I can focus on the good things Leif and I shared."

He sat down in his chair and we studied each other for a long moment.

The sadness had threatened to overtake me, but I managed to tamp it back down. "Finn, I don't want to open old wounds, but I do need to know something."

"Anything."

"Why did you come back to Killdeer? You told me last fall that it was for the job, to be Loy's deputy. But Loy told me you came back because of me. So, which is it?"

My blunt question seemed to startle him. For a moment I thought he wouldn't answer.

When he did reply it was my turn to be surprised.

"I came back for you," he said quietly. "Of course, it was for you. I love you, Marley. I always have."

His words sank in slowly, layer by layer. At first I couldn't believe what he had said, and it took me a moment to realize he'd just declared himself to me. My bruised heart skipped a beat. I wanted to reciprocate, to say the words back, but my emotions were still too fragile. My feelings for Finn were

233

powerful, but saying the words was something I wasn't quite ready to do just yet.

But I also knew that someday I would be ready. After I'd had the necessary time to grieve, and heal.

He didn't seem concerned at my reluctance to reply. His face was open and trusting, and he didn't show a hint of fear.

I tried to speak, but nothing came out.

He held up one hand in a placating gesture. "I don't need you to respond. I didn't tell you how I feel because I need, or expect, something in return. Just one thing, though?"

"Yes?" I managed to say.

"Would you do me the courtesy, in the future, of alerting me when you intend to enter into a situation in which you may be killed? As a potential partner, I would like to be informed of your reckless actions in advance."

In spite of the gravity of the conversation, I felt the corners of my mouth turn up. "A potential partner?"

He seemed to suddenly grope for the correct words. "Ah, that is, if that is a reasonable assumption on my part. I wouldn't want to insert myself where I'm not wanted of course, but . . ."

I waited for him to stop stammering and when he finally fell silent I reached across the table and squeezed his hand.

"Finn, of course it's a reasonable assumption. There are many months of healing still left ahead for me, but I won't be broken forever. If you are willing to wait—"

"Of course I am," he said.

I smiled faintly and released his hand. "When I am able to make promises again, make a commitment, you will be the first to know."

A look of relief flooded his expression and he returned my smile. "Thank God. For a second there I thought I'd gone crackers and pulled a dof action."

I just shook my head at him. Whenever Finn was nervous or upset his South African slang drifted into the realm of nearly incomprehensible. Luckily I was savvy enough concerning the dialect that I understood he was feeling happy he hadn't made a terrible mistake.

That made two of us.

We exchanged embarrassed smiles and the tension that had permeated the air around us was suddenly gone.

I wasn't entirely certain what sort of future Finn and I had waiting for us, but at least we had been able to establish there was a future.

The worry and turmoil between us were finally settled, and that allowed me to get back to the problem of what to do about the Houstons.

And what to do about the damn horse blanket.

Loy and Finn had both instructed me to keep the information about the ransom to myself. As far as I knew, the blanket was still missing. It was a problem that I would focus on next, but at the moment there were more important things for Finn and me to discuss.

"I've been thinking," I said.

"Yes, I know. Smoke has been coming out of your ears for days."

"There is one thing about this whole deal with the Houstons that bothers me."

Finn raised an eyebrow. "Only one?"

"The first thing, then," I said. "Even though Butch took the blame for Peter's murder, I'm not sure he really did it. I think he covered up for someone else."

"I can tell you that Butch's cane did not have any of Peter's blood on the handle, or anywhere else for that matter," Finn said.

"So Butch lied about killing Peter with his cane?"

Finn nodded. "That is correct. He did not know what was used as the murder weapon. Everyone we questioned knew that Peter had been hit with some sort of heavy, blunt object, and Butch fabricated a story about using his cane."

"So where is the murder weapon?" I asked.

Finn looked unhappy, but he responded. "We have no idea."

"Do you know where Peter was killed?" I asked.

"Presumably, somewhere on the Lazy Ox Yoke Ranch."

"That narrows it down to about ten thousand acres," I said.

"But we do know only six people were on the ranch at the time of the murder."

"The three hired hands, Vern, Ned and Butch," I said. "What about Felicia?"

"She was in Killdeer filling her car with gasoline at eight o'clock that morning. We can verify that."

I sighed. "So that tells me one of the two Houston brothers is guilty."

"Why do you dismiss the other three men so easily?" Finn asked.

"You mean the three guys who work for the ranch? Why would Butch Houston cover up for an employee?"

Finn seemed to ponder that question. "So he confessed to the crime in order to protect one of his sons."

"The old man gave Felicia all of the water rights to the ranch. She was close to her brother Peter. If he told her to do something, even if it was against the best interests of the other two sons, I am pretty sure she would have done it."

"And you believe that control over water is something a man is willing to kill for?" Finn asked.

"Here in Montana it is," I said.

"If you say so."

"It's the only thing that makes any sense at all," I said. "Butch would never lie to protect someone who was just a hired hand. But he would sacrifice himself to protect a son."

"So, one of his sons is guilty," Finn said.

I nodded. "And one of them is innocent."

"But which of the two sons is the killer?" Finn asked. "On the morning you drove up to the Wilson ranch and saw the two brothers fighting, you had no way of knowing how long either one of them had been there. There is no way to determine which one of them arrived first at the head gate, and which one arrived later. When Loy questioned them, they both answered evasively and seemed reluctant to cooperate."

"That sounds like a typical Houston thing to do."

Finn folded his hands on top of the table, looking irritated. "Unfortunately, Loy has not been able to gather enough evidence to arrest either brother, for any crime. There has been no physical evidence located linking either of them to the kidnapping, or the murder. We have our speculations, but no proof yet."

"Both Vern and Ned are still free to go about their business?" I asked incredulously.

"Until we can find something to tie one of them to a crime, yes."

"But you think you know who the killer is," I said.

Finn sighed with frustration. "The same one that is responsible for the burglaries. So I surmise."

I shifted in my chair. What I had to say next was pure speculation, and I wasn't sure how he would take it.

"I think it could be Vern."

"You mentioned that he is not truly Butch Houston's son. Do you think he was aware of that fact?"

I shrugged. "Probably, otherwise why would he be so willing to kidnap someone for ransom? If it had come out that he was not Butch's heir, his inheritance would be lost."

"It is not enough evidence to lead us to that conclusion," Finn said.

"There's more," I told him. "Remember that Nick Wilcox showed me a photograph of the man who was probably responsible for the burglaries. Butch mentioned that Vern is the deer hunter in the family. He even said that Vern dresses head to toe in camouflage, so I sort of made that leap at well."

Finn leaned back in his chair and rubbed his chin while he thought about what I had said.

"All this time, you and Loy were chasing motives that probably weren't even there in the first place," I said. "The sapphires had nothing to do with Peter's death. I really believe, based on what Butch told me right before he died, that one of Peter's brothers killed him because he could convince Felicia what to do with the water."

"That does not explain the kidnapping and ransom," Finn pointed out.

"Unless the blanket was sort of like a plan B," I suggested.

"Explain."

"Well, what if Vern killed his brother in a weak moment, a moment of rage, because of a fight over the water?"

"Perhaps."

I shrugged. "Now what is he going to do? Hide the body, most likely."

"But he is interrupted and he cannot do so without being seen, or he simply panics and flees."

I went on with my speculation. "Butch discovers Peter dead. He realizes that one of his other sons has committed the murder and he covers it up."

"Logical," Finn replied. "Where does this blanket enter into things then?"

"Maybe it's worth something. A few thousand dollars? Who knows what collectors will pay for old artifacts. Vern knows he's going to eventually have to make a run for it, because Loy is going to get a warrant and will probably find evidence that Peter was killed in his cabin, or in the family house. In any case, sooner or later it will all come out."

"It seems unlikely to me that a man would be willing to kidnap a person in order to secure a blanket worth a few thousand dollars," Finn said.

"What if it's worth close to fifty thousand, or more?" I asked.

He looked unconvinced, but he seemed to be mulling it over. "I could be persuaded of his motive if the blanket appraised at something close to that amount."

"My friend John Taylor is coming to Killdeer tomorrow and he will be going through the rest of the artifacts. Hopefully that blanket will turn up and he can take a look at it. If we can't find it with the other artifacts, I would imagine my father probably knows where it is."

"Your father?"

I smirked. "He is always cleaning up after me. He was in the barn the day after I left the blanket there, and he's the one who hung the little saddle up on the wall. I would guess he stashed the blanket someplace and if I ask him about it he will be able to tell me where it is."

"And hopefully your friend John will be able to determine if it truly is valuable," he said.

I sighed and leaned back in my chair. "I'm not sure how to help you figure out which one of the boys killed Peter, but if I was a betting woman I'd put my money on Vern."

"It is not your job to establish the guilt of a murder suspect."

"No, you're right. I'll leave that to you and Loy," I said.

He fixed his eyes on me. "And until we do establish his guilt, it would be prudent of you to avoid the Houstons. Agreed?"

I offered the most sincere smile I could muster. "Agreed."

CHAPTER 22

"Are those your horses?" John asked.

We stood together beside the gate leading to my father's pasture.

Lil Nipper and Peanut ambled over enthusiastically to greet us. The mustang hung his head over the gate and tossed his nose eagerly. The Icelandic pony eyed John cautiously before muscling into position and shoving Peanut out of the way, just in case there was the possibility of a sugar cube.

As I stood looking at my father's barn in the bright morning sunlight, it occurred to me how idyllic the scene looked. Golden light streamed down from a clear sky, wildflowers were beginning to bloom, and everything looked peaceful and serene.

And so far no one had attempted to break into the sheriff's impound garage. It had sat unmolested for two nights. No one had broken into my house, or my father's house either. It was almost as if things were finally on the verge of returning to normal.

John Taylor, the arrowhead authenticator and my friend from Wyoming, had come to Killdeer as promised to help identify and appraise the collection of Peter's artifacts. He'd telephoned my house and I'd given him directions to my father's barn and asked him to meet me there instead of down at the impound garage. There were a few things I wanted to warn him about concerning the collection he was about to look at, and I'd felt more comfortable doing it someplace isolated so no one would be able to eavesdrop.

As we stood by the gate, I gave him the details of the situation.

I half expected John to turn right around and leave town after discovering the things he was supposed to appraise belonged to a murder victim, but he didn't seem put off at all, and said he would stay to complete the job.

As we spoke, I noticed John watching with amusement as both horses jostled each other for position by the gate.

"I guess we could feed them a treat," I said.

John tilted his head. "They do look hungry."

"They always look hungry. And be careful. The smaller one bites," I cautioned.

"I see. In that case, you go first."

He laughed to let me know he was joking, and without any hesitation he opened the gate and stepped through.

Lil Nipper laid back both ears and took a run at John with his head down.

"Watch it John!"

I needn't have worried.

He deftly stepped to the side and used his forearm to deflect the bite, and the pony tossed his head with irritation that his surprise attack had been so easily thwarted.

I hurried over to help him shut the gate, and by the time I had the latch fastened John was scratching the pony on the neck affectionately.

And, astonishingly, Lil Nipper was letting him.

"He likes you," I said with surprise.

The pony leaned into John's arm like a shameless farm cat getting a good scratch.

We went inside the barn and I noticed the hay had not been put out yet. But my father had come at some point and put a fresh coat of paint over the graffiti that had been spray-painted on the inside wall.

You couldn't even tell the words had once been there.

I wasn't exactly wearing grubby work clothes, but I managed to get a couple wedges of hay out for the two horses without getting filthy.

On a whim I decided to scoop out a can of oats.

"That's the smallest saddle I've ever seen," John said.

I turned and looked up. The little saddle for the pony still hung on the wall where my father had put it.

"It's just for decoration," I said. "I don't let anyone ride Lil Nipper. I guess you could say he is a really expensive lawn ornament."

"Hornilla del heno," John said with a chuckle.

I shook my head. "What does that mean?"

"It's Spanish for hay burner."

I shared his laugh. "Well he does manage to do that."

My nice jeans were already getting smudged, but I bent next to the oat barrel and grabbed an empty coffee can to scoop out some oats anyway. I was already dirty, might as well get covered in horse slobber too.

When I unsnapped the lid on the oat barrel and set it aside, a flash of black-and-white wool caught my eye.

"Well, there you are," I said.

The source of all my troubles had been found at last.

I reached inside the barrel and ran my hand over the heavy wool horse blanket.

It was neatly folded and had been stashed on top of the oats out of sight.

No wonder I hadn't managed to find it.

"My dad," I said out loud.

"Excuse me?" John asked.

"Nothing."

Always picking up after me. He'd probably stashed the blanket in the oat barrel so the mice wouldn't chew on it.

I reached inside and lifted the blanket out.

"Say, John, while you are here could you take a look at this and tell me if it's worth anything?"

He turned towards me.

"It's a little bit dirty," I said apologetically.

When I lifted the horse blanket John's eyes widened noticeably.

I pulled the heavy striped fabric the rest of the way from the barrel, and when I turned back to give John a good view of the blanket, he was laughing.

John shook his head back and forth. "Wow."

"I know, it's covered in oats," I said, blushing.

The corners of the blanket were sturdy and I gripped them hard. I let the fabric unfold until it nearly touched the ground. I got a tight grip and lifted my arms, intent on giving the blanket a good shake to clean off the oats.

John shouted, "Marley stop!"

I froze, looking at him.

He moved forward carefully and took the blanket from my hands.

"Do you know what this is?" He eased my fingers from the corners and gently draped the striped fabric over his arm.

"I haven't any idea," I said.

When he looked up at me, his eyes were shining. "This is a First Phase Chief's Blanket. Some people call them Navajo First Phase, but technically they are Ute Chief's Blankets. There are probably only about a hundred of these left in existence today."

"So, it's historically valuable?" I asked. "But it's so plain-looking."

"Back in 2012, a blanket similar to this one sold at a John Moran auction for a tidy sum."

"What's a tidy sum?" I asked.

"One point eight million dollars."

My knees practically buckled. "How much?"

"I can't say this one will be worth the same amount, but there is little doubt that it will be close to that."

My stomach flip-flopped. "Unbelievable."

I didn't even want to touch the blanket now. I was afraid that I'd hurt it in some way.

John regarded me, his eyes still shining. "Is this part of the collection you asked me to look at or is this yours?"

I stammered. "Felicia Houston gave it to me, but how much did you say it's worth again?"

"We should determine who is the owner first, before we get this appraised," he suggested.

I stood there staring at the blanket, my mind a whirl.

John prompted me again. "Marley?"

When I answered him, my tone was resolute. "It's Felicia's."

John turned his head. "Are you sure? I think you may have a right to it, if you have witnesses who will attest that she gave it to you."

"What would you do in this situation?" I asked.

He ran a hand over the plain fabric and sighed. "Well, she obviously didn't know its value. I'd be tempted, but I think the right thing here is to let her know what it is actually worth and the two of you decide together what to do about it."

"I don't need the money," I said.

"That's not an answer. You need to be sure about this before we proceed."

I lifted a corner of the blanket and ran my thumb over the blue and black stripes carefully. She'd just lost her father and her brother. It didn't take me long to make up my mind. I didn't always make the best choices in life, and sometimes I made mistakes that could be considered epic.

But nobody ever had to tell me the difference between right and wrong.

I just knew.

The blanket should go where it could do the most good.

"It's Felicia's," I said.

A gleam of approval sparkled in John's eye as he carefully folded the blanket. "Alright. In that case, let's get this back to the rest of the collection, for safekeeping."

"Which is precisely where it belongs anyway," I said.

John looked down at what I'd considered an old horse blanket, a look of utter disbelief on his face. "I never thought I'd see something like this come out of a feed bin," he said.

I felt a mixture of relief and shock as I climbed inside my father's old pickup truck. I'd destroyed the back end on my SUV and it would be in the repair shop for a while. Until it was back in service I was forced to drive the ancient truck my father used for ranch chores.

In a funny way, the old truck was a comfort to me. It reminded me of my days spent building forts out of hay bales and hunting for frogs in the creek barefoot. We'd had the truck since I was eleven years old. It was amazing the thing still ran, so to speak. It blew a cloud of multicolored smoke out the back end every time it started.

Finding the blanket was the first good luck I'd had since the ordeal with the Houstons had begun, and I let myself imagine the possibility that fortune was finally starting to favor me again.

With any luck, John would be able to catalogue Peter's collection and discover that many of the items were valuable. I had absolutely no sympathy for Ned or Vern, but if Felicia could benefit from the artifact collection that was good enough for me.

We left the barn in tandem and John followed as I drove to the sheriff's station. I left the valuable blanket with Finn for safekeeping, delighting in his reaction when I told him its true worth, and then I led John over to the impound garage so we could get to work.

John began examining each of the artifacts in Peter's collection. The work was tedious and time-consuming, and promised to take nearly all day. I'd taken the afternoon off from the library and had ample time to work, so I stayed in the garage to assist him.

He stood at a table and I ferried objects to him so he could jot notes on a pad of paper, and if the item was heavy, like the big stone bowl, he would come lend me a hand.

"Does this bowl have a pestle with it?" he asked. "It isn't as valuable unless they are together as a set."

I went back to the spot where the stone bowl had been sitting and searched around. "Not that I can see."

He made a disappointed face. "Too bad. A bowl this big would probably have a very large pestle and it would be worth a great deal more if they were still together."

I frowned and looked at the bowl. "How big a pestle?"

John tilted his head from side to side as he thought. "It could be close to twelve inches long. Heavy too. Maybe we will run across it as we work."

I recalled loading the bowl into the horse trailer back at the Lazy Ox Yoke, but I hadn't seen a large stone pestle anywhere with it. I was certain of that.

Maybe Irene had loaded it without my knowledge. Or worse, maybe my father had thought it was nothing more than a stupid rock and had pitched it behind the cabin.

John catalogued the bowl and helped me place it back with the other artifacts, and we continued on.

I did what I could to help him, but my thoughts were distracted and something was nagging me for attention. I kept making mistakes, and though John was too polite to say anything, I was starting to get the feeling I was slowing him down.

The conversation I'd had with John in the barn had set off a tiny earthquake in my mind, but try as I might, the reason behind it wouldn't come into focus. Something that he'd said, or something that I'd thought of at the time, was causing a cascade of uneasiness in my mind. After a few hours it was obvious I was doing more harm than good when it came to assisting John in his efforts, and I decided the best thing I could do was drive home, call Felicia on the phone and give her the good news about the blanket.

I wasn't sure if she would be happy to hear from me or not, but at least I was delivering some good news for a change.

It wouldn't bring back her father or her brother, but it might console her a little to know that she was going to be a millionaire soon.

But there was also a selfish reason for telling Felicia about the blanket. Once she knew it was locked up in a safe back at the sheriff's station, she could pass that information along to her brothers and hopefully I'd get some well-deserved peace and quiet for a change. I doubted very much that Vern was desperate enough to break into the station with Finn standing guard.

I told John goodbye and left him to work unencumbered by my fumbling assistance.

As I drove towards home the nagging feeling that I'd overlooked something only grew worse. I couldn't help but think there was something staring me in the face but I couldn't see it. Whatever it was, the feeling that I'd missed some vital clue plucked my brain like a guitar string. But no matter how hard I tried to puzzle it out, the reason behind my unease wouldn't come to the surface of my addled mind.

No matter.

If it was really so important, eventually I'd figure it out.

CHAPTER 23

I shut off the engine. The truck backfired as it died and it sounded like a gunshot.

I rolled my eyes as it coughed a couple of times before finally dying, and I slammed the door as hard as I could so it would latch shut.

As I walked up the steps to the front door it occurred to me that the forest was unnaturally quiet.

I went inside and called Felicia, but she didn't pick up. As I hung up the phone someone knocked on the front door and I hurried back through the kitchen to see who it was. Expecting to see my father, or perhaps Loy, standing on my front porch, I was surprised when I pulled open the door.

Jackie Miller greeted me with a polite smile.

"Miss Dearcorn," he said. "How are you?"

"Jackie. I didn't expect to see you. Is Felicia home? I called to tell her some good news but she didn't answer," I said.

He peered around the doorway and seemed to be looking for someone. "Felicia is in Billings."

"I hope everything is alright," I said.

He shrugged. "Something to do with the estate. I think she is talking to an attorney."

I wasn't sure what to say. The seconds dragged by and he seemed more focused on the house behind me than on me.

"So," I said at length, "when will Felicia be back?"

He hardly gave me a glance. "Tomorrow. She is spending the night there to save driving back after dark. You know. Deer."

I nodded my response. The deer between Billings and Killdeer were legendary. If you didn't see one it was considered an event. Hitting a deer with your car at night was a most unpleasant experience. I didn't blame Felicia for not wanting to drive home after dark.

He finally turned his attention back to me and smiled again.

"Was there something I could do for you?" I asked.

"What was the good news? I can give a message to Felicia when she gets home tomorrow."

For a moment I considered telling him about the blanket. But then I thought perhaps it was best if I didn't. "Just let her know we are almost done having Peter's collection appraised."

His eyes widened. "That will make her happy."

"Turns out something in Peter's collection is pretty valuable after all. I thought she should know."

He was paying very close attention to me now, and I found his sudden interest a bit unsettling.

"That is good news," he said.

A flicker of worry flashed through me. Something wasn't quite right. He was acting strangely.

I started inching the door closed. "Well, it was good to see you. Let Felicia know I will give her a call tomorrow."

"Do you know what it is?" he asked, putting a hand on the door. "Was it one of the pieces of pottery or something?"

My instincts were screaming at me that something was wrong. The nagging feeling I'd had earlier became a frantic shout.

"John didn't say. He just told me to deliver the message," I said.

What was happening? Why was he acting so strangely?

At that moment I realized what it was that I'd missed. I took in his Iowa-farm-boy blond hair, his blue eyes. His Midwest accent was unmistakable.

It was the way Jackie had referred to himself once. What had he said? Something that he'd mentioned, back when he'd showed me the bag of sapphires in the parking lot at the sheriff's station. The words were slowly bubbling to the surface of my memory.

John's sudden use of a Spanish phrase to describe my pony back at the barn had prompted my thoughts, but I hadn't put it together until now.

I looked at Jackie with an innocent expression. "Where did you say you were from?"

Jackie gave a faint smile. But the smile was brittle. Almost like he regretted my question. "Milwaukee."

I studied him for a moment.

Vaquero. That's what he had said. I'm just a vaquero.

How many cowboys from Wisconsin used the Spanish word for cowboy?

John had said the term hay burner in Spanish when he'd talked about the horses, and at the time it seemed so odd that a man from Wyoming would do such a thing.

It seemed so out of character.

Out of place.

Exactly like the word vaquero.

I pasted a smile on my face. "Thanks for dropping by, Jackie. Tell Felicia I'll give her a call tomorrow."

As I reached for the door Jackie stepped in front of it and pushed it wider.

"If John tells you what he found that's so valuable, promise that you'll let us know?" he asked.

I backed up a step and felt my pulse speed up. "Sure."

"Marley," Jackie said quietly. "I forgot to tell you something."

He moved inside the house, still talking, still behaving as if he had every right to be there, but his look was anything but normal. It was predatory.

"Thank you for the way you supported Felicia through this whole thing. Her brothers never were able to do much, other than shout and tell her how stupid she is. I think it meant a lot to her, having someone like you around."

His words were kind and gentle, but something in his eyes seemed alien. Almost vacant.

"I was glad to help," I said.

Every one of my senses was yelling at me to get away from him as quickly as I could.

His hands balled into fists as he appraised me. And as quick as a snake strike, all of his pretense was gone. "You just couldn't leave it alone, could you?"

"Jackie, wait," I managed to say.

I lunged backwards but he moved so fast it stunned me.

The last thing I saw was his fist swinging for my face.

Then everything went black.

* * * *

My nose ached intensely.

So did everything else.

I opened my eyes and saw a pool of blood staining an old wooden floor.

It was almost impossible to focus my vision. I tried to sit up but my arms were bound together behind my back and the pain in my head was so intense moving was unthinkable.

At last I managed to blink away the tears and saw Jackie sitting a few feet away, watching me. He sat with his legs crossed, resting his chin in his palm casually.

The blood on the floor was coming from my nose and I tried to inch away from it, which sent a shock of agony through my skull.

As I focused on him, panic rose in my chest.

He simply sat looking at me with what seemed to be curiosity. "How did you know?"

I tried to concentrate on slowing my breathing. "How did I know what?"

"How did you figure it out?"

The rough wooden floor didn't look familiar, and when I managed to focus on the rest of the room I realized where I was.

A wave of sheer panic shot through me.

I was in the fire lookout tower.

Jackie was asking me how I'd discovered it was him behind the burglaries.

And that meant he didn't care if I knew it was him, because he was going to kill me anyway.

I tested the rope that bound my arms.

"Don't bother," he said, watching me. "I used to be a calf-roping champion. You won't get out of that."

"Jackie—"

"By the way, nobody is going to come looking for you, so put that out of your head. They don't even know you are missing yet. It will be easier if you just work with me here."

He reached inside a duffel bag and began pulling out pieces of clothing. A camouflage shirt, pants, and mask came out of the bag and he stripped down smoothly. I watched as he put on the gear and soon he was dressed exactly the way he'd been in the photograph Nick had shown me. He pulled the mask on like a hat, but didn't bother to lower it over his face just yet.

He was preparing for something.

Something that didn't include keeping me around as a witness.

There was no way out of this.

My first thought was that my death would be really hard on my dad. And Irene. She would be heartbroken.

My second thought was that it would be best for everyone if I found a way to get out of this.

And then I realized that my legs were still free.

"You said you were nothing but a vaquero," I told him.

He frowned and shook his head. "So what?"

"That's Spanish for cowboy," I said.

His face registered understanding. "Ah. Stupid. Never should have said that."

"Not a word you would normally pick up," I said, "living in Wisconsin."

"But something I would learn if I lived in the Southwest at some point," he replied. "Sure. I can see that."

"If Peter was helping you hide a bag of sapphires in his cabin, you probably spent a lot of time in there looking at all of his stuff. Someone who had spent time in the Southwest, Arizona, or New

Mexico maybe, might know what a Navajo chief's blanket was."

I managed to inch away from the pool of blood and tried to focus on him.

A shotgun was beside his feet. Within easy reach.

"What I didn't figure out," I said, a wave of nausea forcing me to hold still, "was how you managed to convince Butch that it was one of his sons who killed Peter."

He shrugged. "I didn't have to convince him. When he saw Peter he came up with that scenario all on his own."

"And he covered up the murder thinking he was protecting his boys."

Jackie gave me a wolf grin. "Saved me a lot of trouble."

"But it kept you from getting to the blanket," I said. "Why didn't you just take it after you smashed in Peter's skull with the stone pestle?"

I was guessing, but from his expression I'd hit the mark. The stone pestle was missing from the collection because Jackie had gotten rid of it after he had used it to kill Peter.

Jackie frowned. "Yeah. It wasn't my best moment. I wanted to grab the blanket right then, but there was a lot of blood on my hands. I wanted to wash and change my shirt before I touched the chief's blanket, so I just shut the door and walked to the bunkhouse. When I came back, the old man was already inside the cabin."

"He moved Peter's body. And then he locked the door," I said.

"I wasn't in a hurry, but I should have been. The sheriff showing up an hour later, and then you and Irene came the next morning and it turned out to be a huge pain in my ass. I still can't believe no one on the ranch knew that a million bucks was just hanging over the back of a chair."

I moved my right leg, testing it. It was a little sore but seemed fine.

Now the left leg.

"Where is the blanket, Marley?" Jackie asked, all trace of humor gone from his voice.

"It's in the impound garage," I said.

He lifted the shotgun and pumped it once.

Then he aimed it for my head.

"I already looked through all of that stuff so I know that's a lie. Where is it really?"

I looked down the barrel of the shotgun and everything else in the world seemed to disappear. I felt a sudden clarity.

"It's in the oat bin at my father's barn," I said.

The shotgun lowered slightly.

"Now that wasn't so hard, was it?" he asked.

I wiggled the toes on my left foot. They responded, and I dared to hope.

Then I tested the rope around my wrists and I realized it was tied to the stove Irene and I had managed to push over.

The stove weighed as much as I did.

I wasn't going anywhere.

Jackie shifted the shotgun to his left hand casually. He looked down at me almost like it was an afterthought. "If it isn't in the oat bin, then I'm going to shoot you when I come back."

He took a step and reached for the door.

With a crash the old wooden door exploded and a black shape tumbled into the room.

Jackie lurched sideways but not fast enough. His shotgun spun wildly in the air. It sailed through the glass of the observation window, shattering the pane into a thousand shards, and fell from sight.

A man had kicked the shotgun away and followed the attack with three deadly punches to Jackie's face.

Jackie rallied and aimed a devastating low kick that knocked the man from his feet.

I pumped my legs and managed to slide away from the chaos but the rope grew taut and I stopped like I'd come to the end of a leash.

The man lurched to his feet and grappled with Jackie furiously. Both men lost their balance and the struggle spilled through the door and onto the deck of the tower.

Jackie bull-rushed the man with his shoulder down, slammed into him with powerful force and toppled him backwards. Just as he was about to fall over the railing I realized who it was.

"Finn!"

Jackie had momentum on his side.

Finn waved a hand frantically, trying to steady himself. But it was too late. He somersaulted over the wooden rail and dropped from sight.

Jackie was already sprinting down the stairs madly. He didn't look back at all and disappeared.

I struggled to my knees and tried to crawl forward.

The only sound I heard was Jackie's footfalls as he thundered down the steps.

The sound I hadn't heard was a body crashing to the ground below.

Maybe he was still alive.

"Finn!"

It seemed unbelievable, but as I called his name I saw a single hand gripping the bottom rail of the banister.

"Hold on!"

I jerked against the rope feebly, not taking my eyes off of his hand.

A second hand swung up and he managed to snag another rail.

It was agonizing. I could see him struggle to hold on and there wasn't a thing I could do to help. I pulled against the stove and managed to drag it a few inches but I wasn't nearly strong enough.

My legs gave out and I slumped to the floor. Tears stung my eyes and I watched helplessly.

Finn's hands tightened on the rails and I saw a flash of black as his legs swung into view.

One moment he was dangling on the other side of the railing and the next he was standing in front of me.

The only sound I could make was a sob.

"Hold still," he said.

"I thought you were dead," I said miserably.

"So did I."

He snapped open a knife and in moments my arms were free.

I collapsed with my back against the wall and flexed my fingers, willing them to come back to life.

I could barely feel my arms at all.

"Can you see?" he asked.

My injuries must have looked bad. I managed to nod. "Well enough."

Finn pulled an automatic pistol from his holster and placed it in my hands.

"If anyone other than me comes through that door," he said, "shoot them."

"Where are you going?" I asked.

He stood up and repositioned the knife in his hand before moving towards the door.

"Finn, you can't. He's wearing camouflage and you won't be able to see him."

He walked through the door silently.

A sudden flash of anger surged through me.

If Finn was going to sacrifice himself for me, the very least I could do was try and stay alive.

I backed up in the corner of the tower and gripped the pistol in both of my hands. I made sure the safety was off and pointed the barrel straight at the door.

And then I waited.

My ears strained to hear something, anything. But all I could discern was the quiet and ordinary activity of the forest.

The minutes ticked by and the only sound I could hear was the soft creak and groan of the old tower.

"Finn, where are you?" I asked in a whisper.

All I could think about was the possibility that Jackie might have retrieved the shotgun, and Finn only carried a knife.

Everybody knew how that scenario usually turned out.

I forced myself to take in deep, slow breaths, and concentrated on the door.

My face felt sticky and I used the hem of my shirt to wipe it off, and to clean my eyes so I could see more clearly.

My heart was hammering in my chest with worry. I should have heard something by now. A shot. The sounds of a fight. Something.

It was too quiet, and just as I was about to stand up and peer out the window I heard footsteps on the stairs.

I squared my shoulders and aimed the pistol straight ahead.

"Marley, it's Finn. Do not shoot me."

I lowered the pistol and a sigh so deep it sounded like the wind escaped my lungs.

He came through the door and I saw that he wasn't carrying his knife anymore.

"Did you find him?" I asked.

He knelt down and gently ran a hand over my cheek. "I think your nose is broken."

"Did you?" I asked again.

"Of course."

"What happened? Can we get out of here now?"

Finn nodded. "It is safe to leave."

"But how?" I asked. "How could you see him?"

He eased the pistol out of my grasp and replaced it in his holster. "I told you, camouflage does not work on everyone."

"I don't understand."

He held out his hand and carefully helped me to my feet.

"I wear black because colors are a problem for me. Camouflage doesn't work on me because I can see right through it," he said. "I'm color-blind."

He took my hands and led me down the steps without bothering to check for danger.

EPILOGUE

Debbie Pritchett used the right heel of her classy patent leather pump to cram the For Sale sign into my front yard.

She was the top real estate agent for Falcon Realty, and I'd just listed my home with her, putting a fair market price on it, which meant it wouldn't sell for another two years, but that was fine.

"I will bring you regular updates for times and dates when we intend to have an open house," she told me. "But I don't expect any activity for a while."

"It will give me a place to stay until my new house is built," I said.

I walked with her to her gold minivan and she waved happily as she drove away.

Loy Shucraft, back on active duty once more, stood on my porch and waited for me to climb the steps.

"Are you sure you want to sell this place?" he asked. "It's like a palace."

"Which is exactly why I want to sell it," I told him.

We sat in small patio chairs on the porch and Loy had to shift his gun belt around so it wasn't wedged underneath the armrest.

The old property where my former house had once stood was now a construction site. The place had burned to the ground shortly before Leif's death, and until now I hadn't had the heart to do anything other than hire a crew to clear the debris away and haul the remnants to the dump.

The huge mansion where I currently lived was way too much house for one person. So I had hired an architect and he was working with a contractor to erect a new house on the site of my former home. It would be a modest three-bedroom, two-bath cabin-style bungalo with no stairs and only one garage stall.

Much easier to clean.

"You heard that Irene is taking on Judy Isley as a business partner?" Loy said.

I smiled. "You don't say."

He didn't look at me when he spoke, but his voice was thick with suspicion. "Seems that Judy isn't so keen to handle cash the old-fashioned way, and it turns out she is sort of a whiz at technology. She's planning to upgrade Lil's café with a whole new payment system, and modernize things."

"That's nice."

Loy looked at me out of the corner of his eye. "Judy wasn't ever going to go work at Lil's again because she and Irene always bumped heads about how things should be managed. But now it seems that she has the financial backing of a silent partner here in Killdeer. Some wealthy widow bankrolled her investment, and she bought half the business."

"Hey, that's good news," I said.

I was a wealthy widow, but Loy didn't bother to point that fact out to me.

He eyed me speculatively. "Now Judy can have some input about how the business is run and

Irene can have some free time. Irene is talking about going to Barcelona with your dad for the winter."

"Good for them," I said with a genuine smile.

We sat beside each other in silence for a moment.

It had been three weeks since Jackie Miller had abducted me and taken me to the fire lookout tower. He'd subsequently met a sudden and violent end.

My bruises were almost completely healed.

I was alive to have bruises, and so I wasn't complaining about them.

Jackie had managed to retrieve the shotgun after he'd fled the tower, but somehow Finn had bested him in spite of only having a knife. I didn't know how he had accomplished that feat and I never would.

Unless I asked, I knew Finn would never tell me the details about it, so it wouldn't upset me.

It was my sincere intention never to ask him. I knew one thing for certain.

I didn't want to know.

After he'd found me in the lookout tower I had asked Finn how in the world he had known I was in trouble, and how he could have possibly known it was Jackie instead of Vern who had killed Peter.

Finn explained that shortly after I'd delivered the chief's blanket to him at the station, he had put Vern in an office on the pretense of asking him some more questions, and he'd purposefully left the blanket draped over a chair next to him to see what Vern would do.

Vern looked right at it and never flinched a muscle. Finn had concluded that unless Vern was the best actor in the world, he had no idea what the presence of the blanket truly meant.

Finn began to worry that he'd been focusing his investigation on the wrong man.

Loy had already run a background check on all the hired men from the Lazy Ox Yoke and come up with nothing special. But Finn persisted, and he discovered that Jackie possessed two social security cards. One with the last name of Miller, and one with the last name of Wagner.

Jackie Wagner was wanted for questioning in connection with a string of burglaries that had occurred at several ranches in New Mexico over the past eight years. All of the items taken were small antiques or vintage collectables, usually described as a family heirloom that had a fair amount of monetary value. And all of the items had vanished without a trace. They had never ended up in any local pawn shops and none of them had ever been sold over the internet on auction websites, so Finn had surmised that Jackie had been a professional collector of some kind. Most likely, he'd had a regular buyer he supplied, and had taken jobs at ranches rumored to have valuable relics.

It was even possible he'd come all the way to Killdeer after hearing stories about an old woman who had taken a huge cache of antiques with her to Montana, years and years ago.

He must have thought he'd stumbled across his biggest score ever after finding the chief's blanket in Peter's possession. It was a prize too tempting to resist.

But Peter had spoiled his plans.

No doubt, Jackie had been caught trying to take the blanket, and had resorted to violence in a moment of panic.

To Jackie, a million dollars had been worth killing for.

I was lucky he hadn't managed to make me his second victim.

Thanks to Finn.

When I'd asked Finn how he had known I was missing in the first place, he'd described driving to my house and finding the door open, seeing blood on the floor inside the entryway and realizing I was gone. He said it had been the most distressing, and the most galvanizing moment of his life.

He knew exactly what to do next. He was wearing a badge, but when Finn wanted to get inside the mind of a criminal he was capable of doing it. No doubt he had thought of the fire lookout tower because that was the place he would have taken somone to do away with them.

I'd persisted. "But Finn, how did you know where he'd taken me?"

He'd shrugged and looked at me with an unreadable expression. "I just knew."

I smiled at the memory.

Loy cleared his throat and interrupted my thoughts. "I didn't come up here to talk about Lil's."

"You want some iced tea?" I asked.

"Marley, can I get this out, or what?" he asked.

"Sure, Loy. I didn't know you actually came out here for a reason."

He hesitated for a moment before speaking again. He seemed to be trying to find a way to say what he wanted to without getting it wrong.

His brow was furrowed with concentration. "I know you like working at the library," he began.

"Oh, no. Are there going to be state budget cuts again?" I asked.

"Not that I know of. This isn't about the library," he said.

"You want me to waive your overdue fees, don't you?"

"I want you to resign," he said.

I frowned and turned to face him. "Why?"

He leaned towards me and used his hands to emphasize his passion about the subject. "Marley, the library isn't keeping you busy enough."

I shook my head. "I'm sorry, what?"

He pressed on. "You need to have a job that challenges you, or else, well, you get into things."

"Get into things," I echoed. "What things?"

"Like, asking questions until it leads to you being kidnapped and beat up," he said. "And this isn't the only time things have happened as a result of you meddling."

I looked at my hands. There was no arguing with that.

"I know most of what happens isn't your fault," he said quickly. "But I was thinking. These past few years you have gotten a great deal of experience dealing with situations that require a certain skill set."

"Skills like not getting killed?"

He beamed. "Exactly."

"So, what did you have in mind?" I asked.

"There is a summer intern job opening up with the Forest Service here in Killdeer and I want you to apply for it. I already talked to the local supervisor over in Parkman who handles the pine beetle study group and he said he will look for your application."

I made a face. "Loy, pine beetle mitigation study? I'm not much for bug hunts."

"No, now just listen," he said. "It's a summer job, but it gets your foot in the door."

"For what?" I asked suspiciously.

"The wildland fire investigator job in Killdeer Valley is vacant, and if you get the beetle job, you will be eligible to apply for the investigator position in September."

I considered his suggestion, noticing the entire time he stared at me without blinking once. He obviously wanted this very badly.

"Why me?" I asked.

He proceeded cautiously. "You have a lot of energy. I think it would be productive to channel it someplace where it could actually do some good for a change."

I gave him a look. "For a change?"

"I meant to say, it would be good for the valley if you were actually wearing a badge, while you were getting shot at, for a change."

I had never considered it before, but the more I thought about it, the more I liked how it sounded.

"I'll think about it," I said.

Satisfied, Loy stood up, pulled me to my feet, and gave me a crushing bear hug. "That's all I can ask."

He headed for his truck and pulled out of my driveway, giving me a hearty wave as he disappeared through the trees.

I sat in down the patio chair and thought about what he'd suggested.

Killdeer valley was where I belonged, and even though it could be challenging to live in such an isolated place where the locals sometimes made up the rules of life as they went along, I knew I'd never leave it again.

Maybe it wasn't such a bad idea to spend my time and energy doing what I could to make sure it was looked after.

Life in rural Montana wasn't easy. I'd made plenty of mistakes, but I knew as the years passed my memory for the bad things would fade. As long as I worked hard to build things up instead of tear them down, it would all work out.

Living in this little valley, surrounded on all sides by tall mountains and whispering pine trees, I knew I'd never have to walk any hard journey alone. The people here were a tough, loyal bunch who didn't shy away from responsibility, or accountability. They were my friends and neighbors, and were my family of a sort.

If I had one true hope, it was that someday I would be worthy of them.

The prospect of holding a job where I could have official sanction for asking questions and pursuing the truth intrigued me. It might be nice to have a little training, too.

Maybe it was time for a career change.

I could settle into a new life as an investigator and do something that gave me a true sense of satisfaction.

I still missed my husband and always would. But for the first time I felt as if my life was on the verge of giving me a real sense of purpose again.

My future in Killdeer looked pretty good after all.

And then there was Finn . . .

FOR TEACHING ME IT'S NEVER TOO LATE
TO DO THE RIGHT THING—
THANKS JEB.

ACKNOWLEDGEMENTS

Many thanks to my editor, Sean Murphy, who
turned me upside down and shook me until the good
stories fell out, and whose patience and perseverance
helped immeasurably when it came to shaping the
Killdeer series into something readable.
And to Paul Spragens, who did what he could to
clean up after my spelling mistakes and never
seemed to lose hope that I would be able to
hyphenate correctly someday.

My gratitude to Peter Honsberger, who managed to
juggle my multiple requests while dealing with this
thing called life, and made the books come alive with
his imaginative and artistic work while
taking a chance on an untested new author.

For the original members of The Wrecking Crew,
Jeb Taylor, Milt and Karen Mydland and Michelle
Mueller—you tore apart my manuscripts so that I
had to rebuild them from scratch,
and I can't thank you enough.

For Bill Matteson, who literally gave me the shirt off
his back to use as a rope before I fell off a cliff in
Hell's Half Acre, thank you for providing the cover
for book six, it's my favorite.

For my dear husband, Glenn, you are a true patron
of the arts and without you this series would have
never been written.

David Hartschuh, who built a fantastic website for me in the amount of time it takes to brew a cup of coffee, saving me from working on it over the next twenty years, thank you again for lending me your spare time and considerable skills.

Thanks to the Independent Booksellers who allow me to take up valuable space on their shelves, particularly in Wyoming and Colorado, where I am a "local" author.

And for all the librarians at Sheridan County Fulmer Public Library in Sheridan, Wyoming, particularly Michelle Havenga, who nurtured in me a love of reading, thank you for making writers feel welcome, and encouraging all of us to treasure the written word.

A fourth generation Wyoming native,
Jessica McClelland is a librarian, avid archer and
spent a decade hunting dinosaurs in the
Jurassic formation in the foothills of the
Bighorn Mountains, a stone's throw away from
where the Johnson County Cattle Wars occurred.
She is the author of the Marley Dearcorn novels,
a series of murder mysteries set in
South Central Montana.

www.ingramcontent.com/pod-product-compliance
Lightning Source LLC
Chambersburg PA
CBHW020245180626
46810CB00006B/2369